It Started with an Itch

Alkanet & Kester

Published by
Alison Hughes

Published in 2013 by Alison Hughes
1 Says Lane, Langford, North Somerset BS40 5DZ

ISBN: 978-0-9576341-0-7

Cover illustrations by Alison Hughes and Tania Young

ACKNOWLEDGMENTS

To Mark West for his tireless technical help
making this book a reality.
To my husband Tony for his patience and
grammatical advice.
And to my daughter Tania for her help with
the artwork.

PROLOGUE

The year was 1532 and Peter's wife was about to give birth for the fifth time.

Another scream rent through the cottage to where he sat on a log outside the door followed by another. He could stand it no longer.

He pulled his old grey cloak about him and swept off down the lane; walking fast to dispel the anxiety that was burning in his mind and shortly found himself outside the tavern. Automatically he turned in at the door and, unusually for him, went to sit in a corner by himself. He was usually a gregarious man who loved company with a ready wit that could cut like a knife as he suffered fools ungladly. He usually looked on the bright side of life and was seldom down in the dumps. But today his world was full of pain and he found it difficult to deal with.

When Gwen, the barmaid, came to him and asked what he wanted, he barked out,

"Ale!"

She scurried away to get his order.

He sat slumped in the corner, his usually jaunty red felt hat, was rammed down on his head with the pheasant feather hanging unhappily at the side. His once-white shift cuffs poked out from his brown doublet which hung loose from his shoulders. As he pushed his feet forwards the irons on his clogs scraped the stone floor. Gwen arrived with his ale, but, unusually for him, he did not make any remarks about her comely body or slap her plump bottom as she left his drink before him.

He downed it in one gulp and ordered another, then another, but the agonising sounds of childbirth echoed around in his head. How could women go through such pain and still love the baby that was the cause of it?

He was 34 and had lived on the manor all his life. He had three living children and his wife was about to give birth again. He wanted to stay and help her but the women had chased him out and anyway, what use was a man in that situation. So he just sat and tried to drown the sounds that he did not want to hear. He found it much more difficult to bear someone else's pain than his own.

Before he knew what was happening, his head started to swim and he realised that he had not eaten that day. The alcohol had gone straight to his head. He got to his feet and slapped some money into Gwen's waiting hand. His speech slurred and his legs would not walk in a straight line. He staggered home but still he seemed to hear his wife's screams. He stumbled on the road and fell. His leg hurt but he was not sure why. All he wanted to do was sleep and shut out the memory of the last 24 hours.

The next thing he knew it was daylight and there was a bird singing in the hedge nearby. He was cold and damp but the sun was warm on his back. He sat up and rubbed a painful knee. He must have fallen on it the night before. Then he remembered Lydia, his wife, was about to give birth. Was he a father again? He must go home and find out whether it was a boy or a girl. He knew that she was having trouble but she had the women around her and they knew what to do. He had been shut out and told to keep out of the way. He could not remember the night before, he felt as though he had been in a fight. Someone was playing a drum inside his head. He was not used to getting drunk and he had never been as bad as this before. He staggered home.

His cottage had one room and was built of wood and plaster with a thatch roof. The Master could not afford glass for the windows but in the winter cloth was hung across the mullions and it kept out most of the wind but it also kept the smoke in.

When he got to his door he felt a little better. The exercise had done him good.

He was met at the door by one of the women who shook her head sadly. His wife was not there.

"Where be my wife? Where be Lydia?" He demanded.

The maid hung her head, then looked at him with big sad eyes. "They have taken her body to the church," she said.

"Dead?" Peter questered.

"Aye, sir", she answered. Her eyes were red with crying and there were black circles under them as though she had not slept.

"No, it can't be true." He rushed out of the house and ran to the church. Tears blinded his eyes.

There he found Lydia's body laid out. He bent down and kissed her lifeless lips. He could not believe it, but he had to. There she was, in front of his eyes. He rested his head on her chest and sobbed. His heart was broken and his world had come to an end.

A hand rested gently on his shoulder. He looked up and the priest smiled at him. He looked back at Lydia and held both of her cold hands. Mr Medlock pointed to the silver ring on her left hand and said "'Twould be best if thou take that off rather than leave it for the grave robbers."

Peter eased off the ring without difficulty. She had lost weight as well as being so cold that her hand was smaller than when he had put it on all those years ago.

"Why? Why doth God let it happen? She did never harm a living soul. It's not fair. I am never going to trust God again."

"My son, you have the baby to look after." Mr Medlock. The priest was a kindly man and understood grief. Peter had forgotten the baby.

"Was it born alive?" he asked.

"Aye, Maria do have it, for she have milk to feed it." Peter took one last look at Lydia and rushed off to Maria's house to see if anything needed to be done for the baby.

"It be a little girl," said Maria showing her to him. The baby looked very small and wrinkled. "What will be her name?"

Peter considered for a moment then said, "Lydia said that if we had a girl we should call her Peg after her Grandmother and so she must be called." He took some comfort from seeing that her will was done. He felt that he was being torn apart with this great loss.

Over the ensuing weeks Peter's anger against the death of his wife subsided. He gradually got back his sense of humour and began to work with a will with the woodsmen and builders. The baby thrived with Maria who was engaged to look after her. He paid what he could for the care she took of his new daughter.

Peter worked hard during the day and enjoyed his family when he got back to the cottage in the evening, but the nights were lonely and he searched around in his mind for another woman to warm his bed and his heart and mother his children. He could think of no one on the manor who was not already married and who would take on his family. Except perhaps Gera, she was fair of face and motherly. Her man had left to fight in France and not been heard from for a year. Daily she sat beside the log fire with goodwife, Tibia toiling over a large cauldron of seething tallow. The candles they made grew larger with each dipping. Over the fire hung a great cauldron in which cooked the pottage for the group of builders working outside. It was vegetables livened up with herbs from the garden and the occasional hare or pigeon.

Three times a day Peter took logs to the fire to keep it blazing and to exchange glances with Gera. Her soft brown eyes searched into his very soul as their eyes met across the flames in the Great barn where they both ate. On the third day he was to work upon the large oaken timbers that they fashioned into beams to build the cow byre, he took and offered her handfuls of sweet smelling fresh oak chippings, which came from his labours as a joiner.

By chance one chip from his adze formed into a heart shape, and he offered it to Gera, bidding her to place one half of it in the embers of her fire before going to bed. The scent so sweet would scent her hair and clothes and rid her hovel of moths and worms. The other half he bade her place beneath her pillow and she would dream of her true love, if one there be.

Next day in the Great barn he found a shaft of sunshine striking downward to the threshing floor. He took his leather apron from the nail on which he hung it and laid it upon the golden patch on the floor. Dust and insects filled the shaft of light, but as he attempted to pick it up, the patch of light slipped back to the earth. He tried again and this time he raised it to waist level. He held up the golden ring in the direction of Gera. He then asked her approach him as he dare not move in case the spell was broken. She advanced slowly to embrace him - twining her fingers about his neck as she stared unblinking into his eyes and kissed him so tenderly.

He wondered if now was the time to ask her to marry him. It would be good to have her to warm his bed and look after his family.

"Wouldst thou marry me Gera and help me with my family and warm me at night?"

"Nay, Master. I cannot forget my man. He may yet return to me."

She was not prepared to wed another, at least until she was sure she was free. That could be some years. Peter felt sad but they parted good friends.

Peg grew and thrived and joined in the family fun but Peter was lonely at night and continued to look around for a mother for his children.

1 ~ IT ALL STARTED

It was the year of our Lord 1535 when he first saw her gathering wool from the hedges and fences where the sheep had rubbed themselves. But now it was summer and the sheep were shorn and the fleeces were being carded for spinning, there was no need for hedgerow wool gathering.

Mary sat daily carding and spinning with Tilly in the woolshed above the cow-byre and often walked 5 miles a day going back and forth across the wooden floor as they spun the wool on the 'great-wheel'. A wide wooden stairway wound its way up the side of the building and the platform at the top led to open doorway. It was used to store the hay in the winter, but now the shed was nearly empty except for the women spinning the wool.

It was a pleasure for Peter to see both of them walk to and fro across the mullioned window which of course had no glass in it, for the master had barely enough money with which to buy glass for the manor, let alone for his workers in the woolshed. Tilly was short, just five feet tall and only the top of her head peeped above the sill whereas Mary was fully head and shoulders above it and in view to Peter.

As he mowed the grass to make hay in the field below, he made as if to sharpen his scythe

with his stone but was really watching and
admiring the tall dark-haired elegance of Mary as
she peeped out above the half door to take in
some of the summer air. He also admired her as
she walked daily past his cottage, her long blue
skirt sweeping the dew and her old yellow cloak
wrapped around her shoulders for warmth. She
glided by with a gentle air of inner confidence.
Her cottage was further into the village but Peter
always watched her going to work at the manor
and sometimes followed her at a distance up the
lane across the sheepfolds and up to the
woolshed.

He found that his scythe needed a new
handle. This kind of scythe handle took a lot of
bending and so he went off into the coppice to see
Kit. Kit said he would be able to make a new one
but would take three days. At this Peter asked to
borrow one from Kit's brother Mark so he would
able to work and not lose any pay, as 2 pence a
day was a great deal to lose. Peter walked back
towards the hayfield and as he did so, he saw
Mary enter the coppice. He waited on the path
that she would have to use hoping to get a chance
to talk to her.

They were both the same height and age,
bronzed from the years of the open-air life on the
manor. She came back out of the coppice and
walked towards him. A magical aura seemed to
exist between them even from those first close
glances. Peter felt the need to say something but
held back, so unlike him, for he had a sauciness
that won him favour in the tavern as well as with
his work folk. He was hardly ever known to be
downhearted and cheered many a downed soul
with his humour. Like the time when Ben lost his

leg. Peter told him that his two uncles had both come through the last stage of the war in France together, and each had lost a leg - one the right and the other the left one. He told how that at each Lamas fair they both came to the village to buy a pair of shoes between them. It did not cheer Ben much but the rest of the tavern rolled about in fits of laughter.

Peter accompanied Mary as she walked back towards the woolshed. He turned aside into the woods hoping that she would follow him, for he wished to get her on her own where they would not be disturbed, but she did not. She waited for him on the path and when he turned, she pointed out to him that he had unwittingly broken off an orchid. Mary was so sharp of eye and keen not to harm any plant. He said he was sorry that he'd destroyed the flower. As he stood up Peter caught his doublet on a briar bush and tried unsuccessfully to remove it. Mary saw his problem and reached behind him and deftly pulled it aside. Their eyes met, she smiled at him and his heart skipped a beat. He turned to see the briar and plucked a rose from it, took off the thorns and leaves and tucked it down her inviting cleavage. She blushed and thanked him and turned away and they walked to the end of the copse.

Peter stopped at a bush trying to think of a way to get Mary to walk off the path with him. He tried to rub his back where the thorn had been as it tickled but he could not reach the spot. Mary came close and scratched the area between the shoulder blades.

Oh! How it felt.

What bliss.

She hit the spot right first time. It felt so

9

good. How could an itch start such a feeling?

"That feels so good" said Peter "I'll give thee two whole days to stop". Mary said nothing but continued to rub the spot and, taking off her coif, shook her head making the sun dance on her black hair. Vibrations shot hither and thither like sparks from a charcoal fire when it is puffed with bellows. As his arms encircled her waist she seemed to hesitate for a moment and then she put her arms about his neck and hugged him back. He let her go but kept hold of her hand and drew her into the undergrowth. She went with him dragging her feet a little. He pulled her to him and kissed her fiercely. She pulled away from him and said "Treat me gently". He kissed her again more gently this time. The eyes of both of them were closed in a dream of ecstasy. Time stood still and a breeze stirred them to pull apart.

"Oh thou art lovely" said Peter.

"Why should I love thee?" She questered, misunderstanding what he had said. He repeated what he'd said more slowly.

"Oh pardon" she replied and he drew her close again and kissed her until they both grew quite breathless. She turned aside and as he began to speak, she placed a finger to his lips and pointed to the undergrowth where Tilly and a woodman were cutting branches from which to make the 'wicker man' for the summer solstice. It would be burned, as tradition had it, the moment the sun went down. 'Twas, midsummer day.

They moved deeper into the undergrowth.

"I know not why I am doing this with thee Peter" said Mary. She was a married woman and had not considered any other man. She had been very happy with her marriage in spite of the fact that her husband had a liking for the ale house.

"It must be the summer air and country life" said Peter. He sat down and pretended to retie his boot. She sat on the sun-dried grass beside him. When he'd tied up the lace, he gently pushed her backward placing his own felt hat beneath her head as it came down to the ground, lest the thistles should cause her pain. She shifted her position and removed her drop spindle from her waist as it was pressing into Peter as he held her close upon the ground. He smothered her neck, ears and bare shoulders with eager kisses. She remained motionless letting feelings flood over her as life seemed to flow from his very finger tips and mouth. She was uncertain what to do. She should not let this continue but she seemed powerless to stop him. She felt that she should not be there. Her husband would be very angry if he found out.

"I can feel thy heart Peter." She said hoping to break the spell.

"I should hope thou canst, else would I be in very trouble." He replied and then continued to kiss her.

"I beg of thee, make no marks upon my neck with thy mouth lest my husband should see."

"I'd never do that, nor have I ever done so before."

"Oh, so thou hast been at this afore sire?" She questered, mocking him.

"Of a truth I have, canst thou not tell. I do live but for two things. For love and good food are the best things any man could wish for, and if God ever made ought else better, then I do say that he kept it for himself. I'm good at my trade as a cook in the manor kitchens, and I wish only to please thee in any way I am able. The journey in love is better than the arriving, especially when I can give pleasure as well as getting pleasure, Mayhap I can give pleasure as well as get it. They not be at the same time".

She wanted this man but she was already married and had made a vow in church that she would sleep with her husband only. Her husband had recently taken to drinking more than usual and staying out late with the wenches in the tavern. When she complained, he only said that he was fed up with her and that he was going to sell her to whoever would give him a good price. Should she tell Peter what he had said?

"My husband doth say he would sell me" she suddenly blurted out, her face calm one minute and a well of tears and grief the next.

"Sell thee?" Peter questered.

"Aye at the next Michaelmas Fair in September upon the village green" she wailed. She buried her head in his chest and sobbed as if her very heart would break.

"How many childer hast thou borne this man?" Peter asked.

"Three", she sobbed, "I would have as many as ten, but he sayeth if I want more then he has had enough of me and wills to sell me at the fair, as his income would never stand such a sized family."

"My wife did give me four childer" said Peter much concerned and with a tremor in his voice. "I will seek out thy husband and bid for thee afore he goeth to the fair. 'Twill save him the trouble and me some money. I will avoid having to pay the agent at the fair. If thou wilt have me I would wed thee indeed, so with thy three souls and my four we would thus have a goodly family without any more trouble to thy body. My wife did die in child bed these three years since, so this doth make fate to come and save us both".

'Twas a good offer this man did make but she must think about it a little. Mary knew the reputation of this man. She did think that he was a good man at heart but she knew that she would not be the only woman in his life even if he did wed her. She knew his childer and they played games with her own. It would be good for them to live in the same cottage. He had a good wage and as far as she knew did not over indulge in the ale. Her husband seemed determined to sell her and she could do a lot worse than Peter.

"Oh sire, if thou wouldst buy me 'twould be the end of so much grief my house do suffer. When I do attend my husband in the coppice I must wheel his woodworkings to the village for to sell, then when he hath made his sale he do repair to the ale house and becometh drunken. I must then wheel him back home in the barrow."

The sun was fast going down and the evening chorus of birds began - thrushes, doves, blackbirds and the odd chaffinch. The copse grew cool and the cough of a pheasant in the bush beside them told them they had tarried to long. They must be away, as supper would be on the board and if they did not hurry they would go without. The master made sure that the workers on the manor were given some food if they needed it.

A breeze caused them to shiver and pull apart. She stood up and Peter picked off every scrap of grass that had attached itself to her gown. In turn, when he stood, she picked him clean also. With one last deep kiss they walked out of the copse and past the woolshed where

Tilly saw them as they walked together to supper.
She was the soul of discretion as she had also been
in the copse with Peter the year after his wife had
died, and she would keep silent. She had found
herself another man to support her, and she
treasured that new love for him. From supper
Mary and Peter left the manor separately and
went homeward a quarter of a mile apart.

2 ~ THE GREAT STORM

Next day was the village dance and the
burning of the wicker-man at Midsummer Eve. It
was cut short as a great darkness came over the
manor and all but a few revellers made haste for
home as a storm was clearly coming. As they
stood upon the hill overlooking the village a great
play of light came upon the clouds both in sheets
and repeated forks going down the same path in
the sky. Great flashes and rumbles rent the air
and a great wind did rise up rocking the tall oaks
like as to corn within the fields. Many people
were afraid and scuttled to their houses and shut
the doors tight. The priest went straight to the
church and knelt to pray.

On the road to the village Peter saw Mary
with her cloak not about her shoulders, as was
usual, but with an embroidered shawl. He caught
her up and she smiled at him as if she had found
sanctuary. She felt a warmth just from his
presence. They stopped and watched the play of
lights on the blackening clouds, the high gusty
winds blowing their clothes about but they
seemed to be oblivious to it all. He took off his
great cloak and put it about her and they walked
on until she stopped at a tall and stately oak tree
that she had great affection for. She placed her
hands upon its trunk and stood a moment

absorbing the strength of the tree. He shot her a questioning look and she explained that she met her husband on that road and accepted his offer of marriage on that spot.

A few paces on and she stopped again beside an even larger and much older oak, for this was the Great Hollow Tree. There were many legends about this tree and it was spoken of in all the villages round about. It gave shelter to a great many folk from storms and from robbers. It was also an ancient witness to a great many trysts and rituals not the least of which were the losses of virginities. Indeed four sisters with their lovers, all lost theirs on the same night and that was how it was well known to be able to accommodate eight folk at one time - a tight squeeze but true. Mary showed Peter this was where she would like to have lost hers but it did not happen that way. However she still placed her maiden garland inside the hollow tree, but of course it was long ago and the garland had turned to dust. The garlands were offered to the great tree spirit in the hope of fertility and long life. Several coins had been buried in the rich fertile soil inside the hollow tree by the men from these unions, also as a token to the tree spirit.

They left the hollow tree and the first splashes hit them. The wind in the coming storm had begun to tear off branches from the trees in the lane back to the village. Peter picked up a slim whippy branch, wove it into a circle and placed it upon Mary's head. She smiled up at him and tugged his hair. The freshness after so long without rain made them gasp, but it was with joy that they did so as if new life was about to be born. This was to be the grandfather of all storms in many folk's lifetimes. As they passed the paddock a great limb came crashing down breaking the gate and making the horses scatter. The horses screamed like some demented spirits about to leave a body. Hand in hand they hurried on towards the village. The rain came faster as they passed the church. The sky was black as soot now and the flashes continuous.

"Hurry" said Peter, "We might just reach my cottage ere it do come." They walked fast, there seemed no need to run and as the spots turned to a flood they came to Peter's cottage, went in and closed the door behind them.

Peter's dog came to him and licked his hand, gave Mary the once-over then returned to his sack-bed under the chair, curled up, and went to sleep.

"Oh, I'm wetter than I thought" said Mary as she took off her coif and Peter's cloak. She kicked off her wet shoes and luxuriated in the feel of the sheepskin rug that she was standing on. Peter had popped his red felt hat on his chair beside the fire and hung the cloak on the hook behind the door, then put a couple of logs on the dull fire.

"Would you take some mead, Mary?" asked Peter.

"I'm not one for such drinks, and not good with scent and tastes" she said. "But have you a posset of raspberry or perhaps of lemon balm?" He opened a drawer and took out a small wooden box and threw a handful of balm leaves into the pot on the fire where it simmered.

"Rebecca, my daughter, always sees that I have a pot on the fire to come home to. She is a good girl for all her nine summers." He judged the time it should brew and poured the balm posset into a tyg for them both to drink from. He set it down on a crude table made from a couple of split logs.

Mary sat on the floor watching him in the firelight. She carded the sheepskin with her fingers, relaxed, and let out a sigh of comfort as the brew made her feel wonderful.

The fire started to die down so she rose and took up the bellows and began to blow up the embers and put on another log. Peter gazed at her as she swayed to and fro. After a while he came behind her, put his arms around her placing his hands on hers as she pumped at the fire. She gasped as she felt his codpiece nudging between her buttocks.

"Oh Peter" she exclaimed "what are you doing?"

"Just helping to light your fire mistress" he said. She dropped the bellows on her foot, stood up and facing him, encircled his neck with her arms. He pulled her close and pressed his hips hard against her. The storm raged outside. The wind whistled under the door stirring the straw on the floor and the rain beat against the cottage wall and swirled in through the window. Peter let her go and moved a stool away from the window lest it get wet. The fire grew brighter and a golden glow lit up the barely furnished room. She sat on the sheepskin rug while he sat on the low truckle bed, untied his boots and sipped the balm brew as she passed the tyg to him. They gazed at each other for what seemed an eternity, their flickering shadows on the cottage walls. The smell of the rain steaming from their clothes lulled them into a kind of trance. The fire cracked and stirred them from their waking slumber and she shifted round so that her back was between his knees and leaning against the bed rail.

The storm had blown itself out - it must have gone on for about three hours as the first cock had begun to herald the dawn. Mary rose and made towards the door. "I would stay but you know my husband will miss me so I must go now".

"Then take my cloak as the rain is still quite heavy. You can give it me when I see thee at the manor on the morrow."

With this she kissed him and in a moment she had closed the door behind her and was gone. Peter pulled the blanket over him and went straight to sleep.

It seemed he had only just lain down when the door opened again and the morning sunlight streamed in across the floor. It blinded him as he tried to see who had woken him. After all this was the day he went to the kitchen late as he would have to be at the banquet late into the next night. He cursed as he tried to see who it was and could not.

"Oh Peter what have I done?" said Mary, crossing to the bed to calm him.

"Tis well that it is thou that doth waken me Mary, I was to sleep on this morn as I do work late this night at the manor banquet. But feel not that thou hast caused me distress, for thou art ever welcome whatever the time."

"I've returned thy cloak to thee lest thou hast need of it later."

"I thank thee for it." Peter rose quickly to stop her from going out of the cottage feeling badly. "Haste not away Mary, I would that thou dost not feel badly at waking me." He kissed her tenderly on the cheek and she turned to him, flung her arms about his neck and kissed him deeply as she had done the night earlier. With that she turned away and sped up the lane to the manor.

He dressed and followed her half an hour or so later.

After midday lunch had been carved and served, Peter cleaned his knives, sharpened them and put them away ready for the coming banquet in the evening. He washed and gathered cherries, a portingale and some pears, put them into his hip pouch and took a slow walk across the butts where the archers were practising, to the barn and woolshed. First he saw Tilly teaching a maid how to card and spin so he gave each some cherries for which they gave him a kiss by tradition. Tilly winked as she chewed on her cherry. Mary sat at the top of the stairs going up to the woolshed, weaving a braid belt for Jack the bronze founder. He'd asked for one the day before to be made in sombre colours to decorate his new hat. She rose and went off on her way to give it to Jack and appeared to ignore Peter.

She had not really snubbed him but wanted not to make her feelings for him too obvious. When she came back she set up another braid warp in colours that seemed to Peter to be familiar. It was sky blue and grey and had a red thread running down the centre. He asked her what it was for and she just looked him straight in the eye and said - 'Tis for thee. The sky is for the colour of my gown, the grey is thy doublet and the red the felt hat thou dust wear. I have started it as a round one but I like it not and have make it a flat braid for thy waist. I will finish it round so it doth match the other end."

They sat beneath the oak tree in the shade and Peter offered Mary a portingale and a few cherries. She glowed and kissed him and ate the sweet cherries but said that she could not accept such a costly gift as a portingale and bid him return the exotic fruit to his pouch.

It was getting on towards evening when they went inside the woolshed. There was a bed there on the wood floor, where Tilly took the nap she often felt in need of after midday dinner. Mary and Peter both looked at it but both cast its purpose from their minds as there were several maids still spinning even at that late hour, so they would not be alone at all.

The stairs creaked as footsteps were heard coming up to the shed. It was the husband of Mary fresh from the coppice where he had slept all the afternoon from his excesses of the night before. Mary took up a spool of thread and started to wind it around the warping loom ready to be used on the morrow. Peter engaged Jonah in small talk while Mary tended to the threading. It grew dark, the sun was nearly gone and as she could no longer see, Mary wound up the last threads and gathered the spindles and tidied all away.

They went to supper and parted without a word between them save for "Good night". Sadly Peter went slowly back down the lane to the village, bought a loaf and went to his cottage. He had taken out a fresh shirt and apron for the evening's banquet and after a wash at the well put them on and went about his nights duties with a heavy heart.

After midnight he returned to the cottage where a light in the window made him start. Becky had placed a light there to show there had been a visitor who promised to return. Peter went inside and tidied up the room. He was just making up the fire when the door opened and Mary stood in the doorway. She crossed the room in silence to be with him by the fire.

"I'm so sorry I could not bid thee good night earlier, but as thou didst see my husband was there and maids also. I had to keep silent. I must go back to the manor soon with these victuals for they are to fire the potters kiln and stay in vigil there all night. I just had to come to comfort thee for thou were so sad at supper but there was nought that I could do to bid thee cheer. I am so sorry."

"That be the hand of fate" said Peter "but thou didst come when I had need of thee most. Hast thou not slept?"

"No. I did watch these two hours for thy return, that I might come forth to bid thee good night".

She kissed him long and slow.

Then she left the cottage, closed the door behind her and disappeared into the darkness.

3 ~ GLORIOUS AUGUST

Mary called Peter from the field to where she and Tilly sat and worked. He had not been to see them lately. It was a warm August evening and Mary had another braid for Peter that she had worked on when she had finished her day's work. She had woven a message into it that Peter would have the task of deciphering if he was clever enough. She had been to the well and taken a fresh new shift and kirtle with her and changed into it just before she called Peter over. He was hot from hay cutting but she was fresh and clean. Her hair she had garlanded and had the scent of roses about her. When Peter saw her he could do nought but hold her hand gently like a young maiden - she looked so different, so much younger, in fact as he put it "Mary thou dost look like unto thine own daughter." She looked so pure, so virtuous and with her garland and a different bonnet she looked like a bride. Indeed this was her intention.

It had been a glorious day of summer sunshine with work finished to perfection all over the manor. Once the spinners had left the woolshed, Mary had busied herself clearing a path across the floor to the back and laying out two wool sacks.

After the evening meal, Mary motioned Peter to follow her and she led him across the green in

the evening's fading light and up the steps into the
woolshed. She had said nothing to him of her plan
but as she led him across the floor she warned him
to mind his cloak on the spinning wheels lest he
knock them over and they become damaged. The
gnats and dust danced in shafts of late golden
sunshine that streamed in through the windows.
He peered out of the open half door from where
he'd seen Tilly and Mary so many times from the
hayfield. He was unwittingly part of her plan and
followed her dumbly, as he seemed to fall under a
spell. She gave him the braid, a beautiful mix of
autumn colours of leaves and fruit, of the season
on the doorstep of time.

   She was deft with her fingers, could card,
spin, weave and make her own clothes. She was
good with sheep and goats and looked after the
orphan lambs and kids. She helped slaughter and
butcher them for the Manor and cured their skins
for use at home. She had a billy-goat skin on the
floor in her cottage. It was her favourite because
of the long silky hair and a slightly musky odour
that still clung to it. She loved the smell of these
animals and without him knowing it, Peter, after
he had toiled all day, had his own similar air, but
it was exquisitely different, his own attractive
maleness. Oh how she would miss this if ever he
had to leave the manor. If he could change his
trade to work in the coppice and she could join
him there. One of her favourite things was to sit
astride the shave-horse, there to shape green
wood for the lathe. Jonah had gone to work with
the carpenter, and the manor was in need of
another to work the green wood.

   She gazed out of the half door with Peter,
watching the last of the sun's last rays over the

trees. They drank in the sweet smell of the hayfield and that of the pigs in the byre below. He moved around behind her and held her with his arms about her, his chin on her neck and shoulders. He chewed her ears and sucked them making her twitch and shiver as she enjoyed this previously unknown pleasure. His hands loosened her bodice as he cupped each gorgeous breast in turn as he released them from their prison.

Her nipples already stood out and goose pimples showed on her skin. He kissed her shoulders as he kneaded her breasts in a gentle, loving and caring way that she could endure for hours.

She felt his manhood nudge her buttocks and wriggled to get closer to him. The scent of her hair and the garland set his mind reeling and in a fit of passion he tore open his breeches and entered her from behind were they stood at the open half door. In a flash he had spent but she did not suspect and pulled away and taking off her gown and kirtle she pulled him down to the wool sacks. Once again they coupled in a slow rhythm that brought Peter to a near peak. Mary savoured all he did with her and to her, trying all he knew or dreamed up to bring about her zenith. Waves of sensation washed over her and she was lost in a world of passion. Then he found the very centre of her love nest and she threw caution to the wind and let the moment of pure joy run its course through her. She felt at one with this man. She sent up a silent prayer thanking God. The next he knew was that she was silently sobbing against his shoulder in her relief.

"Oh Peter I dared not have asked thee for this

but I needed thee so much about me, in me, and filling me. I must have thee. How can it be that I am able to love two men so different and yet in many ways so alike? Forgive me if I speak selfishly or vainly but I would bear thee a son, the best that has ever been. This I do believe as I do love thee so."

"Mary, thou hast overtaken me long since and I am helpless to have refused thee. How would I do ought else but serve thee as thou wishest? I too care nought that the Manor folk or indeed the world do know of our love. I want thee; I sleep little without a woman beside me, for I am so alone these days. I would have thee in my bed."

"Nay, thou shouldst not say such things," cried Mary. "We must tell no-one of our doings, else there will be talk in the village and it will reflect badly on the childer. They must be able to hold their heads up and not suffer the shame of it."

They lay together fused as one soul for a long time and both nodded off into a light slumber until a cool breeze blew in on them through the half door. He made as if to rise but she sensed it and held him fast, her arms about his neck and her legs hooked over his so he could in no way leave her. Her love passage pulsed and he began to stiffen a third time. Peter laughed and said "how many times would you have me Mary. Dost thou wish that I fill thee to the brim?"

She said nothing but increased the pulse to a rhythm which did bring him to yet another wave of wondrous relief. She was like a fire but his back by the open door was like ice. As he slid from her he said,

"Let me go Mary, for I needs must piss." She reluctantly let him go and he walked out of the woolshed, feeling his way in the dark.

Mary felt suddenly alone.
He had gone.
The darkness weighed heavily about her,
pressing in on her and cloaking her body. It was
as if she was in a grave. Above her was a square
of sky showing through the open half door. It was
like the last thing that she would ever see. She
felt as though the priest was saying the last
service over her and shortly the lid would be put
on the coffin and the soil would be replaced and
she would be all alone in the dark damp earth to
face eternity. A figure blocked out the moonlight
and she closed her eyes waiting for the first shovel
full of earth to fall upon her.

Peter had hurried back into the woolshed,
something was wrong. He could feel Mary calling
to him. She was facing an eternity of loneliness.
What was wrong?
He bent down and kissed her mouth. Her
eyes were shut and she was as cold as death. He
lay down next to her and covered her with his
cloak. She cuddled into him and held him so tight
that it hurt. She clung to him with a desperation
that he had not known before. He could not
understand what had happened. He had only left
her for a minute. He held her to him and
gradually she relaxed and they drifted off into
sleep.
The moon watched over them from the
velvet black sky that was sprinkled with a million
stars.

The piglets grunted as they suckled the sow and disturbed the sleeping couple up aloft. Dawn was breaking and the first birds were just starting their chorus.

Mary rose and shook out her crumpled gown then replaced the wool sacks to their proper place. They picked off the straw from one another and quietly stumbled down the woolshed steps sleepy and tired but satisfied. She had planned it all and taken such care to arrange their tryst and blissfully had obtained all she desired.

Whatever happened between her and Jonah would have to be seen, but at present she was so happy that she was certain she would have the son she desired. So much did she want this man and to have his child, and now she would. Already she was working out in which month he would be born. She even toyed with a name for him. Peterkin was the name that she was sure that Peter would want for him but as she felt that she had conceived in the earliest breath of time, she felt she should call him Adam. She had been into the very Garden of Eden and she was right in between two phases of her moon.

Her mind went back to a time after she first knew him, when, on a gorgeous sunny afternoon, he had led her off the path from the coppice into a glade. She had gone all coy and teased him, as she knew he liked to entice, whereas she liked to tease and tantalise. While they were becoming engrossed with each other they could see people passing by. She would have ignored them but each time Peter was put off and became nervous and indeed irritable.

"Oh, Peter," Mary said in despair. "When a man

would take a maid into the bushes to spoon, he ought well to find a more discreet place." She was laughing at him while he was trying to be serious. He cast about but his search brought them only scratches and rose thorns and they both lost the initial magic of the venture. Disappointed and a bit forlorn they had left the glade and gone back to work their separate ways.

4 ~ KNIFE

It was late, and Peter was exhausted by his night's labour attending the gentry at high board. His thoughts never strayed from the previous two days and the golden glow of Mary. The night of the storm had left memories that nothing now, or in the future could erase.

The cook had stuffed the choice neck of lamb with marjoram, savoury, thyme, and parsley chopped small, and the yolks of two eggs, pepper and salt, stitched closed and boiled in lamb and vegetable broth.

Twice, whilst carving, his knife slipped on the butter sauce that had been poured over the lamb. The first time was when he saw Mary serving at table. She brushed against him and he gashed his hand. She felt as if the knife had run into her own flesh as he did it and it took her great courage not to faint. She turned away as the blood ran from him and ran from the banquet hall for she felt that she had caused it all. He quickly covered it with his apron. No one saw this and he continued carving. The second time, he knocked the lamb off the plate onto the floor making the head steward much enraged. He left the banquet sore but not really having lost face.

He was well thought of as a cook and was rapidly forgiven by the steward. The meat that had fallen onto the floor was no good to eat and it was suggested that Peter should take it home to feed his old dog. He wrapped it in a cloth and made his way up to the stillroom where he found young Pog, still working even at this very late hour. She washed his left hand and applied honey and several mint leaves. She finally bound it with a strip of white cloth.

In two weeks the wound had healed leaving no scar. During this time he was unable to work and, as if a punishment had been put upon him, his youngest daughter, Peg, was found drowned in the manor moat. The simple service in the village chapel brought everyone who Peter knew on the estate to witness the burial of the tiny coffin. Peg had been just three years old.

Mary was disappointed when she did not see Peter at work after the banquet but she was very busy during the next few days as her husband was ill. He was confined to his bed for three days and Mary was forced to go to the coppice and help Kit to make the hurdles and earn enough money for food. When she returned to her work in the woolshed she still did not see Peter. He was not at work in the Kitchen and she did not see him in the hayfield. She asked Tilly if she had seen him. She had not. She asked the folks within the Kitchen and they said that he could not work as he had injured his hand with a knife. Then, when his daughter died, she knew that she must find some way to speak to Peter alone.

Peter returned to work after the two weeks that it took his hand to heal. On the first morning as he left for work he met Mary when she came past his cottage. He did not go out to meet her but literally walked into her as he emerged from his front door. He had made no effort to see her or indeed anyone else. He had been so struck down by Peg's tragic passing and he had been grieving by himself. She had gone frantic worrying and wondering why he had not been around the manor. She had thought that perhaps he did not want to see her anymore. She had not dared call at his cottage for fear of who might be watching but on this particular morning she had decided that she had to know how he felt and what was in his mind.

"Oh, Mary, how wonderful to see thee. I have missed thee so much. I could not work and the space that Peg hath left in my heart has hit me so hard. Please forgive me but I have not hid from thee, I had so great a grief........"

She wished not be seen in the lane talking to him so she swept in through the cottage door past him. He followed her in and the door swung shut behind him. She flung her arms about him and kissed him in that deep way that made him go weak. He clawed her hair and her sensitive back. She nibbled his ears which sent shocks to his brain, whirling, whirling into a misty, dreamy sensuous weakness. As he sank to his knees he pressed his head to her belly and in a trice he was raising her gown to expose her white thighs. She moaned and moved away breathing fast and sat on the bed. He eased apart her legs burying his head between her open thighs. He found the spot with his eager fingers and played with her centre of desire with his tongue - something he had seldom done with his wife before she died. Mary's musky scent put his senses into a further whirl as she clawed his head. She grew breathless and shifted

his head directing him to the exact places she
wished stimulation. She bit her lips and in one big
movement of determination pushed him from her
and stood up.

"Mary what have I done to offend thee" he
questered in dismay.

She said nothing but pulled him up by his arms
and changed places with him so that he sat on the
bed. Facing him she went on her knees between
his legs teased undone his codpiece laces with her
teeth, removed his manhood, kissed its head and
sucked deeply upon it. He looked down and saw
her cheeks hollowed as she sucked and caressed
him, her eyes closed in concentration. She felt a
naughtiness come over her as she teased and
sucked him to a peak of hardness and desire. He
bade her to slow down and even stop while he
composed himself. The pleasure she gave shot up
his spine and thumped him on the back of the
neck. Again and again he had to motion her to
slow down as he neared his coming. She got as
much from giving him pleasure as he did in
receiving it. She remembered how he had smelled
to her what seemed so long ago before Peg died
and he cut his hand. Wood smoke, good honest
sweat and maleness. Oh how she needed all of
these things.

"Peter, do tell me if I do right to thee in my
lovemaking. I do what cometh naturally to me and
copy the caresses by thee of my body. The only
thing I would ask is that thou dost not mark my
body with bruises or bites lest someone should
see."

She rose from kneeling and Peter asked,
"Where dost thou go now Mary?" thinking that she
was once again teasing him to achieve higher

peaks of desire. He thought she'd go full length on the bed but she said no.

"Then where shall we lie - on the ground?"

"Nay Peter, on neither bed nor on the ground."

"Standing up then?" He asked.

"Nay," she said again. Peter was so puzzled that he just stood there kicking off his breeches.

"In this way" She replied, going down on all fours tossing her skirts up about her waist. She lowered her head to her arms. Her breasts touching the sheepskin rug, her arse upward towards him, open, hot and ready for him to enter her. She was so wet and hot and turgid that he found the entrance deep and easy and he gasped as she swallowed him fully up to his throbbing balls. At each thrust Peter made, she moaned quietly in joy as he panted and drove on towards his peak, deriving blissful pleasure from her innermost depths. She used her muscled passage in time with him. He raced up the hill this time with ease but she was still far behind him but catching up. Balanced on one knee he reached forward and down to grasp her aching breasts taking the hard nipples between his middle fingers causing her to crush him within her as he tweaked them. He shuddered as he spent his seed deep inside her and she tried so hard to echo it but not quite. Anyway she had given her all and so had Peter and neither expected more. He slipped away as she rolled over and lay on the rug panting hotly and blushing.

"Oh Mary, that was so good, I feel as if I have run about five miles, but fresh as a daisy."

"'Twas good for me also Peter, I do love thee so much I want to cry, for love's depth and width are so vast for me to enjoy. Each time we make love I enjoy thee, even just thy fingers in my hair, clutching my teats, brushing thy beard over my back, my arms, my ears. Just thy touch doth send me into pimples. When thou dost begin I am powerless to stop thee. I want it to last for ever. If we could just lie and touch I would deem it such pleasure as thou dost when inside me. Thy seed do warm me so when I do feel it rush from thee. I do hope that one day we can wed and I can have a child for thee. Methinks that would be one of the best things that we would do for each other. But I have tarried too long. I am already late for the woolshed and if thou art to go to the field or kitchen we had best part now."

With this she washed herself in his bowl, smoothed her skirts down over her shift and swept out of the door.

Jonah had been busy during a period of being sober and had made a good sale of the master's old furniture and a pair of old ploughing horses at the fair in the market. This had set his stock much higher than it had been for years. He had been just passed off as a local drunk who neglected his wife and children. He had schemes to better himself on the manor. He had served at the banquet, at the Master's bidding, the night Peter had gashed his hand and dropped the meat on the table and then to the floor.

5 ~ BANISHMENT

When Peter returned to work the next day, he was in for the greatest shock of his life. In the great kitchen stood the head cook, the Steward and the Constable.

"Peter Meade," began the Constable, "thou hast been charged with the theft of a joint of meat from the Master's table yester eve. The Master hath said that you will not be taken to a court for the sentence would be, we do know, three years in the jail, and he do wish not to have thee languish in any prison. He hath spoken that thou be banished to the Abbey of St Benet in Broadwells, for the same period. How say you to this charge?"

Peter grasped the table in shock and steadied himself. The kitchen maids burst into tears. The head cook blew her nose and was visibly shaken and also wiped a tear from her face. She was a large woman with a temper but even she was taken aback.

"I be innocent of this charge." said Peter, his voice hardly more than a whisper. "The meat was no good for a man to eat after it had fallen upon the floor into the rushes. Thou knowest the awful mess of the floor at this time of the year, for flies do breed their maggots there, the dogs do dung upon it and men do piss there for want of the jakes. How would I steal the meat for to eat? I have worked hard here these seven years. The meat I did take, aye, but to feed my old dog not to feed myself or my young ones, though God knoweth that they could well do with....."

His words fell on deaf ears as far as the constable was concerned. He had said that he had taken the meat and that was enough. Without another word from the assembled company, Peter was led out to where a tumbrel stood waiting with Daniel, the carter, holding the horse's head. They took him to his cottage where he was allowed to collect what little he owned, what little money had been saved and his old dog. His children knew nothing of his leaving as they were at the woolshed carding wool with Tilly. Mary had run along behind the cart and waited to see what they would do to Peter. They were caring men who seemed to act as if they were playing an unwilling part in the scene. They all knew Peter well and this arrest was so out of character for the players of this macabre tale.

As they came from his cottage Mary stood rooted to the ground, she followed all that went on unable to speak. As Peter was helped up to the back of the cart he had his hands free as he clutched his clothes bundle and the dog's collar. As they moved off Mary found her voice and screamed;

"No........." Her voice tearing her throat as if she were witnessing an execution. Peter heard her and turned to face her. Her white face the picture of misery. He took his eating knife from the scabbard and put it up to his neck.

Again Mary screamed out

"No......" but she need not have worried for

he was not about to seek to end his life but to cut the thong about his neck that held the leather pouch. He hurled it in her direction and it landed at her feet.

"Use this, it be all that I have, for to keep all our childer in food and warmth. Remember me; I love thee with all my h......" His voice trailed off into the distance and if he did say any more she could not hear him.

In the pouch Peter had about two crowns, five groats, a few pennies and the wedding ring taken from his wife's hand after she had died giving birth to Peg. He had not even remembered that it was with the money, and even if he had, he had not the time to tell Mary that she should use it for to sell if they fell on hard times. So much did he have to say but the cart was well out of earshot, and the day was getting greyer by the minute. Rain clouds were gathering and Daniel drove the old horse as fast as he would take them on their way to St. Benets Abbey.

It took nigh on seven days to get there; what with stops for the horse for feed and to be shod when he threw a shoe. Also Daniel had sales to make on the way and Peter helped him unload the carpentry that Jonah had arranged buyers for. What irony, that Peter should even have to handle work that Mary's malevolent husband had made. For he was sure that it was he who had denounced him.

They reached the Abbey at nightfall on a Thursday evening. It was a large grey forbidding building with a high wall running away in each direction. They were met at the door by a young man dressed in a long dark grey habit. The habit had seen better days and was faded in places. He had a leather belt from which hung a pouch and a knife in a leather sheath and he looked at them with a kindly smile on his face and welcomed them in. Daniel handed a paper to the Prior, who was the Abbot's deputy, explaining why Peter had come. They were fed by the brothers and Daniel went on his way.

Peter was seen by the Prior and told what was expected of him as a lay-brother. He was given a cell, a heavy grey woollen habit and some used sandals. He would not have chosen the monastic life but now he had to obey all that he was bidden to do, even to making confession. After confession he was lashed by a fellow brother for the sins he had admitted, in particular those concerning Mary and their lovemaking when she was still wed to another man. Each night he was woken by a brother to attend mass and worked alongside them both in the abbey kitchen and in the fields - not a lot different, he mused, from being on the Manor.

St. Benets in Broadwells got its name from the relics of Saint Benet that were seen to bring back to life a child that had been crushed by a wagon, after the parents had prayed to the Saint. Broadwells was the local name for the expanses of water that flowed from the wells making lakes in the wet season. Fish were in abundance and the area grew many rushes and all the cottages had enough reeds for thatch.

After the day's work had been done, Peter, who was allowed to keep his own name, was befriended by Brother Joseph who was of the same age. Joseph was patient and showed Peter how to care for bees in the Abbey gardens and to make skeps in which to keep them. These were made from straw twisted into a rope and held together with strips of blackberry or bramble stems. This craft Peter picked up very quickly. He also learned how to make mead that the monks drank with their evening meals. Peter slept so soundly after his first taste of mead that he could not be roused from sleep and bore the weals of the lash for days afterwards.

The next that Peter began to learn was, for him, not so easy. He was good at anything with his hands but when it came to writing, he failed miserably at first. Joseph sat with him into the late evening many times and after two weeks he could write his own name and begin to read some of the simplest writings that the monks had shown the town's children. He took courage in both hands and begged that Joseph ask for permission for him to write a letter to Mary to tell her what was happening to him and where he was. He knew she must be beside herself wondering if ever she would see him again. Already he had the semblance of a plan in his mind for getting home. But as fate would have it, each time he thought of it the leering face and coarse laugh of Jonah came into his mind and shut out all positive thoughts. He was convinced that it was he who had been behind his banishment.

The permission was granted for the letter to be written but all would have to be seen by the Prior before it could be taken by any carter to Briarmeade.

His first letter was quite short. It reached Mary and she, of course, was not able read it. She had to find someone to read it to her. She cast around in her mind to try to think of someone who could read it and be trusted not to use the information for any bad purpose. Eventually she thought of Brother John. He was a Friar who lived not far away and was often seen about the Manor helping people with their problems. Indeed Mary had already talked to him about the problems she was having with her husband in the hope that she could find some answers.

She was overjoyed when he said that he would indeed read the letter to her and keep her secret. She had him read it to her five times - she just could not believe that Peter had found the way to get this message written and sent to her.

The children from both Mary's family and his were all living under Mary's roof. Cramped, but just enough room, the children sleeping four to a bed.

Jonah was hardly ever to be seen, on or off the Manor and he seemed to take little interest in either Mary or his children or even the job he was paid for. He was going blind from the pox and had so many falls that he was often covered in bruises. No man laid a hand on him but it often looked as if he had been in fights in the taverns where he spent all of his money.

Mary had found the ring in the pouch and had kept it safe on a thong around her neck. It fitted her perfectly but she would not dare to wear it else she would have to explain to all her friends how she came by such a costly gift. She was trying to build up a good reputation on the Manor so that the children could be proud of at least one parent and so that she could earn enough to feed her growing family. She did not expect, or get, any help from her husband.

With the help of Brother John, Mary answered the letter to Peter and although limited in content the yearnings were as strong as ever.

6 ~ MARY'S STORY

It was September and the Master asked if Mary would accompany the young Master to Broadwells to help him sell the cloth to the merchants. He said that he wanted someone to go who knew how it was made. Mary suspected that it was more to do with her charms and that he wanted her to 'be nice' to the merchant. She reluctantly agreed to go. They would get up very early in the morning and take the fast carriage and be in Broadwells by the next day.

She asked Alys if she would look after the children for her and was ready when the ostler came to collect her.

The drive was rough and bouncy but she tried to keep up a conversation with the young Master to make the time go quicker.

They pulled into a small Inn for the night and had a good meal and were shown to comfortable rooms for the night. The maid woke Mary early in the morning and after a meal of bread and cold mutton and a cup of small-beer they were on their way again.

They were late arriving in Broadwells and the Merchant was not pleased so Mary tried to smile her best for him and tell him all she knew of how the best wool was used and how the cloth was made. She was sent to wait in the carriage whilst the men talked over the money which was to be paid.

When the young Master returned to the carriage he was flushed with success. He leapt into the conveyance. Then he drew the blinds and started fondling her.

She jumped out of the carriage and ran.

She did not know which way she was going she just knew that she had to get away. After she had turned the corner she found that he was not following. She thought that she ought to walk so that she did not attract attention to herself. She had heard stories about the city and how there were a lot of thieves and violent people about and there were indeed a lot of people. They looked strange and spoke in a strange accent.

There were men in dirty rags and children playing with hoops and sticks. There were beggars on the street corners sitting next to piles of rubbish. The centre of the street was running with dark brown liquid which the carriages were splashing up as they dashed past. The occasional large cart would come lumbering past pulled by large heavy horses carrying goods to some warehouse perhaps. Everywhere was noise and bustle.

She walked briskly on, clutching her pouch, in which she had put a penny with which to buy a loaf of bread for her hunger. She had no idea where she was going she just had to get away from the young master.

Someone emptied a pisspot out of an upstairs window just missing her. She looked up and the old woman laughed at her. She looked at the ground and realised that it was covered in filth and, as it had not rained recently, the stench was almost overpowering. The hem of her gown was smeared with 'mud' and her shoes were in a dreadful state. She was lost and did not know what to do. She thought that she ought to try to get back to the stables where the horses were having their rest before the long journey home. Otherwise how else would she get back to Briarmeade Hall? She knew that she would have to ask someone but she was frightened because they would then know that she was a stranger and may take advantage of her or try to rob her.

She could feel the tears pricking behind her eyes but she knew that she must not cry or else she would not be able to see her way and she would show other people how vulnerable she was.

She was tired and did not know which way to turn.

She stumbled on and the houses seemed to crowd in upon her, their upper stories hanging over the street. People shouting foul language at each other. She had never seen so many people at one time and was very frightened. She saw a flight of steps and a sign over the door which looked like an inn. She thought that they might be used to travellers and would direct her to the stables.

She walked up the steps aware of two pairs of eyes on her from people lounging in the doorway.

Were they going to pounce on her?

What would she do if they spoke to her?

She walked up the steps trying to look as though she was used to this sort of thing and had done it many times before and pushed open the door.

There walking towards her was Peter.

She could not believe her eyes.

He looked very different dressed in his monk's garb. She fell into his arms and he caught her hand and made as if to usher her out of the door. She could not face the street again just yet and she just clung to him unable to believe that she had found the sanctuary that she most craved. The tears fell and he held her close until her sobs had subsided. Then he took her hand and led her out into the street and walked with her around the corner and held her again. She could not believe that she had found him, she felt safe and protected from the noise and people of the town.

He asked her if she had eaten and she told him no. He took her hand and led her to a place he knew where they could buy a loaf of bread and some cheese and then took her to the town square where they could sit and eat. She had brought an apple with her and she cut it in half and gave him half. They were sat in a quiet corner where not many folk walked and he kissed her and held her.

The abbey bell tolled for the early evening service and she realised that she had got to find her way home. She did not want to travel with the young master. She was concerned that he might ask for only one room in the inn on the way home. Peter took her to the stables. He knew where the place was and he walked with her and showed her the way. She gave him the bunch of herbs that she carried to ward off the plague.

The carter, Daniel, was there ready to leave. He said he would take her back home if she did not mind the slow journey. The Ostler was there also, harnessing the Master's horses, so Mary told him that she was going to travel with Daniel. Daniel helped Mary aboard and she took her place on the box beside him. They drew out into the road and as she pulled her shawl about her and waved to Peter, she bit on her finger to hold back the tears. She tried so hard to smile at him but it would not come. Her thoughts were so jumbled and soon she was whisked away.

Peter could not make out her face as she looked back again. He waved to her. It seemed as though he felt rain on his hand, but when he looked down it was not rain but his own tears dripping from his beard. He wiped his eyes on his cuff but when he looked again, she was gone. He sank to sit on the stone steps, his head in his hands and sobbed his heart out. His pool of misery had returned.

7 ~ THE APPLE

Peter felt a tug at his sleeve but ignored it as there were so many beggars about the town. The tugs grew more insistent and he raised his head to see who it might be. A child in ragged clothes was pulling at his arm and Peter looked at the pale, dirty face of a small girl.

"Good day," he said, "what is thy name, little one?"

"I be called Meg." Was her answer.

Peter's stomach churned over. She looked so much like his own daughter that had recently drowned and the memory was too raw for him to ignore this beggar. It seemed that everyone he loved was being lost to him. He put his arm around the girl and crushed her to him. She cuddled close and more tears fell from Peter's eyes. Then he caught her shoulders and held her at arm's length and looked at her.

"How many summers dost thou have" he asked.

"Summers?" she questered.

"Aye - how many years since thy birth?"

"I be 5 - I think" she said, "Would'st have an apple sir?" She thrust a bruised red apple into his left hand with her small grubby one.

Peter wanted to thank her but could in no way find his voice. He choked, coughed and muttered his thanks. This was a present indeed from one who had so little. He must be dreaming but the apple in his left hand and the sprig of herbs that Mary had given him still grasped in his right, made him believe what was happening.

"Be this your dog?" asked the small girl. She reached out to pat Rags. Rags looked up at her with his liquid brown eyes and gave her a kiss with his long pink tongue and nuzzled his head into her hand. She put her thin arms around his neck and hugged him and when she let go he lay down heavily on her feet. His long brindled fur warmed her and tickled her legs.

Peter looked at the apple and instead of biting it as usual he cut it across the core making a top and bottom. Why he did this he knew not. He had not done such a thing before. Each half showed as a star at the core and there were three seeds nestling in each star. He gave her the stalk end and bade her hold it steady.

"Wouldst thou like to have a wish?" Peter asked.

"Oh aye" she replied; a smile breaking out on her face and her eyes brightening.

"Thou must know then that each star in the night sky be a fairy that hath died from our lack of care for them when they were upon the earth. But they did good deeds when they lived here and are fixed for ever as jewels into the velvet of the night. Dost thou believe in fairies?" Meg shook her head but had a doubt upon her brow that made Peter continue.

"See this star in each half apple - in there be fairies wishes for us." She gazed in wonder at her apple half as Peter prised up a seed onto the flesh.

49

"Now close thine eyes Meg and wish hard."
When she shut them tightly Peter flicked the seed
away with the point of the knife and told her that
her wish had been taken by the fairy standing at
her feet, and if she believed in him the wish
would come true. She must not tell anyone what
she wished until it came true, so that they too
would believe in fairies.

"Can I open them now?" asked Meg.

"Aye, Meg." he said. She smiled and it seemed
to Peter that the sun came out as she did so.

"Now wish two more times." Peter told her.
"Thou hast two more seeds there to use up and
the fairies at thy feet are waiting." She wished
again, twice more and Peter felt within him that
he could read her mind and what she had asked
for. First she asked for the love of parents,
second she wished for a roof over her head, and
last she desired food.

"I will also make three wishes. Meg." said
Peter for I too have three seeds in my half apple.
He closed his own eyes. He held his breath and
wished so hard his face creased up as if in
torment. Meg saw his grief and held on to one of
his free fingers. His spirits rose and he opened his
eyes. "I must believe - I must believe - I must
believe" he said inwardly to himself and to the
fairies, as they stood around his feet in a ring.

He looked down and saw Meg's small, smooth
hand nestling in his broad rough brown one. He
ate his half of the apple slowly savouring its
juiciness. He made as to adjust his girdle but
could not shake off Meg's grip on him. She stuck
to him like glue. She smiled up at him as they
rose to walk away from the inn, her rosy cheeks
aglow. Her battered hat a little askew over her

matted hair. She looked like both urchin and angel.

This-wise, joined hand in hand, they walked the length of Binstead-in-Broadwells main street to the water trough and fountain, that had been placed there for travellers and their horses to drink. They both drank their fill. Peter took his muckinder from his pocket, wetted it and wiped away some of the grime from Meg's face and hands. She held the sprigs of herbs in one had while the other was washed. Never for an instant letting Peter go lest she lose him forever.

"Where dost thou sleep at night, Meg?"

"Under a tumbrel or carriage, if I cannot get up into the stable. One whole month I did sleep in the stable hayloft. It was grand and sweet and warm till the farrier found me and did turn me out."

"What hast thou eaten of late then?" asked Peter anxious to know about her habits.

"The odd crust, hard and sometimes mouldy. A bit of cheese, the odd egg I do find under a market stall. Apples in the autumn. I get the ague when it be cold."

"Can'st thou remember ought of thy kin, or a bed, or a home life?"

"But a little ...." she began and then Peter felt her go heavy on his arm as she fainted. He caught up the frail bundle of rags like a child's doll. She was still clutching his fingers. He sat down on the worn stone steps of the fountain and gathered her to him and pulled his gown about her. Her shoeless feet were filthy, scratched and thin. Rags licked her face and she revived, her hand held his so tightly the knuckles showed white. Her grip on him reminded him of the leeches that fixed themselves to his arms when he soaked the osiers in the pond. The monks had taught Peter to make fish baskets but first the willow had to be soaked to make it supple. The monks called fish their Friday-meat.

Meg's colour came back and she gazed up at Peter's face. She smiled and nestled in his body warmth and went to sleep. It grew dark and chilling as the sun went down. Peter rose and carried his treasure along Mill Street, where the Abbey had its corn mill, and walked up the Abbey steps to the slype. Brother Benedict and Brother Dominic, the cellarer and trader monks, saw Peter and the bundle. When he showed them what he held so carefully, they motioned him past them. They were good brothers who gave food and drink to the poor and to travellers and also traded with the merchants at the slype.

Peter went to his cell. A small square room with a bed and a rough chair and a low cupboard. The bed was a simple wooden frame with ropes pulled tightly across it and a mattress stuffed with straw. There was a neatly folded blanket on the bed. He told Rags to lie down outside in the place that had been made for him and he laid the child on his bed. He picked up a bowl and went to the lavatorium, took two towels and filled the bowl with fresh clean water. When he returned to the cell, Meg had woken and when she saw him light the candle she flung her arms about his neck and hugged him long and hard. As he had often done before with all his own children, he washed her from head to feet and dried her and combed the tangles out of her yellow hair. He then made some covering for her small thin body from an old gown he had as a spare garment. He took a piece of bread and some cheese from his cupboard and, with a little water, they had their simple supper. He folded the garments that she had been wearing into a bundle and put them under his bed. He blew out the candle and they both fell asleep.

That night brother Joseph did not awaken Peter for he had been primed about Meg's presence by Brother Benedict. They slept on. The deep sleep of innocence, only to be stirred by the morning bell, calling all to service. Peter woke to find Meg curled up in a ball in his lap as he lay on his side, still in a deep sleep. He went to gather her up but changed his mind and slipped from the bed leaving her wrapped in his old habit. She mumbled something about Rags and went on sleeping. After matins had been said, he took bread and water and sat watching the child as she slumbered on. She looked so much like his child that had drowned, but much thinner. His own child had been raised with much love and care after his wife had died in the agony of birthing her. Perhaps this child had been sent for him to love in her stead. He knew that he should not have brought her to his cell but he did not want to be parted from her now.

Then a tap at the door called him back from dreaming. It was Joseph, who had been told of the events of the previous day and had come to see the child. He smiled as he saw Meg asleep and drew forth a jug of milk and some bread, fruit and a hard-boiled egg from beneath his habit. She stirred, yawned, and opened her eyes as the early morning sunlight came through the small window. She started when she saw two monks peering down at her. Joseph placed the food on the bed before her in the small stone cell. Her eyes grew wide.

"Be it for me?" she asked.

"Aye" said Joseph "and for Peter who is thy friend indeed."

She made a grab for the jug of milk but Joseph placed his hand upon hers to steady it and also that he could bless her and say grace for them all. Peter broke off some of the new bread baked that very morning, dipped it in the milk, and gave it to her. She ate like an animal, for that was what she had been the last two years since she had been left as an orphan near the town fountain.

When she slowed down Joseph spoke to Peter and said, "Prior Matthew would see thee in his lodgings with this child for he hath much to say to thee. Fear thou not Peter for 'twas I who did hear thy confession in the box when thou did'st first come to us, and I do mind the woes and story of thy past that thou didst tell. Matthew do know of thy past for I was obliged to tell him as it was my duty. He did speak to me in the Chapter House the next day after thou didst arrive here and he would hear from thine own lips what deeds thou hast done concerning this child."

This said Joseph brought forth also paper from his voluminous sleeve and two candle stubs.

"Thou hast, I feel, great need now for these, and no longer need me to write for thee. Thou hast laboured hard and long to learn to write, now do so with thy heart and may God speed thy words to thy family. Prior Matthew would see thee at noon - may all go well with thee both." Peter pinched his leg for he thought he was still asleep - was this true? He felt no longer one imprisoned in

the Abbey but embraced and comforted by all
about him. He felt a real warmth even to being
overheated and pulled the habit from about his
neck to gain air. During the time they had talked
Meg had demolished almost all of the food save
for a little milk. Peter finished it off. Then she
slipped off the bed and pawed at the closed door
like Rags did.

"What is it Meg, what dost thou wish to do?"
asked Peter.

"I must go" she said.

She became agitated and danced about, but
Peter recognised the signs from his earlier family
life, of a child wanting to relieve herself. Peter
opened the door and led her out to the
necessarium behind the Frater. She tripped over
the rough material of the old habit that he had
put around her. After a few steps she put most of
it behind her and it dragged out like a bride's
train. Peter knew that he would have to get her a
better garment to wear.

"Do not leave me," she wailed as he drew
across the fustian curtain.

"I'll not leave thee Meg for I am here and do
wait for thee." He sat on the stone bench by the
jakes and mused over what today might bring and
his audience with the Prior at midday. He
wondered how he would explain. How and what
would be his punishment for transgressing the
Abbey rules about visitors in the cells? What
penance would he have to endure? His insides
churned over.

Meg's call to him to say that she was ready to
leave the jakes, roused him back to reality. He
took her to wash and then gently led her to the
place where they kept the clothing that the

brothers gave to the poor who had nothing to wear. Brother Clarence, who was in charge, gave him a warm shift and a small gown of sunshine yellow that fitted Meg with a little to spare. She put it on and hugged him in gratitude.

They went through Abbey church and into the grounds in the winter sunshine. She asked, "Why do all these people stand so still and look unhappy?" She pointed at the stone statues that she had never seen anywhere before.

"These be carved in local stone and be the memorials to those people who are to be remembered by us for their good deeds here." The effigies stared down at her tiny form and scared her. She clung tightly to Peter and hid behind his habit. They went back into the church.

"See also these brass plates in the church floor - These too are to remember the folks of the past." Her eyes widened when she saw the coloured glass figures in the great rose window, over the altar. He told her what little he knew of the Saints and he pointed out Adam and Eve in the Garden of Eden.

A cold hand wrapped itself about his heart.

He felt a great crushing in his chest.

He gasped for breath as Mary's face blotted out the great rose window. A voice from within his head said, "Peter, thy son shall be called Adam." Then the fear and pain left him and Mary's face smiled. He became very warm and the face melted away and left just the great rose window with Adam and Eve standing in the beautiful garden.

Meg shook his hand but got no response. She shook it again and called repeatedly "Peter, Peter, Peter wake up." He stared down at her and enquired what was wrong. She held his hand tightly as ever and led him out into the open air.

He showed her where he had made the bee skeps in which the bees were living and the one which he'd made for Rags to sleep in, for he was not allowed inside the cell with his master.

"Tell me about the bees" said Meg.

"If I have good or bad news, I do tell the bees for they do fly unto the ear of God and he hears all that they would tell."

"Are they like the fairies then" She questered, "and my wishes they took from the star in my apple?"

"Aye, Meg, just like that - it be true." He sighed and accepted that she was close to his very soul, closer to him than had been anyone apart from his wife and his small daughter who passed away those two years since. He could not abide the thought that he would leave her in any one's care save Mary's.

Whilst Meg and Peter were in the garden with the beeskeps, Joseph came in haste and found them and bade them hurry to Prior Matthew's lodgings, for noon approached. He showed Peter and Meg both the time on the stone sundial in the grounds by the fishponds and his own one that he carried about with him on a golden chain. The one he carried was a piece of metal, about the size of his thumb, and with it was a short metal rod that fitted into a hole at the top. When held up to the sun it cast a shadow onto a some marks that told the time of day depending on the month of the year. Joseph was never late for the church service if the sun was shining.

It was nearly midday.

8 ~ THE AUDIENCE

As they walked to the lodge Peter remembered that all the time he had been at St. Benets Rags had been with him save for night time when he slept in his straw skep. Meg liked to see Rags. He had licked her cold sore feet the day before when Peter found her, or rather she found Peter. As he sat on the cold stone step he had felt so lonely and she had given him her apple, the only thing she had.

Rags stayed outside but he was old and his body wasted despite Peter's efforts to feed him what little meat he could beg from the kitchens where he worked. Meg patted Rags as they went by his place on their way to the lodge and they both cheered up a little. Rags wagged his small tail and Meg smiled at him. He stood up stiffly and followed them.

"Peter, why hath Rags so small a tail?" Meg questered.

"'Tis because the wind did blow the barn door shut when he was coming through it and it did catch his tail and the end did die and fall off." Peter still remembered the yelp of pain that the new puppy cried as the heavy door had closed on him.

They waited in the porch of the Priors lodge while Peter composed himself and calmed. He

knocked three times as was the custom of friars.
Monks knocked only twice. A rather small, white
haired servant opened the door and motioned
them inside. His blue eyes twinkled and he
showed them to two joint-stools by a great log fire
in the stone hearth. Meg held Peter's hand tightly
for she feared she would be taken from him. She
shook visibly. The man with the blue eyes and
white hair returned and took them into the
private chapel. All was serenely quiet. Meg
fidgeted and could not sit still, so Peter took her
upon his knee where she settled and gazed about
her. She seemed to have revived a great deal
since Peter found her. It must have been that she
had been fed and had proper sleep but how long
that situation would last Peter did not know. The
door latch made them start and in came Prior
Matthew. Peter rose and with Meg both
prostrated themselves on the stone floor before
him.

"Please rise, brother, sister. Do not do so
before me for I am not the Abbot nor would he
have thee do such. I bid thee come to the rail and
kneel for I would bless thee both." Peter knelt
and Meg copied him.

"Oh Lord," he began, "bless these thy children
who seek thy sanctuary and protection within this
Abbey. We give thanks that this little one hath
been saved from the torment of the streets by thy
servant Peter Meade. For he hath shown mercy
and kindness in his deeds in this community of
brothers as much as upon the streets and the
byways of the town. Pray give him the strength to
continue and the wisdom and patience to restore
this little one to good health by thy grace. Amen."

The Prior bade them to rise and they followed

him into the antechamber. The old servant was bidden to bring food for it was five hours since the first food of the day had been eaten by all in the Abbey. The room had oil-lamps and was warmed by a smaller fire in a stone hearth. The Prior lived well but he did have much pressure upon his time and great responsibilities as the deputy of the Abbot. There was always much work to be done and few hands to do it as their numbers had so dwindled after the last attacks of the great sweat.

Peter sat on the stool with Meg upon his knee - 'twas as if she had been glued to him, for even as the food was brought in, she feared they might be parted. She was so thin and weak it would have taken a mere puff of wind to blow her over thought Peter. White manchet bread, wine, cheese, and more milk were set down on the board. Peter had rocked back and forth from paternal habit as the stool stood unevenly on the flagstone floor and Meg had drifted off into yet another sleep. He shook her and she again made a grab for the food even before Matthew could say grace. Peter stayed her hand and after grace had been said, they all ate in silence.

When they had finished Peter was called upon to tell of how he found Meg and what he had done since. All the time Peter was speaking Rags whined outside where he had been left in the porch and his yelps sent an arrow through Peter's heart. He could stand it no longer and begged permission to take him to his cell for shelter even if there was no meat for him. It was Friday and not even a dog was allowed meat, but Peter found a morsel in the rubbish outside the kitchen and gave it to Rags as he took him into his cell. Rags hardly had the energy to chew it but somehow he

moved it about his near toothless mouth and it
went down.

"Oh Rags what am I to do for thee" said Peter.
Rags looked up at him and seemed to know that
the next food might not be seen before tomorrow.
Peter hurried back to the Prior's rooms to finish
his story. The great fireplace was a golden glow
after the lightly falling cold rain outside. At least
if Rags was inside, the poor old dog will have a bit
of comfort, thought Peter. His heart was a
mixture of joy for Meg and despair for poor Rags.
Meg had warmed up and was more perky and
chatted away to Matthew as if they had been old
friends. After Peter came in she said, "How fares
Rags now? Do he sleep in his bed?"

"Aye he do sleep, Dost thou like Rags then
Meg?"

"Aye, that I do, 'cos I mind that at home there
was an old dog like Rags."

"Home? When wast thou at home, Meg?" asked
Matthew.

"I not remember where or when," she said,
"but before my kindred died there was an old dog's
face." She curled up on Peter's lap and closed her
eyes, still, even then, grasping his wrist. He felt
her face with the back of his hand and she was
sweaty and hot and her breathing fast and
shallow. She began to shake and Peter looked
into Matthew's eyes and they both knew what was
happening.

"Peter, methinks she be sick and that if she is
to be saved she must go to the infirmary right
soon." Peter placed his hand upon the Prior's arm
to stay him as he rose.

"Good brother." he began, "before we go I
would ask of thee a great boon."

"What is it Peter? Thou seemest as thou hast a great weight upon thy shoulders and thy mind. Pray do unburden thyself."

"Joseph did tell thee at my first confession all those months ago when first I did come here, not by choice, I did tell that one, Mary, would have me for to wed if she were left widowed or sold by her husband. I must return to her as she be cared for by neighbours in our village and the carter did tell me that she be sick of a fever, and do carry my child within her belly. I crave thine indulgence to leave this Abbey for St. Ruth's chapel-of-the-poor for this be situate but one mile from my village in which do stand the manor of Briarmeade. There, I could be of more use than here, to my own villagers and kinsfolk."

"Peter thou art a good and kindly man that would make a good brother here with thine abilities and deeds, but I see thy request be founded upon the greater need for thee at Briarmeade. Mind thee of what I say. If thou thinkest in thy heart that thou can'st make a little more time here to help in restoring Meg to better health I will release thee as thou dost ask. I would feel that thy Mary be better able to recover than this little one."

"I thank thee Prior Matthew, for we shall all ever be in thy debt."

"Go now Peter to the infirmary and find Brother Luke who will show thee what to do with our herbs and treatments. I see in thy face and eyes much trouble but also the truth that thou dost speak. Brother Luke would know what must be done and will do all to make Meg well. I think the lack of food and warmth for so long hath taken her down as much as the sweat she hath upon her. We be all Benedictines here as thou knowest and work for the good of all who come to seek succour."

This said, Peter carried Meg to Brother Luke on the other side of the Abbey estate, the rain near blinding him but he knew his way. He went in through the large wooden door into the anteroom where Brother Luke met him and took one look at the child and led them into the hall. It was lined with beds on either side. There were three brothers there, sleeping on wooden beds. Meg was laid on a bed with a blanket under her and another over her tiny body.

Peter stayed there on a bench beside Meg four days and nights while Brother Luke and Brother William tended her. Deeply asleep Meg thrashed about in fever burning and shivering. Beef broth was fed to her by Peter and the meat from it - little though there was - Peter gave to Rags.

Peter had gathered some cloths and wetted them to apply hourly to keep Meg's fever down. The herbs did their work and the fever left her. He lost much weight himself and it seemed that as Meg recovered his strength ebbed away. One morning she awoke with the winter sunshine falling on Peter's face as he lay beside her. She said just three words, "Where be Rags?"

Peter could not contain his grief and wept silently into his cuffs which he held over his face, for Rags had passed away that very day. The day that she came back into the world. He said in a hoarse voice, "Rags be asleep Meg." But she guessed somehow that he had not told her the whole truth.

"Tell me true Peter, where be Rags now?"
"He sleepeth in his bed - he be an old dog and

faithful - he be at rest now."

"I feel that he be cold, not just old, Peter." she said tearfully, and a tear fell upon Peter's arm as he held her close.

"He be asleep forever," Peter whispered, "he were ever my good friend."
She nodded and then gave a cry, as Peter slipped to the floor in a faint.
Brother Luke heard her and came, pulled Peter's arm to rouse him where he had passed out and fallen beneath Meg's bed. He had succumbed to the cold and lack of sleep and food. The Benedictine brethren were well versed in care for the sick and poor travellers. Their faith and dedicated service to that community had saved many from the cold of the worst winter's blast for ten years. They were all well versed in curative properties of herbs. Peter was put to bed across the aisle from Meg and was there five days before he came to his senses. By fate, Meg now cared for her saviour, as he had cared for her.

9 ~ THE ACORN

By late October Mary knew that she was with child as three moon phases had passed and she had seen no show of red. She hardly dare tell Tilly in their daily wool spinning but she was so overjoyed that she had to tell someone. In confidence, she imparted the secret to her, and together they both wept holding each other to celebrate the joyous news.

When she heard that there was a messenger going to Broadwells she asked Brother John if he would write another letter to Peter for her. She told him that she was with child and as it was Peter's she thought it was right that he should know. Brother John reluctantly agreed and the letter was written.

Mary knew that it was not her husband's child and he would know, for he had not slept with her for a long time. He did not want any more children and had been very careful to make sure that it was not possible for him to give her any. He spent his time bedding the wenches in the ale house.

She could see a lot of problems ahead.

That the child was Peter's she had no doubt and she wanted to give birth to a healthy child for his sake and to bring it up the best way she knew.

Nothing would be too good for this child. She would need some help. She had friends upon the Manor in whom she could confide and who she knew would help her and stand up for her if Jonah got difficult.

One night at the full moon, she decided that it would be good for her to go and ask the tree spirit for help. She saw to it that the younger children were in bed and asleep and asked the eldest to keep watch. Then she put on her cloak and walked down the lane that lay in the direction away from Briarmeade. When she had walked about one quarter of a mile she turned off the stony way and down a muddy track. The nettles were almost as tall as she was and the trees crowded over her and glowed in the moonlight. She felt as if she was among friends. They were all reaching out to greet her. She went up to one which was her favourite from long ago and touched its bark and quietly let its spirit flow into her. She felt her back strengthen as she drew strength from the spirit of the tree and she sensed that her child was going to be a great man one day.

She walked on and turned off down a small path almost hidden in the undergrowth and came to the hollow tree. She peeped inside, not wanting to disturb anyone else that may have come to ask the tree a favour. There was no one there only a patch of moonlight on the ground and a smell of the timeless forest. The old tree accepted her into it and Mary felt that she was entering the womb of Mother Nature herself. It was almost as if the tree had wrapped its arms around her and made her part of it.

She was warm and safe and happy and she did not have to say what was in her heart because the tree already knew. It had already granted her wish that she might have a happy healthy child and was asking her a favour in return.

At first she did not understand and then she remembered that you cannot listen to trees with your ears but must listen with your heart and soul. She stopped thinking and cleared her mind of all thought and became one with the tree.

Time stood still.

The only sounds were the faint rustle of small animals in the undergrowth and the gentle breeze stirring the yellowing leaves above her. A beetle crawled across the rotting wood by Mary's head and a large garden spider dropped from his web and crawled into a crevice.

Gradually Mary came to know what she must do. She had to take an acorn from the branches of the tree and plant it where it would have a chance to grow into a strong new tree. In the darkness of the woods the acorns did not have a chance to grow into trees because they were shaded out. She had to find somewhere in the sunlight on the edge of the woods and as the tree grew so would her son.

She did not want to leave the comforting presence of the old tree but she knew that she had other children to look after and she must get back to the cottage.

As she walked out of the trunk a branch caught in her hair and on reaching up to disentangle it, she found an acorn hanging on the end of it. She picked it off and put it carefully in her pouch. Tomorrow she would look for a place to plant it where it would be undisturbed and she could look after it. When the boy became big enough, she would tell him of his tree and he would be able to look after it himself.

As she turned onto the lane the moon disappeared behind a cloud and she had not gone very far before a light drizzle began to fall. By the time she got home her cloak was very wet and she was glad that she had been wearing it for she was almost dry underneath.

Becky was a good girl and she had made up the fire and Mary was able to hang her cloak up on a nail to dry. Becky said that the children had been very quiet and all was well. She had also put some water in a pot over the fire and it was hot enough for Mary to make herself a drink before she went to bed.

It was still dark but she could hear the children stirring. It must be morning. She turned over in bed. She thought over the events yesterday . . . The acorn . . . it must be planted, but where?   She must think of a place where it could grow and thrive, where no-one would want to cut it down.   It was difficult to think of a place. . .

Then she remembered that there was an old broken bowl behind the cottage and wondered if she could plant the acorn in it with a bit of earth and let it grow there. Then she could decide later where it could put its roots down, when she could think of a good place or when she had asked if she may plant it in the manor grounds.

She slipped out of bed and felt in her pouch. It was still there nestling in its green cup.

Most seeds needed to be planted in the spring and she was not sure when was the right time to plant an acorn. She decided that it would be good to keep it until the spring and in the meantime she wrapped it in a small piece of cloth and put it in an old cup on a high shelf where it would be out of the way.

Peter was so overcome when he read Mary's letter that he missed Mass and took another lashing but this time he had cause to smile under it. He felt ten feet tall and savoured the name Adam. Even brother Joseph had to say that he was pleased that so much joy was to come for them both, though he too saw troubles ahead.

10 ~ BED CHANGING

It was the time of year when the threshing was done and the Master had all the strong male hands that could be spared to help with the arduous task.

It was also when he gave each of the cottagers who worked for him a load of new straw to renew their bed mattresses. The heavy cloth bags that they slept on would be emptied and refilled with new straw for the coming winter.

Accordingly, one Sunday after church Daniel brought a pile of straw on the cart and left it in a heap outside Mary's cottage. The children tumbled out of the cottage when they saw the golden pile outside and leaped on it.

Aaron, Rob and Nem picked up handfuls and threw it at each other. Then hid in among the straw pretending they had vanished. Alys sat down on the sunny side of the heap and pretended that she was a princess and that this was her throne. Everyone who passed by had to bow and kiss her hand. She imagined a handsome prince who came to claim her for his bride and take her away to his castle on the hill, where she would wear cloth of gold and silver, dripping with jewels. She would have servants to do her bidding and all the food that she could eat.

Aaron stuffed some straw down Alys's neck

and it worked its way down her back and itched.
She jumped up and tried to put some down his
neck and a fight ensued. Kitty intervened. She
had dragged one of the mattresses out of the
cottage and she told Alys and Aaron to empty it.
She went back into the cottage with Rebecca to
fetch the other one from upstairs. Rob got the
small knife out of his pocket and cut the stitching
on the end of the mattress. Nem crawled inside
it, stuck his head out of the end and said that he
was a snail with his house on his back. He put his
arms up like two stalky eyes. Rob patted him and
he withdrew into his shell. Aaron jumped on him
and he squealed and crawled out bringing half of
the old, compacted straw with him. Aaron
crawled in and pulled out the rest.

Alys and Nem picked up the empty bag and
shook it and hung it over a bush to air.

The pile of old straw was carried into the
cottage to spread on the floor so that they could
have warm feet in the winter. Mary had collected
some herbs to strew on the floor also so that the
air in the cottage would smell sweet.

The other mattress came bump, bump, down
the wooden stair and was emptied and hung up as
well. The truckle bed downstairs did not have a
mattress only a heavy cover tucked over a pile of
straw. The straw had worn so thin that Mary
could feel the boards of the bed when she lay on
it. She rolled back the heavy cover and swept the
straw into the floor making sure that the cloth
covered parcel was still safely laid flat on the
wood of the bed. The children brought in armfuls
of the new straw and stacked it up on the bed.
Mary spread it out so that it was of even thickness
all over then reached the heavy cover and pulled

it over the top of the shining heap and tucked it in around the edges.

Aaron jumped on the bed and started to bounce. Nem joined him. Mary told them to get off. She did not want it flattened just yet; anyway she had need of them outside. The mattresses were taken down from the bushes and given a last shake. Mary asked Nem to go inside one of them to tell her if her if there were any holes in it. She fetched her large bone needle and some strong linen thread and a small board of wood.

Nem stuck his finger through a hole. Mary reached inside and gave him the board with instructions to hold it against the hole so that she could sew it. Kitty was doing the same thing with Rob and the other mattress. When the boys could see no other holes and no thin places they crawled out.

Bit by bit the straw was stuffed into the bags. This time Mary encouraged the children to jump on them to make sure they got as much of the straw into each one as possible. Alys was sweeping the upstairs floor of the cottage to get rid of the dust and bugs and mites that inhabited every part of the place. It took four children to pull and push the unwieldy and unwilling palliasses back up the stair and through the hole in the upper floor. Then they were dragged into place ready for the cold nights to come.

For once the children were eager to go to bed. They had barely finished their supper when Rob pretended to yawn and said he was tired and would like to go upstairs. Mary smiled a quiet happy smile. She was glad that she had their company and their love. It was having the family around her that made life worth living. She would see that the boys grew up healthy and strong and were taught a skilled trade so that they could earn a living. She was teaching the girls to be house proud and thrifty and hoping that she would find considerate and skilled husbands for them when the time came. In the meantime every farthing that could be earned was needed to keep the family together.

11 ~ FLAX

The appointed day came. It was fine with an early morning mist heralding a fine day. Mary collected her drop spindle and her cloak and walked down the road to the village. She was going to the house of Mistress Ruth who was to teach her to spin flax. Ruth was an old lady and she had a wealth of knowledge. She was short and wide around the waist. Her gown was usually of a rust colour and her hands were gnarled from long hard hours of work. She had raised many children and looked after the large cottage in which they lived and oft-times helped on the farm as well. She was well known in the village for she taught all the young people how to card, spin and weave. Her cottage was full of the different devices that were used, so that she could show her students all the different possibilities.

Most of the people who went to her were the poor or destitute who did not get any other chance to learn these skills but having learnt them could earn themselves a wage. The parish paid Ruth to teach them and help them to set up a work place. In this way they provided employment for Ruth and work for the poor.

The Master had asked Mary to go to learn to spin the flax so that she could teach other maids on the Manor. For he wanted his workforce to be flexible and to produce all the fabric that they would need to clothe themselves and then he would not have to buy expensive cloth. Mary was a good spinner but spinning flax was very different from spinning wool.

She got there and pushed open the large front door. It creaked on its rusty hinges and she stepped in onto the stone flags. Ruth's cottage had a large high roof built in the shape of an arch. It was very roomy but it was crammed full of looms and spinning wheels of all different shapes and sizes. People had been weaving all sorts of complicated patterns in different kinds of wool on different sizes of loom.

She found that there were two other people there now. They both wanted to learn to spin wool and she was the only one who was learning flax. Ruth first showed them the different kinds of wool and told them how to divide a fleece. Then she showed Mary the raw flax and told that it was called 'line flax' because it was the best kind and that the poorer quality was called tow. Tow had a shorter staple and was quite often tangled.

Ruth put on a dark coloured apron and took a small quantity of flax off the bundle and said that it was called a finger of flax. She tied a braid to one end of it and then tied the braid around her waist. Ruth then sat down on an armless chair and spread her chubby legs wide under her skirt to make a large lap and spread her apron evenly over her knees. On this she spread the fibres in a fine spider's web layer then with her other hand she spread another layer in the opposite direction. She continued until there was no flax left in her hand. She untied it from around her waist and then rested it, apron and all, on the large wooden table whilst she fetched a wooden pole from the corner of the room. The pole had a wooden cage on the top of it. It was called a 'distaff'. Then she rolled the flax spider's web around the distaff and wound the braid around it several times and tied it to hold it in place. Taking a spindle, she expertly spun a fine thread from the bottom of the prepared distaff. Thus the fibres of flax, up to two feet long, were prevented from tangling whilst they are being drawn out to be spun.

Mary knew that she would have to get someone on the manor to make her a distaff. She knew that if Peter had still been there, he would have made her one, for he was good with his hands. She thought she might ask Jonah but he would probably say that he was too busy. Maybe Kit from the coppice or the toymaker would fashion one for her. Maybe she would have a go at making one herself. It should not be too difficult. She would ask Kit if she could use the shave-horse to smooth a piece of wood but first she must learn how to spin.

She took over the distaff and drop spindle from Ruth and tried to make a yarn that looked like Ruth had made it. It went too thin and broke. Then it pulled down too much line from the distaff and got very thick. Ruth explained how the fingers must be kept wet all the time so that the flax could be made supple and the ends could be tucked into the twist. She told Mary that she must never sit by the fire and spin but always stand in a place that was damp or keep wetting her fingers. If linseed was boiled in water, in the same manner as the ostlers did for the horses, it produced a slimy liquid that was good for wetting the hands when spinning.

The maid prepared a hot posset but Mary was too busy trying to tame the recalcitrant line to be able to stop for a drink. It came time to go home and Ruth asked if Mary would like to borrow her distaff to practice with. Mary refused because she thought that she would not be able to carry it home and it looked easy to make. Ruth gave her some flax to take home with her for practice.

Mary gathered up her things and put her sun-coloured cloak about her shoulders. It was beginning to get cold in the evenings now. She trudged home trying to remember all the things she had been told. She went over the lesson in her mind so that she would not forget.

When she got home she found that Kitty, with Becky's help, had tidied up the cottage and put the pottage on to cook. Mary had prepared the food earlier in the day knowing that she would be home late and with so many hungry mouths to feed it took time to cut up all the vegetables. She blessed the children for their thoughtfulness and kindness. The children were getting on together very well and she was happy to have them all around her.

She found that there was only enough bread for them for one meal. That meant that she had to go to the baker to get some more for them to eat in the morning. So when they had finished eating and washed the plates and the children were tucked up in bed, she again put on her cloak and went to the bakery at the manor. She knew that the baker sometimes stayed by his fire after he had finished for the day. It was a place where people gathered in the evening telling stories and drinking homemade beverages. As the evenings progressed tongues got looser and the stories more farfetched. If the baker had any bread left after the day's baking he would sell or barter it to whoever wanted it.

Mary walked wearily up the lane in the dark. She knew the way well and although there was little moonlight she found her way without difficulty. Sure enough there were several people in the bakery and a player had brought his instrument with him so songs were being sung and everyone was getting merry. There was still some bread on the board and Mary went around the back of the people and found the baker and asked if she could have some bread for the children.

The baker looked at her and said that of course she could have some. He gave her the loaf and she wrapped it in a cloth. Then he asked her what was she going to give him for it. She had brought some money with her and she offered it in payment, but the baker refused and said that as it was for the children he would only charge her a kiss. She was not sure that this was a good idea but money might be hard to come by in the winter months to come so she agreed. He gave her a warm hug and a brotherly kiss.

She thanked him for the bread and walked out of the bakery into the dark night. Just as she was leaving the bakery door she tripped over a large log which had been put there to sit on when the sun shone. She fell full length and rolled over. She lay there for a moment trying to gather her wits and then she got up. She heard someone in the bakery say "Someone has fallen". She retrieved the loaf which was undamaged and still wrapped in its cloth and then the baker appeared out through the door to see if she was all right and if he could help.

Mary sat on the log feeling a little shaken but she was not hurt apart from some bruises on her shins. The baker sat next to her and talked in a friendly way for a while until she felt well enough to continue her walk home. She wished with all her heart that it could have been Peter that had sat by her, put an arm around her and comforted her. She got up and thanked the baker again for his friendship gathered her cloak about her and walked, maybe a little unsteadily, home.

By now the moon was floating in a sky full of stars and shedding enough light for her to see her way. She remembered a night like this, not so long ago when she had walked home with Peter and they had marvelled at the lights in the sky. Peter was a good companion and he could always make her laugh.

The next day she went to Kit in the coppice and asked if she could have his help to make herself a distaff. She also asked if he would give Peter a reference and put in a good word for him to the Master. He said that of course he would but did she not realise that the cook, if she was asked, could give a full account of what had happened. Mary had not thought of her. She was a bit of a dragon and all the maids were frightened of her, but Mary knew her to be fair. She resolved to go and see her and ask what could be done.

She had seen several different designs of distaff at Ruth's place and had decided on the lantern shape. It was the one that she thought she would get on with best. Kit said that he already had a shaft that had been made for a broom handle but was not wanted. So Mary shaped two wooden disks, one small, for the top of the lantern shape and the other larger for the bottom. These disks had holes in the middle which fitted over the handle. Then she got some thin laths of wood and fastened them onto the disks and made the outer shape. When she had finished she was quite pleased with the result. It would be very serviceable. She found an old piece of yellow cloth in her work box and made a cover for it so that she could dress the flax on it in an even web.

The next day she went to the woolshed armed with her new distaff and her lightest drop spindle and the flax. She sat on a low stool and made a large lap and repeated the actions that Ruth had showed her, dressed the distaff and started to spin. Gradually her spinning got better and she started to make quite a good thread.

12 ~ LATE NOVEMBER

The day dawned cold and a light drizzle was falling from a grey sky. Mary fed the children and made sure that each one of them had a warm cloak about their shoulders to go about their business. Kitty said that she had left hers in the woolshed the day before and, as it was a half mile to walk for her, Mary lent her own cloak to the child to keep her warm and dry. It dragged on the ground but Kitty could kirtle it up and keep it out of the worst of the mud. Kitty took the little children to the Manor cottage on her way to the woolshed.

Mary tidied her small cottage and put the food ready for the evening. Then she made her way to work. She had left her distaff and flax in the woolshed so that it would be ready for her in the morning.

As she walked to work the drizzle settled on her gown and upon the hairs of the woollen fabric making it look an even mistier blue. It also settled on her coif which was made of white linen. The linen soaked up the moisture and by the time she got to the woolshed her head was wet through. She climbed up the steps and when she got inside she shook the water off her gown and it was, remarkably, hardly wet at all.

Tilly greeted her cheerfully and they both

started work, Tilly was spinning the wool that the girls were carding for her and Mary picked up her distaff. A thought suddenly struck her, rather than have to keep wetting her fingers to spin perhaps she could stand outside in the wet air and let nature do it for her. She picked her distaff out of the hole in the seat where it was usually put, and wondered what to do with it. Holding it in one hand and spinning with the other was very tiring and made her wrist ache in a very short time. She thought of pushing the pole into her belt and holding it that way. This seemed to work very well the weight of it was taken by the belt around her back and she had two hands free to spin with. She walked outside.

The drizzle was still falling and it was just right to keep the flax wet whilst she spun it. The line started to run smoothly and she found that she was making a good thread. She filled the drop spindle and started a new one. Then she heard Tilly calling her from within the woolshed telling her that it was time for pottage and that the cooks below them had called them to come whilst it was still hot. She had not realised that it was that late in the morning. She put down her spinning and took her bowl to collect her food.

It had been Simeon's turn to cook the food that day and Mary was pleased because he was good with the herbs and always came up with a tasty meal. He told her to come and warm herself by the fire and, only when he did this, did she realise how cold she was. As she sat by the fire, she shivered. She huddled closer but she could not get warm. Tilly said that she should not have got so wet but Mary did not mind, she had been wet before.

She could not stay by the fire to continue her work so she went back to the woolshed and started to spin again. As darkness fell she put her distaff and spindle back in its place in the woolshed and walked home. By this time she was shaking so hard that her teeth were chattering and all she could do when she got home was huddle by the fire. When Kitty got home she could see that her mother was not well, so she undressed her out of her wet clothes, wrapped her in a dry blanket and put her to bed. Then she told Alys and Rebecca to get into bed with her and cuddle close to get her warm.

Mary woke next morning with a fever and a deep hacking cough. She was mumbling words that the children could not understand. They were not sure what to do. Their father, as usual, was nowhere to be found so they went to the cottage next door where lived an old friend of Mary's called Maria. She came in and looked at the situation and immediately took charge. She praised the children for what they had done and said that it was exactly right and she made sure that they were fed and sent them off to their usual places of work for the day. Then she put some more wood on the fire and put a palliasse of straw on the floor next to it and bade Mary to lie down and wrap herself up and keep warm. Then she made her a medicinal herbal drink and bade her drink it whilst it was hot. She put some more water on the fire so that Mary could help herself during the day. Mary could do nothing but shiver and shake. She felt too hot by the fire as the fever overtook her but she tried to keep warm as she had been told.

In the middle of the day she thought she saw someone come into the cottage and put a drink in a cup for her and put it to her lips. She fancied that it was Peter and felt his arm about her shoulders and drank gratefully. Then the figure left again and she felt destitute. Mary was on her own in a world full of pain and darkness. Her chest hurt with the coughing and her limbs ached.

Strange pictures were whirling through her mind. Pictures of people being hurt and killed and of children drowning and through it all Peter's hand in hers leading her away from all the misery.

In the evening the children all came home to find that Maria had come and made a meal for them. Their mother was lying by the fire but she did not seem to know who they were. She was tossing and turning and mumbling words incomprehensibly. She did not eat anything and they went to bed worried.

The next day their mother seemed a bit better she woke up and directed them to get their breakfast and go to work saying that she would be all right. Her words were punctuated by a deep hacking cough but the children did as they were told and just as they were leaving Maria came again to see if there was anything that she could do.

She shooed the children off to work and made Mary an infusion of elecampane roots and wild cherry bark to try to help her cough.

On the fourth day Mary woke up before dawn feeling much better. Her head was clearer and she seemed to cough less. She looked out of the window and saw the new moon rising in the west. A tiny crescent floating amid a myriad of twinkling lights. The stars gradually winked out one by one as the sky brightened. It turned from dark blue to light blue and then to gold. The cock was crowing in the farmyard and the birds were singing their late autumn songs. Maybe it was going to be a fine day. She could hear no feet upon the cobbles; it must be a Sunday for no-one was going to work. She put some water in to a pot on the fire and tried to control the deep spasms from her chest that tore at her throat while she waited for the water to boil. She made a tisane in the cup that she always used. She took a sip of the warm comforting liquid and looked out of the window.

The moon had gone and a large black cloud had covered the whole sky. She felt a dampness between her legs and found that she was bleeding. She sat down at once as fear for the unborn child clouded her mind. Babies had been lost before by the mother's illness and this stage in her pregnancy was the most dangerous. Rest and sleep were the only remedies that she knew. But how could she sleep when she had to cough every few minutes. Perhaps it would be better for her to lose this child. It would be one less mouth to feed and maybe she would get another chance to have one last child. But Peter was miles away and he may never come back. She did so want to have a child of his.

No, she must do everything that she could, to keep her baby. The Oak tree had said that he would be a great man. She must do the best she could. She must ask Maria if she knew any herbs that might help. She could not afford to ask a physician to help her, for he would demand so much money that she would not be able to feed the children. She was losing money as it was because she could not work and would have to use the money that Peter had left her.

Maria came in the evening to find Mary propped up on her folded cloak looking very worried. Mary asked her if she knew of any remedy for miscarriage and Maria did not understand at first what she was talking about. Mary had not told her that she was pregnant. When she understood, Maria asked Mary if anyone she knew had the pox. Mary said yes but did not tell Maria who it was.

"Then," said Maria, "you may have some snakeroot among your herbs?"

"Yes I have." Mary was not sure what the connection was.

"Snakeroot is what you need to stop the bleeding and keep your baby. Put the powder in some mead and make it hot if you can and drink a little of that night and morning and all will be well. But you must not get up for several days." Maria went home and Mary clutched at the thought that the herb might save her baby.

She reached for another log to put upon the fire; it was nearly the last one in the pile. The wood store had never been so low, not since she was first married. Something caught her eye! Underneath the log was a small whittled spoon, not yet finished. She picked it up and looked at it and then she remembered, Jonah had started carving it when she was big with her first child. He had meant it as a feeding spoon for the baby and had carved beautiful patterns into the handle. He never finished it because after the baby was born she cried frequently and Jonah had started to spend less and less time at home. Finally he had thrown it into the corner in a rage saying that the child did not deserve anything made for it if it was going to keep making that terrible noise.

That all seemed long ago in the days when they were happy. Jonah was gentle and kind and a good friend. They had worked together on the cottage and made it into a nice home in which to bring up a family. She longed for those happy days when life was good and there seemed to be magic everywhere. Now he seldom came home and when he did he would stagger in and fall on the bed and sleep and when he woke he would leave again, often without a word.

Now it had started to rain. A heavy, steady rain that seemed to have set in for the day. It was dripping off the thatch in a steady curtain and making rivers in the lane. She tried to get up to get some food for the children when they got home from their labours but her legs were weak and would not hold her. She lay back down, defeated.

Late in the afternoon she woke from a fitful sleep to find that the children had returned home and made themselves some supper and were sitting around her looking unhappy.

She asked them what was wrong and they said that there was no more food in the house and that there was no money to buy more. Mary thought of the money that Peter had given her and knew that now was the time to use it. So she bade Becky take some and buy some vegetables for the next few days and also some bread from the baker. Kitty was told that on the morrow she must go and take the older boys and Alys to where the farmer had been digging turnips for the cattle, and ask if they could collect the small and broken ones that were left on the field. The two youngest children she told to go to the coppice and see if they could find some underwood or sticks of firewood to help cook the food.

Next day, when Becky returned with the vegetables she said that she had seen some boys kicking a large white ball around the field and they had told her that it was a fungus that had grown there. Mary asked her if there were any more of them. She said that she was not sure and Mary sent her back to look, telling her that they were eatable and, indeed, very tasty.

Half an hour later Becky came back with a large white ball the size of her head and Mary was delighted. She showed the girls how to peel off the outer skin and slice the giant fungus and then they put it on a griddle iron with a little fat that Mary had in her box and fried it until it was crispy brown on the outside but still white and soft on the inside. A little crusty bread with it and they feasted like kings.

During the next week Mary rested as much as she could. She did not go to work and spent most of the day lying or sitting on the bed. She managed to do some sewing that had been waiting to be done for several weeks. She knew that her gown needed patching on the sleeve seams but often when she got home from work it had been too dark to see to do it. Also she did not have any cloth to do it with. Whilst she was resting she had the idea that the gown could be a little shorter without being indecent and then she could use the hem that she cut off to patch the holes. She also had a shift that had seen better days and the cloth had become so thin that it had torn. In this case she had to cut out a large piece of cloth and replace it. She had some linen in her work box which was large enough to do this.

During this time she had been making herself the herb tea out of the snakeroot and put it in some mead, warmed it and drank it twice a day. She saw no more sign of blood and all was well except that she had a deep cough which she could not shake off.

She gradually got stronger and found that she could do more work each day. The next week she knew that she would have to go back to her spinning because she must earn some money. The money that Peter had let her have was going fast and the winter was yet to come.
The girls brought her some wool and she sat and spun by her fire so she did not have to walk to the woolshed each day. She missed the company of the other people there but at least she could earn some money to help the family. Gradually she got stronger and could keep the house and cook the food as she used to.

13 ~ THE COOK

It was getting near to Christmas and the beasts, that were being fattened for the festivities, were to be slaughtered. Mary was asked if she would help with the butchering of the animals. This she readily agreed to because it was a tradition that anyone who helped was given a piece of meat as a token of appreciation. Mary knew that there was little in the larder to feed the children and on such a special day it would be right to be able to give them something good to eat.

She went up to the manor and into the back kitchen where the carcases were hung on hooks from the ceiling and worked all day. When she had finished she was given a good sized piece of beef. It was one of the poorer cuts and was marbled through with fat but she did not mind. It was a great prize and she considered herself very lucky to have it.

She took it home and put it in a box away from vermin. She put the box in a cold place so that it would keep a while. Then she realised that she did not know how to cook it. She had never had anything like it before. She was looking for an opportunity to talk to the cook, perhaps this was it. She would go the very next day and ask her for her advice and also ask for the truth about

Peter and the stolen meat.

Mary awoke early the next morning and busied herself about the house trying to summon up the courage to put on her cloak and go to face the cook. She was a large person and had the reputation for being very hard and beating the kitchen maids if they made any mistakes. Mary thought that if she went to ask her advice she might be able to get on the right side of the dragon and gain her sympathy.

The walk to the manor seemed very long that day and she felt as though all eyes were on her. She knocked politely on the Kitchen door and asked the maid who answered it if she could see the head cook. The maid disappeared and when she came back she said,

"Come you in. Fortune is with you, Mistress Bett be well tempered this day."

Mary walked across the rush strewn floor skirting the large table in the centre of the room and came to where Bett was stirring something in a large flat pan on the charcoal grill. The smells were delicious even this early in the morning.

"What seek you, Mary?" The cook almost had a jovial look upon her face.

"I pray you advise me?" Mary spoke hesitantly, but she need not have worried. The cook called one of the maids over and bade her keep stirring whilst she talked to Mary. Mary explained that she had been helping with the butchering and had been given a piece of meat for her family but that she had no idea how to cook it and she had come for advice as to what she should do.

Bett said that she thought that the best way of cooking it was to marinade it in best ale or buttermilk for a day or two until it was tender.

Then it would have to be roasted on a spit for three or four hours and basted with a mix of herbs, peppercorns, spices and wine.

Mary sat down on a backstool in the corner and put her head in her hands. The tears fell unbidden from between her fingers. This morning had been just too much for her. She did not understand that cooking meat required so many other ingredients and so many expensive things that she would never be able to buy. So much time and so much fire wood.

Bett put a friendly arm around her. For all her shouting and hard words she had a compassion for someone who was troubled.

"What ails thee, Mary?" She asked.

Mary explained that she had little enough to feed her children and, since she was also taking care of Peter Meade's children, she would not be able to afford the expensive ingredients that Bett had suggested she could use to cook the meat. Bett realised her mistake. She was so used to having all the ingredients that she wanted; she sometimes forgot that the poor could not afford to eat in the same way as the gentry. She knew that Mary was looking after Peter's children and understood that this must put a further drain on her resources.

"Peter took not that meat. It was Jonah, your husband, who told him to take it to feed his dog. Peter did not want to have it without permission and he asked me if it would be all right. I could see no reason why not. It was good for nought else." Bett had answered Mary's unasked question.

"Why did you let them take him away, Bett?" asked Mary.

"It was none of my business and I'm not one

for poking my nose in where it's not asked for."

Mary could see the way of it now. Jonah had tricked Peter into taking the meat only to report him to the constable and get him arrested. Jonah had probably hoped that Peter would be put into prison for a long time. Mary's thoughts wandered back to her present problem.

"Bett, how may I prepare this meat with such as I have?"

Bett's expression softened and she looked thoughtful.

"Tell me what thou hast in store that I may devise what may be used."

Mary thought carefully about her dwindling supplies.

"I have apples left from the old tree in the cottage garden and a few dried blackberries and some herbs. Oh! and some very hard dried plums from yesteryear that I near threw out. I may buy vegetables from the market and bread of the baker."

"If thou dost soak the plums for a goodly time thou wilt likeness for the wine. Thou canst soak the meat in some apple juice and it will tender it for thee. Hast thou a spit whereon to cook it?"

Mary lifted her red eyes and looked into Bett's caring face.
"I have nought but a griddle iron and a pot in which I cook the food for the children." Mary's voice was quiet and despairing.

Bett said, "Thou must send a child out to the coppice and get a green stick as thick as her wrist and put that through the meat and it will not burn through until the meat be done."

Mary was about to leave the kitchen when Bett pressed a cloth package into her hand and pushed her out through the door.

When Mary got back to her cottage she looked into the package and it contained some peppercorns and some spices. She knew not why Bett had been so kind to her but they would have a feast at Christmas.

As for the matter of Peter and the meat she knew what she must do, she had to take her courage in both hands and go and see the Master. He must be told that Peter was innocent. She did not want to get Jonah into trouble but could see no way round it. She rarely saw Jonah now and when she did he barely recognised her. She still loved him but there was very little that she could do for him and all her advances were met with gruff words and dismissals.

So the very next day, before she had time to think too much about it, she went to see the Master. The best time to speak to him was when he had just eaten and was in a good mood. The Gentry were sitting out on the courtyard catching a bit of winter sunshine when Mary walked up to the Hall. She curtsied low and asked if she might have a word with Master Robert. He smiled and asked her how she was getting on with the flax spinning. She answered him that it was going well enough and she had now one of the other maids spinning flax as well. She could see that he was pleased. She went on to explain why she had come to see him and plead Peter Meade's innocence. The Master looked thoughtful and grinned. Then he said that he would look into it and dismissed her.

She could expect no more.

14 ~ JONAH

It was early in January and it had been
freezing hard for a week. At first it was just a
white frost on the ground and on the trees turning
everything white. It was beautiful and the
children went Ooh! and Aah! when they saw it.
They were hoping that it would snow so that they
would be able to throw it at each other and play
at snowmen. It did not snow, only got colder.

Mary hung sackcloth at the windows of the
cottage in order to keep the heat in. Firewood
was already short and the cold weather had
pushed up the price of wood. The children had
gone out and collected as many sticks as they
could find but they did not last long on the fire.

One evening just after she had put the
children to bed, the door of the cottage flew open
and Jonah staggered his way in and fell onto the
bed. He was an awful sight. His clothes were
torn and there was a large bruise appearing on his
forehead. His hair was matted and full of straw
and he had no shoes on his feet.

He curled himself up in a ball and hugged his
knees and shivered. At first Mary did not know
what to do. He was like a stranger to her. Then
he asked for a drink. Mary took him a cup of
water. It was all she had. She was about to make
herself a herb drink and she said that if he would

wait a while she would make him one too. He took the proffered cup and took a sip and then threw it at her swearing that if he had wanted water he would have asked for it.

She could see that he was in a bad way. One side of his face and neck was swollen and his feet were bruised and cut from walking on the frozen ground. She got a blanket and covered him up and warmed some water and rung out a cloth in it and put the warm cloth on his forehead. At first he resented her attentions but after a while he relaxed and let her do as she wished.

She ran her fingers through his hair and combed out some of the mats. Oh! how she had loved this man. She felt so happy to have him home but he was in such a state. She took off his wet clothes and wiped some of the dirt from him. He looked so thin and emaciated. She could remember the time when he could pull a 100lb bow with the best of the archers and score many high scores at the butts. Now he looked as though he had not eaten for a long time. His body was wasted and grey and his hands were covered with an angry rash. She treated the many sores that she found with herbal brew and with a salve that she kept for the many scrapes and scratches that the children seemed able to acquire. Then she put a clean shirt on him and wrapped him in a warm cloak. She laid a blanket over him and he drifted off into a fitful sleep.

Mary sat on the edge of the bed and looked at this man. She could remember when he was good looking with an eye for the girls. Was it her fault as he had always said? Had she been a bad mother and let the children rule her life and ruin his? Perhaps she could have kept them quieter.

Perhaps she should not have expected him to act as a father to them. Maybe she could make amends now. She could tell the children to creep about and not to disturb their father. They were older now and she could tell them not to cry when he was near. She still loved this man and would do anything for him. She would do everything for him.

She did not know where he had been sleeping but he looked as though he had been under the hedgerow or perhaps in the stable with the horses.

He turned in his sleep and mumbled. Mary could not catch all the words but he kept saying her name and something else about far away. Then he flung out an arm and pulled the pillow to him and hugged it and started to cry. He sobbed and choked and tears were streaming down his face. Through his tears Mary heard him say, "I love you Mary. I love you." over and over again. She could not bear it. She lay with him and held him and rocked him in her arms and cried too. Finally they fell asleep together locked in each other's arms.

Mary drifted back to consciousness. It was very dark. The fire was out and it was cold. The children were stirring above. At first she thought that she had had a dream but then she discovered that Jonah was lying beside her still sleeping. She slipped quietly out of bed, lit the fire, put a pan of water on to boil and crept upstairs to the children. She laid her finger on her lips and quietly told them what had happened. She said that they must keep very quiet and talk quietly and go about their work. Mary would stay and look after their father and Kitty must tell Tilly that she would not be in to work today.

She crept back downstairs to see Jonah lying with his eyes wide open on the bed. She was not sure whether he was awake or asleep and she went over to him and put her hand in his. He clutched at it and pulled her to him.

"Be it really you Mary?"

"Aye, My love." She answered. Her pregnancy was beginning to show. She would not be able to keep it a secret much longer. Jonah was too ill to notice and she thought it was not wise to tell him whilst he was in this condition. She would wait until he was better and even then she was not sure how she would tell him. She took his head on her lap and rocked him till he fell asleep again.

Kitty got the breakfast for all of them and then the children went to work as usual.

All that day Jonah hovered between wakefulness and sleep and Mary made him some broth and managed to get him to take a little of it. She sat by his bed and held his hand and loved him. She felt so guilty that he had come to this state. It was all her fault; she should have looked after him better. She should have been more considerate, more loving. She should have followed him to the tavern and persuaded him to come home. She should have joined in more with his friends and been more of a wife to him. Her heart ached but there was nothing she could do now but love him, feed him and keep him warm and hope that she could make him better.

She remembered the time when they first made love together. They were lying together in a field of long grass, near to a large spreading oak tree. The sun was shining and the day was warm. A few fluffy white clouds were floating in the blue. He was kissing her and caressing her. A thrush was singing in the topmost branches of the tree and filling the air with its liquid song.

He lay next to her moulding his body to hers and running his hands up and down her spine and round her buttocks pulling her ever closer to him and sending shivers of delight through her. Then he reached up and undid the lacing of her bodice and kissed her neck and shoulders and down over her chest until he was nuzzling her breast. He kissed and sucked and moulded her, sending shafts of delightful sensation through her body. She lay still not knowing what to do.

He ran a hand down her leg and up under her kirtle, moved her shift aside and caressed her mound. She did not know what he would do next but she was enjoying what he was doing now. He stopped and moved aside and took his breaches off. Mary looked at a him and saw for the first time what an adult man was like. She was surprised that he looked like the pictures that she had seen and like the crude drawings that were sometimes put on walls. His manhood was extended and ready to come into her. He knelt between her legs and rubbed it up and down her legs and up her thighs until he was at her doorway. She lay still, a feeling of anticipation and a longing for something she could not explain.

He slipped into her and moved with gentle rhythmic strokes. It felt wonderful and she lay back as waves of sensation rolled over her. Quickly he was spent and he lay quietly on her savouring his joy in her and his love. For her there was something missing. She wanted more but he had no more to give. His member shrank and slipped out of her. He rolled off her and lay beside her, satisfied. He knew that she had not reached her peak and he slipped a hand down between her legs and found her centre of desire. He rubbed gently in the place that he knew gave the most pleasure.

At first tiny shock waves rushed through her. Then she relaxed and let the sensations take over. She opened her eyes and looked up into the blue sky and it felt as if her soul was leaving her and soaring up past the tree and into the blue yonder. The liquid notes of the bird were all about her as she floated on a cloud of ecstasy.

He felt her body twitch and knew that she had reached her zenith so he lay still and just held her. For what seemed like eternity they lay together both completely satisfied.

This was a memory that Mary treasured and would always remember. Nothing and nobody could take this away from her what ever happened.

During the week that followed his home coming, Jonah lay in bed and did very little but sleep. It was a fitful sleep and was often disturbed by bad dreams and bouts of shouting or crying. Mary stayed with him cuddling him and calming his fears. Trying to get him to take some nourishment and keeping him warm. She did not go to work but stayed with him all the time. The children did what they could and kept as quiet as they could and stayed out of the way. The money that Peter had left for them was almost all spent because the little that Kitty and Becky could earn was not enough to buy the food and the firewood that was necessary.

Jonah condition did not improve. The disease

had got too strong a hold over his body and he had no strength to fight back. Mary tried everything that she could think of but she could only offer him comfort and love.

The next week showed some improvement in his condition. Mary managed to get him to take a little nourishment. He spent a lot of time sleeping and when he woke it was usually the result of some violent dream. He cried a lot and held onto Mary as if she was the only person who could save him. Mary did her best. She sat by him night and day but there was very little she could do. Indeed there was very little anyone could do.

A week later when Mary was getting him some food, he sat up and asked for some ale. Mary said that they had none and Jonah flew into a rage. He said that if he could not get what he wanted in his own home he would have to go elsewhere. He flung a blanket about his shoulders and staggered to his feet. Mary tried to get him back to bed but he pushed her aside and wove a path to the door. His eyesight was not good and he banged the door post on his way out and cursed. The door slammed shut behind him and he was gone.

Mary ran to the door and opened it and called after him, but he did not even turn his head. She watched him go, helpless to do anything. He staggered down the road towards the tavern and blundered into a cart that was taking some hay to the cows in the field. As he fell he hit his head on a stone in the road. Mary rushed to help him but there was nothing that she could do. He tried to say something but the words would not come and he died in her arms. She had not been able to save him. All she had done was to make his last week more comfortable.

The body rolled from her grasp and she rose woodenly and walked through the cold morning to the church. There were things to do, arrangements to be made.

The priest was there lighting the candles in preparation for the early service. He saw her come in through the main door and knew from the look of her and the blood on her apron that there was something seriously wrong. He greeted her kindly and sat down with her. She had not come for confession, he could see that. He knew about her misdemeanours and her pregnancy because she had confessed all to him. She blurted out her message. Jonah was dead and she wanted him to be buried with a proper Christian funeral.

The priest did not know what to say. The man could quite correctly be buried by him but it cost a lot of money and he knew that Mary did not have that sort of money spare. He tried to tell her gently that he did not think that she could afford to have him buried in the churchyard. She put her head in her hands but no tears came. She stood up quietly without a word and left the church.

As she left she looked back at the large wooden door and asked God for some miracle to happen. As she looked she saw the round iron handle that was used to pull the door shut. Then she remembered the silver ring. Peter had given it to her hadn't he? He said that she could use it for anything that was needed. Well this burial was needed. She still had it on a thong around her neck. She turned and walked back into the church. The priest was still there. She took the ring from its hiding place and gave it to him.

"Will this pay for the burial? It was with the money that Peter gave me to help look after his family. Will it be enough to buy a burial for Jonah?"

She looked so earnest and so frail. After some thought he said that it would be enough. She knelt down and began praying and thanking God for the means to send Jonah to the next world with dignity. He left her alone with her God and went to make arrangements to bring the body into the chapel where it could rest until the burial service.

She sat in the church all through the early service and through dinner time. Late in the afternoon when the priest came back to the church she was still there. He put a kindly arm around her shoulders and bade her go home. She was cold and stiff but she swayed to her feet and trudged home as she was bid.

When she got home she sat on the bed and said nothing. She did not cry, she just sat and rocked. The children tried to get her to have something to eat but their words fell on deaf ears. They made a hot drink just as she liked it and put it into her hands. She sipped at it half-heartedly. They did not know what to do so they went to bed quietly and left her to her loneliness.

The next day found Mary still sitting staring into space. The children did not know what to do. There were only a few sticks of firewood in the house and there was little food.

They made a hot drink and went to work hungry. It was a good thing that they were given a meal in the middle of the day. This would sustain them in the harsh conditions. Tilly came to see Mary at noon and made her a hot drink but

Mary only sipped at it and seemed far away. Tilly tried to talk to her but Mary seemed unwilling to reply.

She left to go back to work.

Maria came to the cottage in the evening and made a meal for the children.

Mary just sat.

Maria went to see the priest the next day and asked him if he could do anything to get Mary out of her reverie. He went to visit her and spent a long time talking to her but he failed to convince her that Jonah' death was not her fault. She made confession to him but it did not help. She was lost in a world of black despair which had no bottom. She had no emotion left in her. She could not cry and she could not see any way out.

15 ~ QUICKENING

Peter had a letter, written by the Master of Briarmeade Manor and sent to the Abbot, wherein he told the Abbot that Peter had been pardoned and that the cook had told the truth of the incident with the meat.

Rags had been buried in the abbey grounds by the beeskeps that Peter had made and tended.

After a round of the whole brotherhood, Peter and Meg were bidden a safe journey, given a cloth bag of food and a flask with water and they set out upon their road.

The manor of Briarmeade was 5 days walk away, and the two figures, a friar in his grey habit and a straw haired child with a brown cloak about her shoulders, looked a strange sight in both the lanes and byways. Meg was like a terrier dog, in and out of holes in the hedges, round the trees and gateways. She was constantly asking questions about all the things that she saw and all the plants that grew by the roadside. She never let Peter out of her sight for one minute. She often talked about Rags and said that she missed him, then Peter would give her a hug and she would skip away happy again. Hope was on their lips as the miles meant they were closer to Briarmeade, and Mary and the children.

The pardon was the source of a new future,

but what would Peter do for a place to live? Who was in his cottage? He supposed it had been re-let. The road to Briarmeade was uneventful and they made good time. Once they were helped by a carter who was going past to the next village.

When Peter entered the Manor all was quiet. It was the hour after midday when the workers rested from their labours. He felt that eyes were watching him but he could see no-one. He wandered up to the great house and asked for Robert De Vere Ashton, the master. Peter did not know what to expect and waited with great joy in his heart but great fear in his mind. The Master had great power over his future. He was afraid that he would not let him stay on the Manor but that he would be banished. He might lose contact with his family and worst of all with Mary. He had to find a home for Meg and perhaps lose her too - the child that meant so much to him. The one who had loved him and nursed him and given him joy when life seemed so bleak.

Robert gave Peter a stern lecture, telling him that what he had done was wrong. He told him that he should have asked the steward for the meat and not accepted Jonah's word that it was right, just to ask the cook. So he was going to send Peter on a journey to Ashingham Priory to fetch a bottle of holy water to be placed in the newly built chapel on the Manor of Briarmeade. This pilgrimage was yet another punishment. Oh! That cursed meat, Peter wished that he had never seen, cooked, carved, or even touched the joint. But the Master said that in exchange when he returned he would be allowed to stay on the Manor and would be given work to do.

Shattered from this fresh torment but with a little germ of hope in his heart, Peter trudged away and towards Mary's cottage. Meg never left his side. When they came to the lane Peter felt uncertain. He did not know what sort of welcome he would get?

Would Jonah be waiting for him? Peter sat on a stone by the roadside and looked before him in a blank stare. His well of misery had yet again returned and was about to drown him. How would he make the journey after all the recent past? What would Mary do now? He roused himself and put into order the things that were, to him, the most important. First he must get to speak to Mary and find a home for Meg. Next he must see that Mary was cared for as she was getting bigger with child - his child.

He did not know what Jonah was doing to help her now, nor how he had taken the news of her pregnancy. He must, by now, be able to see that she was with child even if Mary had not told him. Although Jonah was not a violent man, he did have a temper and Peter was imagining that he may have beaten Mary when he found that she had conceived by another.

He must talk to her.

He summoned up some courage and taking Meg's hand they walked wearily up to the cottage. They knocked and after a long wait a very pale Mary opened the door. She asked them in but she was like a shadow of herself, someone with all the cares of life heavy upon her shoulders.
For that was just what she had.
The cottage was untidy and there was very little fire in the hearth, in spite of the cold weather. The firewood pile was small and seemed to consist

mainly of sticks such as the children could gather.
Peter kissed her on the cheek and she did the
same to him, but little of her former fire or life
seemed to exist. Meg held tight onto Peter's leg
and seemed to have a fear of something. Mary
offered them a posset and Peter tried to draw
from her what had occurred since her last letter.
She seemed too tired to do or say much and was
full of melancholy. He wanted so much to cuddle
her but, even when he tried to, she was stiff and
unresponsive. He tried everything he knew to get
through to her but she seemed to have drifted
away from him. Apart from her obvious bulge
about the waist she was thin and looked much
older than she was. It seemed that there was
nothing he could do for her. Was he going to lose
Mary as well? The black despair clutched at his
heart again and the spark of hope, that he could
come back to Briarmeade and live as he had
before, died with it.

"Hast thou money still that I did give thee
Mary?"

"Aye, but little now for the wood and food do
take nigh all we can make from spinning."

"Do the childer help thee?" Questered Peter.

"They do work hard, both at home and in the
woolshed - thine as well as mine."

"Do the childer get on well together?" Peter
wanted to know all but Mary seemed not to want
to talk.

"Aye. Though we are cramped and they do
sleep four to a bed, they do fare well enough."

Silence descended in the small cottage which
had once been full of fun, laughter and warmth.
Peter wanted to ask about Jonah but he did not
really want to hear the answer. Mary did not

seem to be ill she had just drifted off into a melancholy world of her own where she could not be reached.

Was it Jonah' fault?

What had he done to her?

Should Peter ask?

She did not seem to want to tell him.

Meg clung tighter to Peter's leg and whimpered. She did not like this cold, unhappy woman and was frightened that Peter would leave her there.

Peter did not know what to do. He could not stay and help as he had hoped. He would just have to explain to Mary what had occurred and hope that she could understand his feelings.

"Would that I could stay and help thee to earn more. I would also work to stand by thee and supply thy needs but I am not yet ended my tasks for the master. He do send me away again. For he doth tell me that although I be pardoned I must still perform one more punishment for that cursed meat. I have to go to Ashingham Priory for some holy water for his new chapel. As a friar of St. Francis, I must do this before I be allowed to remain at Briarmeade. Oh! I wish so much that I could find a way to get out of this task, but I have to do this. Mary I beg thee, stay strong for our childer and our new son for I will do the task and will return to thee. On the morrow I will ask the steward if there be any way to resolve the matter but I do know in my heart that I alone must do what I am bid, or I shall never be permitted to live here again."

Mary would normally have burst into tears, but she had no tears in her head. Life had drained all grief from her and she took life with a

numbness that made even her children almost
strangers to her.

Meg was the one to cry.

She expected so much to be ready to start a
new chapter in her small life, but it was not to be.
Her saviour, Peter, had to go on still more physical
torment as well as mental agonies. She sobbed
for Peter to cuddle her as Mary just sat by the fire
drained of all emotion.

Peter saw that there was nought that could
be done or said to change matters, so he kissed
Mary as she sat there, pressed her shoulders
warmly and went out of the door with no more
words said between them. Outside he leaned on
the door post and just sobbed his heart out,
banging his head on it - he felt so rejected. Meg
hugged his legs and tried in her own small way to
comfort him. He seemed to have no choice but to
take her with him. He bent down and scooped her
up into his arms and walked quickly away from the
cottage. Then he hesitated, put Meg down, ran
back and tucked his pouch under the door. He
turned back to Meg and they carried on their
journey. Now they had not a penny in the world.
At the Manor gate there were only beggars to see
them leave as they walked sadly away.

Mary's face ashen and drawn kept coming
before him and it tormented him that he was
powerless to comfort her, to hold her, to feel his
son move inside her. He felt that he should be
lying beside her in bed each night. Oh! why was
life so cruel to them? She was now nearly six
months in her pregnancy and he should be there
but fate had other plans for him.

Mary watched him leave and through the veil

of depression something of her left with him. A little hope had entered her heart when he had come in through the door but she was unable to respond even to him. She had her husband's death upon her conscience. She felt that it was all her fault that he had died and that there was now nothing that she could do to make amends. She sat down again. The fire was getting low and she put a few sticks onto it to try to get a little warmth into her aching bones. As she leant forward Adam gave her a kick. She straightened up in surprise and he kicked again. She had forgotten that she had another life to look after. She had only been thinking about herself. Some of Peter's words filtered through the mists of depression. What was it he had said?

"Stay strong for our childer ...... and our new son."

Our new son!

She was carrying a child that was part of Peter. She would not lose the man that she loved completely. She had part of him inside her. She must look after this baby and even if Peter never came back she would have part of him to look after and nurture.

Jonah was dead.

There was nothing that she could do for him. Now she must look after the living and the growing baby within her.

She stood up and suddenly realised how weak her legs were. She looked in the food box to get something ready for the children when they got home from work and found very little food there. There were a few turnips that the children had gleaned from the fields and a few dried herbs. There was half a loaf of stale bread and a small piece of mouldy cheese. She went to the water bucket and broke a piece of ice from the top of it and set it in a pot over the fire. She prepared some of the turnips and added them with a few herbs for flavouring. It was not much but it would have to do. Maybe she would toast the bread and they could share it.

When the children came home they saw the change in their mother immediately. She gave them a slow smile and when they hugged her, she hugged them back. It was a change to come home and find a fire in the hearth and some food cooking.

Aaron was dragging behind as usual but as he came through the door he bent to pick up something and then called to his big sister to come and see what he had found. Kitty took it from him and went to Mary to ask what she should do with this money that seemed to have landed on their doorstep. Mary recognised the pouch as the one that Peter had been wearing when he came to see her and knew that he had left the money to help her and the children. She would use it to buy some food and some wood to keep them warm.

The next morning when the children had all gone to work Mary sat by the fire wondering what she should do. Her world seemed so full of grief and heartbreak. She started to cry quietly at the blackness of it all. Gradually the tears fell faster until she was sobbing like a child who had just lost her first puppy.

The tears began to subside and she felt a little better but the world still looked very bleak. She seemed to be losing every man that she loved.

Then she felt the infant within her move again. A tiny leg pushed at her telling her that she must bestir herself. She knew that she must feed the baby that was growing within her. She looked around the cottage as if she was seeing it for the first time. There was very little wood and the fire was low. There was even less food in the box. She knew that she had to go to work to earn some money in order to buy food for the growing baby. That which Peter had left her would not last long.

She stood up and wrapped her cloak around her shoulders and staggered to the cottage door. She had not realised how weak she had become. She leaned on the door post for support and braced herself to meet the icy blast of the north wind. She opened the door and an eddy of wind brought a drift of snow into the floor. She dragged herself through the door and fastened it behind her, leant into the wind and walked to the woolshed.

Tilly greeted her and bade her sit down and brought her a hot drink. Christy, the maid that Mary had taught to spin flax, was using Mary's distaff and making a good thread. Tilly said that Mary must spin the wool today for they had need of it. Mary knew she could spin sitting down and indeed did not think that her legs would carry her another step.

At the end of the day Tilly said that she would walk home with Mary and make sure that she got there safely. She suggested that Mary should take some fleece to her cottage and spin by her fire where she could keep warm. It would be easier for her than having to walk through the bad weather each day.

16 ~ A NIGHT AT THE SWAN INN

Meg and Peter had two days when they had found nowhere dry to sleep and the rain had dripped down on them from the trees. They were both cold and tired. They trudged along dragging their feet and when they came to yet another stile Peter did not think that Meg would have the strength to climb it and he did not think that he would have the strength to lift her over. But fortune did indeed smile upon them. As he bent down to pick her up he found a small leather pouch in the mud beside the gatepost. There was no mark upon it to show who it had belonged to and in it was a half crown and three groats.

As they plodded on along a rutted lane, Peter wondered who had lost the money and what he should do with it. By the time they came to a small hamlet he had decided that he should use it to buy a good meal and a bed for the night. There was an inn in the village with a sign outside, with the picture of a swan on it. Underneath were the words 'THE SWAN'. Peter realised that not only could he understand the picture but he could also read the words. It was a wonderful gift that the monks had given him.

The innkeeper was a large red faced man wearing a dirty white apron. He was a bit drunk but when he saw that they had money he took them in and after a good meal of mutton, root vegetables and mulled ale, they settled by the fire.

There was a long table on one side of the room with benches at either side where travellers sat to eat and at the other side was a large fireplace with a roaring log fire. Another bench was near the fire and a few backstools to sit upon.

There were two other groups of travellers at the inn. At one end of the table sat two drovers drinking large quantities of ale and talking in loud voices. There was also a widow with a younger woman who could have been her daughter. The two women ate a good meal and then went up to their room. There was a small ragged boy strewing some more straw on the floor and there was a comely wench of about 30 clearing the table and tidying up the remains of the meals. Peter thought she was probably the innkeeper's daughter. She hovered near to him and removed imaginary spider webs from the shelf above him.

Meg saw nothing except the Inn's long legged, white dog in the corner by the bar counter. She went over to it and it licked her hand, wagged its tail and followed her back to Peter. The young woman still hung about their area seeming to entice Peter to look at her. Peter was wearing his grey friar's habit and she seemed uncertain as to whether she should talk to him or not.

As she reached about she brushed his arm with her hips and he saw those ripe firm breasts against her partlet. He could no more ignore her than could a dog could ignore a gate-post. She was fresh and clean, her grass green gown had the scent of lavender as if just taken from a linen chest. She wore a white apron and a white linen

115

coif on her head and used a goose-feather duster
along the carved wooden panels beside the fire.
Her body scent too was so appealing that Peter
drank it all in like a good ale. She stood in front
of him and picked up the duster she'd dropped
deliberately at his feet. Again Peter could not
help but see the gentle quivering of her teats as
they hung in her bodice. He shifted on his chair
and got more comfortable though heaven knows it
was not to relieve his arse on the hard seat but
the hardness in his loins. She saw that he was
getting uneasy and roused as his breathing
deepened and his nostrils flared. He gripped the
sides of the backstool making the knuckles go
white. She walked away from him, duster in
hand, her firm hips rolling and swaying, like a sack
of grain on a miller's shoulders.

Meg played with the dog as Peter rose to go
and order some more ale from the counter. The
wench was called Ruth, as he heard her answer
the Innkeeper, when he called her to serve a man
at the table by the door. She drew a tankard off
the barrel bending away from Peter displaying a
beautiful rounded bottom that left little to his
imagination. She took it to the customer and
returned to where Peter was waiting for the ale
and she leaned forward on her elbows awaiting his
order. Oh, how he would like to plunge his face
between those globes of soft delight, those
gorgeous fruits which she shook before his eyes.
Poor Peter, how could he hold back any longer?
She was firm, about his height, almost his age he
guessed and obviously in the market for what
Peter most needed right there and then.

"What room do I have for the night?" he asked.

Ruth said, with a twinkle in her eyes, "I'll

show thee Sir, when thou art ready to go to bed."

Those velvet brown eyes set between long dark lashes. He always went a little woozy when he looked into brown eyes. They were not as dark as her hair which came below her shoulders in waves and curls. There seemed to be something about her that told him she had foreign blood in her veins. When she spoke her full cherry-red lips showed teeth that had been cared for from youth. Often folk would clean them by chewing the end of a twig and using it like a brush. Willow stalks and leaves were also chewed to cure toothache and the diet of ordinary folk was much better than that of the Gentry who ate many sweetmeats and white manchet bread. Peter forgot about the jug of ale and yawned falsely.

"Meg" he called "I shall find my room now, it be time thou wast abed also."

"Can I not stay with the dog, I be not sleepy yet. I shall find me somewhere to lie down when I be tired enough - maybe outside thy door."

"Why outside the door? Thou wilt get cold again. I have paid for thy bed, now go......"

Ruth cut in. "I will find the child a mattress that she may lie beside the fire and sleep with the dog if she do wish."

"Oh please may I?" Meg was not used to beds and she did not want to sleep on her own.

"I give thee thanks, Ruth. That would be well" Peter said. Ruth disappeared upstairs only to reappear a few moments later carrying a straw mattress. Peter moved a backstool and a bench to make room for Meg to sleep near the fire. They put the mattress on the floor near the wall and Meg sat down on it and the dog joined her. She smiled up happily at the two watching her and they knew that she would be content to sleep when she got tired.

"Sleep well, my daughter, and may God watch over you."

With this he followed Ruth up the creaking stairs on to the landing. The lantern light flickered across several doors that he assumed led to guest rooms. Ruth opened one of them and hung the horn lantern from the hook on the low beam. She lit a candle from it and placed this on the dresser under the window and drew the curtains. Peter sat in an armchair and watched her gliding about the room.

He sat like a monarch on a throne, his hands draped on the arms of the oaken chair. The room was sparsely furnished. It had a large bed covered with warm blankets and pillows with white covers on them. The dresser was a rough table, its top worn shiny from much use. It had a jug and wash basin on it and some other things that Peter could not make out. There was some clothing hanging on the wall and a rug on the floor by the bed. Over all there was a faint smell of lavender mixed with other herbs and the wood smoke from the fire below.

Ruth poured out water from a jug into a basin and carried it across the room to beside Peter's chair. She handed him a soap-ball and he washed his face and hands in the cool fresh water. It felt so good. There was a hint of herbs in the water. He thought it came from the soap-ball. He smelled the soap.

"Dost thou like the soap-ball Sir?" She asked in a lilting voice that had a sort of sing-song tone.

"Aye I like it right well Ruth, but do call me Peter. Dost thou make them?"

"Aye, Sir - Peter. I have made them for years from when I was a young girl at my Mother's knee. They be made from wood ash from our hearth, fat, bran and the many herbs we do grow in our garden. This I do sell to the travellers to make me some money in the hope that I may marry and have some dowry. For I be over 30 now and though I have tried no man hath yet come to this Inn that I would wish to live with."

She took a cloth and a small rag from the dresser, took off Peter's sandals and washed his aching feet. He felt like a King.

"But why be there woman's clothing hanging on the hooks on that wall?" Peter asked, "Be this not a room for travellers?"

Ruth crossed the floor and slid the door bolt across - "Nay Peter this be MY room." He made to rise but she placed a hand on his arm, bending low and letting her bodice bulge open displaying its rounded contents. He could resist no longer. He pulled her on to his lap. With his left hand he pulled undone the laces as he kissed her head. His right hand fondled her ears and then came to rest on those cool white mounds of glorious human marble. Little blue veins traced their symmetry just like a statue in the abbey church he had seen so long ago. He thought he must be dreaming but Ruth made sure that he was fully awake. She tasted so good, smelled so sweet and felt so pliable. He took hold of his feelings and curbed his desire so as not to rush things as he had so often done in his youth, putting the wenches off. His heart pounded and she knew it. Her breath came in little shallow gasps as he tweaked her erect pink nipples. They were still pink, so he guessed that either she was still a virgin or she had avoided pregnancy somehow.

She had not avoided it, as she had taken many lads to bed; it was that she was barren. Ruth wanted children more than anything as she had been one of only two children. Her brother was given every choice and favour because he was his parents pride and joy. She was kept as a nurse for her mother when she was ill but left too long, like a plant that had been given no nourishment. She had seen her early years of youth slip away. This man who seemed so lowly but was so attractive to her, could he be the answer to her needs?

After so many months at St Benets in enforced celibacy, and on the road with little Meg in his care, he so longed for Mary that this goodly woman must have been sent to him to stop him going mad. He was just flesh and blood like any other healthy man.

She rose from his lap, his eyes following her as she walked to stand between the lantern and the candlestick, lighting herself like an actress in a play upon the stage. She hummed a folksong about "Poor Robin" and swayed to the rhythm. As she swayed Peter felt the need to join in and got to his feet, their heads only just missing the low beams. As she swayed and hummed she slowly peeled off her clothes until, in three movements, she stood and swayed naked as Eve in the candlelight before the man of her desires. She came to him, blew in his ear and poked her tongue into it and made him squirm. She kissed him full on the mouth, hers open and inviting. Each tongue wrestled for supremacy. Neither won. Loosing his girdle rope he helped her to tug off his habit and cowl which they cast readily on the floor. He spun her around to face away from him, his hand caressing her teats. Taking the stiff nipples between his fingers to roll them until she could stand it no longer.

She reached behind her and took his stiff manhood in her hand moulding it, running her hands up and down its length, and kneaded it to a peak of hardness. His hands slid down her plump belly. Oh how Peter loved a belly on a woman - none of this bony hollow hipped type for him. He liked to get hold of something. His hands teased her slowly as they wrote tiny circles, gradually sinking down to land on her thighs - not her mound or crease like the eager lads did, but like a real man who understood that a woman liked to have the feelings eased from her, like a musician playing an instrument, with delicacy and finesse. She wanted him to rush but she also wanted him to bring her on slowly. As her nipples grew tingling again she took his hands and placed them on her breasts and as he touched them with tenderness she threw back her head in ecstasy banging Peter on the cheekbone.

This time she turned to face him, she pulled his head down to her breasts and made him take them fully into his mouth, pulsing, sucking, teasing, until she felt her love-nest run with moisture. It trickled down her inner thighs. He licked each nipple then blew on them with cold air giving Ruth even more to cope with.

They both bent down together colliding faces as he went to stroke her calves and knees and she to kiss his manhood. He let her win and as they stood up again they wrapped their arms about each other and just stood moulded together. They were still humming. She rose up on her toes to try and get him to enter her standing up, but to her surprise, he held her off. He was ready and oozed as she did but he wanted to give her pleasure before the journey ended. He did not want a quick knee trembler. She held his head as he lifted her and placed her gently on the bed face down.

"Why face down?" she asked Peter. He remained silent and straddled her hips placing his warm hands on her shoulders and began kneading the flesh under his fingers. She wilted and melted as he sent waves of power through her upper body. She became clay in his hands. He continued along her arms, elbows, wrists, fingers, spine and bottom. As he came to her arse he pressed down slightly causing her to open a little and ooze more moisture. He was pressing, rubbing, touching, walking on her body like a big butterfly and she loved every bit of it.

Then he reached over to the dresser and picked up the feather duster from where she had put it and ran the feathers up and down her spine. This was a new sensation that she had not felt before. Whereas his hands had touched every part of her, the feathers touched a wide area all at once and made the nerves in the surface of her skin tingle and cause little goose pimples to appear under the long sweeping strokes of the feathers.

She turned sideways to breathe deeper and he saw how flushed her face had become. He lay full length upon her and kissed her ears and neck and shoulders, his hardness lying throbbing in her arse-crease.

He went backwards and playfully tidied her hair with her hairbrush, then, to her surprise he went down her back with it which caused her near convulsions as she was so sensitive there. His hands smoothed the skin and kneaded the flesh of her buttocks, her knees, but she jumped up and turned over grasping his head and wildly ordering his face to her mound. He saw that this was not the dark brown of her head but like spun gold as his was. He found her scent irresistible and traced her outer then inner lips with his fingers then with his tongue. She heaved upwards to meet his face that ploughed into her and she moaned, grunted and gasped as she neared her peak. Ruth then surprised Peter. She swivelled round beneath him bringing her head to his stiffness and his face to her love-nest so they were head to tail. Peter felt the tell-tale tingle in his back as they both used their mouths to stimulate each other and as it had advanced too far he rose quickly, placed his arms beside her head as she guided him into her hot turgid moistness. They lay motionless for quite a while as they were both on the cliff-edge.

She was the first to move - a fluttering in her inner depths of her love-nest. The flutter grew too a pulse and then to a squeezing action which they both enhanced by a slow rhythm, Peter felt the nerves of his pelvis becoming too great to endure. His spine flexed in jerks and his nostrils flared. Again his heart pounded so loudly he thought it might burst from his body. How long would they keep this going he thought?

Finally using her love muscles like the hands of a milk-maid, Ruth rippled inside and they both burst in a cloud of misty delight, spurting, pulsing, pushing and sucking. Their panting echoed around the room. The lantern had gone out and the candle in the window fluttered and died in the draught from the cracked windowpane.

They rested together, two hearts beating as one. He rolled off her and she reached a blanket and put it over them both. She lay next to him with her warm back against his chest and snuggled closer. They fitted, like two matching spoons in a box. He put his arm round her, held her close and nestled his face into the fragrant softness of her hair. Thus entwined in a golden glow of happiness they drifted off into sleep.

Peter awoke feeling pleasantly warm and rested, his back and shoulders told him how much effort he'd put into making love with Ruth. The bed was empty beside him but he saw the hairbrush on the table with some long brown hairs on it. No, he had not dreamed it all, the lantern had gone out but the stub of candle in the window candlestick was still there to remind him of how much Ruth had tried to please him.

Mayhap she had ideas to keep him and get him to wed her.

She was lonely and had tried to get herself pregnant by several of the village lads. She wanted so much to get away from that inn and its comparative slavery. Peter seemed the best choice and possibly the last chance she could have for years. She wore green as part of her clothing which was usual for a girl who was both free with her affections and sought a husband or just fun, in or out of the bedroom.

He heard a knock at the door and bade them enter. There standing in the doorway were three folk - Ruth with Meg in her arms, and the Talbot dog they called 'Chaser'. She was in pup and obviously had not long to go to drop her litter.

Meg thought the world of her, and she had curled up on the mattress that Ruth had found for her, and the dog had stayed with her all night. Chaser was nearly all white with rusty marks on her face and ears. Meg wriggled down and ran across to Peter, jumped on the bed and hugged him tight. She radiated happiness like he had seldom seen in her.

"What hour of the clock is it?" Peter asked rubbing his eyes.

"About nine I'd say - art thou rested Peter?" enquired Ruth.

"Aye and right well - be there food on the board?"

"There be bread and cheese, milk too, if thou wishest, or ale. There be apples and some pears from the cold cellar." Ruth stood shuffling her feet about as if she wanted to say something but held back as the child was there. Ruth's eyes were wide and her face was flushed, her breathing heavy and fast as it had been the evening before when they fell asleep. She was obviously still a little turned-on after being with Peter the night before and was in some distress.

Meg was on the bed and Peter hugged her back, but thrust her from him to take a look at her face and neck. Her arms too he examined. "I have had my breakfast" she said joyfully.

"Oh Meg thou hast spent the night with that dog, be this not true? For thou hast been bitten by fleas. These red marks be the bites of dog-fleas. I must find some fresh rue and a brand for to rid thee of them." Ruth sent the bitch out and went even redder in the face.

"I'll fetch some rue from our herb plot, and bring a brand from the hearth for thee." Peter took off all Meg's clothes and opened the window. The hinges were rusted and broke away in his hands. It nearly fell right out of the casing but he held it and pulled it inside the room and placed it on the floor. Then he pitched the gown out of the window and gave it such a shaking that the sleeve seam stitches tore away a little. He had a hatred of dog-fleas from his childhood when he had caught them from his father's farm dog.

Meg shivered but Peter put his own gown round her until the herbs arrived. He turned his back on her and put on his worn-out shirt as Ruth came in with a big bunch of rue and a burning branch from the hearth downstairs. Peter took the brand, blew out the flames and got Ruth to turn Meg's clothes inside out and hold them so he could run the heat up and down the seams. The fleas crackled as he progressed. The smell of scorched cloth and fleas hung in the air. It soon subsided as the missing window allowed the wind to blow about the room.

Then he took the rue and split it into three sprigs. One he tied with a cord about her neck to hang down her back. Another he hung to be at her chest and a third to be about thigh level. The clothes had another good shake and then Meg put them back on before she got too cold. Peter would have washed her all over with crushed rue but there was no water to hand. He did not think it prudent to stay too long at The Swan as he felt events were closing in on him. He kept a couple of sprigs of rue for himself to ward off any 'visitors' that might jump aboard his body. Meg wriggled and whined as the herbs tickled her and the stalks pressed into her.

"I Thank thee Ruth - we shall not be about

strange dogs again - shall we Meg" said Peter
sternly and almost angry. He was put out and was
reminded of those hateful days when he was a
lad.

"Nay father," she said, looking at the floor in
disgrace. Peter saw her rub her eyes - her
preamble to tears. He stooped and picked her up
before they began and hugged her. He loved her
so much, and showed her again just how much.

Ruth stood looking lost and alone as Meg was
the centre of Peter's attentions. She said...."Did I
hear thee call Peter 'Father' Meg?"

Meg put her hands to her lips as if she had
uttered a blasphemy or a foul word.

"Oh pardon" she cried..."'tis as if thou art my
father Peter, for we have been together so long
since thou found me on the streets." He pulled
her to him and crushed her to him yet again, like
he had just met her after parting.

Ruth covered her eyes. Peter saw her distress
and said...."She hath the same eyes, hair and
looks as my fourth child Peg the which did drown
in the manor moat. Providence did send this little
waif to me when I was at my lowest ebb, and I did
care for her. After she was ill from lack of
nourishment and I too became ill, she, in her
young years, cared for me. We did each lean
upon the other. I too find it difficult not to be as
a father to her Ruth. I have been a widower these
6 years or so since my wife Lydia passed away
whilst bringing Peg into this cruel world. We were
so very much in love like the two halves of a pair
of scissors, each useless without the other. My
grief was great, but made much greater when at
three years old Peg was taken from me also."

He looked at the floor as his voice cracked up

into silence. Ruth felt her inside churn as she came and joined them in their mutual moment of remembered sadness. She put her arms about both of them. Oh so much she would like to be wed to this dear man. Oh so much she wanted to have a child like Meg by him. But what would fate give her? What did it have in store? She wanted motherhood more than life itself when she saw such love and paternal care as was before her now.

"I love thee more than anything father" said Meg burying her head in his lap as he sat in the oak chair.

Ruth could take no more and burst into a flood of tears, she felt so empty, so alone and that Peter would never be for her. He stood up and tried as he could to comfort her. But what could he do, what could he say. He read her mind and knew her torments. He sensed that she wanted him for more than just one night of ecstasy. She showed so much that she cared for him, for Meg, and although she'd not said a word, it was clear that if only he asked, she would have gone anywhere with him.

He said..."Ruth, I think it best that we part as soon as I have eaten. I feel that I could grow very fond of thee. I be of a mind that I must return to my village, for I must stand by the woman I love and who doth carry my child. I bid thee all good fortune and that thou dost meet and wed a good man and right soon."

"I would bid thee come to our manor at Briarmeade, if thou dost not wish to live here as thou didst tell me. There be several good men on our manor that do seek a wife just like thee. I would have thee for my wife on the morrow had I not been already promised. Briarmeade be but two or three days walk away, if thou hast a mind to come."

He partook of a monk's breakfast, but cheated, as he took milk instead of water with his morning bread.

Peter rose from the board, wiped his mouth on his cuff and put away his knife. He beckoned to Meg to come from the fire so they could depart.

Ruth came to him and gave them both a hug and tearful kiss. She pressed into Peter's hand a scrap of green cloth from her gown as a memento. He put it in the pouch with the coins he had left.

"I shall come to Briarmeade to see thee Peter as thou dost bid me. The things thou didst tell me of thy village, and life on the manor do tempt me. I feel that I could fit in with thy folk there."

She regained her composure and brightened with the thoughts of her possible better future that could lie in wait for her at Briarmeade manor as Peter had bidden her.

With this, she followed them to the door, keeping a tight hold on the talbot lest it shake off more 'travellers'. She took the payment that Peter gave her for their lodging and clutched his hand not letting it go free till he had given her one last long deep kiss. He almost had to force her grasp from his arm.

They walked away from The Swan without looking back.

He could only imagine the despair that he had left behind.

17 ~ THE GOAT

It was early March and Mary was spinning by the cottage fire when Maria came in to tell her that she was bidden to go and see Ruth Weaver the goodwife who had taught her to spin the flax. Mary put her old yellow cloak around her shoulders and trudged out into the cold clear sunlight of the morning. All the land was still. There was not a breath of air to stir the twigs on the trees. The sun felt warm on her face and the ground was dry beneath her feet. A bird sang from the top of a tree and it seemed to put a spring in her step. She almost felt human again.

When she got to Ruth's cottage she was surprised to find the door ajar. She knocked and pushed it open. Ruth was sitting hunched by the fire warming herself. She looked up as Mary entered and smiled weakly and motioned her to sit near her. Mary saw no-one in the large room and the looms seemed to be unused. There was an air of neglect about the place.

"Wouldst thou help thyself to a hot posset from the pot over the fire, Mary." said Ruth. "Then I pray thee come and sit with me awhile."

Mary was surprised that Ruth did not pour the drink for her, as was the custom. Then she noticed Ruth's hands. They were swollen and looked like sausages that the cook made in the intestines from the sheep. The ends of her fingers were white and one of them had an open wound on it.

"I have a gift for thee, Mary, which, by the giving, will lift a great load off my mind. 'Tis well known that thou art with child again and that thou dost have many mouths to feed in thy house. I would that thou take my goat as a gift to the new baby." Mary was overwhelmed by such a gift. It would certainly be a useful animal to have as it would provide some meat in the form of kids and perhaps some milk too. She could comb its coat in the spring and perhaps get some fibre to spin as well. But she could not understand why Ruth would be giving away a useful animal. Then Ruth explained that it was getting more and more difficult for her to milk the animal each year and that she had hurt her finger this winter because she had no feeling in it. She did not want the animal to be neglected as she was a good milker and was in kid. She was due to have her kids in the middle of April.

"Thou doest me a great service, Ruth. But how can I repay thee?" Mary knew that she could not give Ruth anything that had the same value.

"Canst thou give me some of thy time? Now that I can no longer spin or weave I am left alone here and I would have someone to talk to on occasion. If thou couldst bring thy spinning here and sit with me and give me news of the Manor, I would be more than grateful." Mary could see that Ruth did not like her enforced idleness. She had formerly been a very busy person.

"That I will, and gladly, but canst thou still walk away, Ruth?" asked Mary.

"Aye, a little."

"I would that thou might come to the woolshed and sit with us and give us thy advice and help with our work. If thou canst not walk that far I will come and sit by thy fire to spin, or maybe, if thou wouldst wish, come to my cottage for I do spin there on cold days."

Ruth shifted on her stool. She was a big woman and the stool looked too small for her. "That would be very well. It will be well to be among friends again and enjoy banter."

Mary went quiet and sipped her posset. She was thinking about the goat.

"May I leave the goat with thee a while until I do find somewhere for her to live?" Mary could take the animal to the common land to graze but she had no-where to put her at night. Ruth said that she could manage her until she kidded but could not milk her. Mary stayed with Ruth a while and told her of the things that had been happening on the manor and then she walked home. Everything seemed to be good for her at the moment. This goat was just the animal that she needed to ensure that Adam and the other children had enough good food. Now she was sure that they would grow into strong adults.

18 ~ FIRST DAY HOME

Peter sought the keeper of the holy spring and told him of his quest. The keeper was used to such requests and gave him some water and instructed him to go the priest and have it blessed that it might have the power to heal.
This done, they left Ashingham Priory with a small glass phial wrapped in wool and hung on a thong about Peter's neck. It hung inside his habit right over his heart.

The first day of March dawned, cold and frosty but there were no clouds in the sky. They had slept the previous night in a hay barn which had been warm and sweet smelling. They were just outside a small village where he had found a baker and bought Meg a small gingerbread man as he remembered his Peg's birthday would have been that day. It was brown and crusty and had small currants for its eyes and mouth and a small dimple in the centre of its body.

"Why had he a hole there?" Meg was curious.

"Have you not a hole there, Meg? Said Peter."
Meg lifted up her gown and had a look.

"Aye I have. What be it?" Peter laughed at her innocence and told her the story as it had been told to him when he was little.

"When God makes all the little babies he has to be sure they be done so he doth poke them all.

In this way we have a belly button."

She was so excited to have the gingerbread man that he had to explain that she could eat it and not carry it about like a doll. She bit it and he saw blood on the ginger bread and on the child's mouth. It was as if the baker had put life into the biscuit and Meg had done it some terrible injury.

Was this an omen for the future?

Was this child going to do some terrible deed in her life?

Peter knelt down beside her just as she spat a small white tooth into her hand. Peter sighed with relief. She had shed her first front tooth. She cried when she saw the blood, thinking that she had done something to hurt herself. Peter gave her a hug and explained that baby teeth have to be lost.

"Put thy tooth into thy pouch and save it for the tooth fairy, for they do need them and will leave thee a gift if thou dost look in the morning." She laughed, not really believing him.

Peter had persuaded a cobbler to mend some sandals he was about to throw away so that Meg could have something to wear on her feet. To pay for them Peter swept his shop out for him. He reminded Peter of Brother Andrew, the cobbler monk, at St. Benets at Broadwells who was a shoemaker and cordwainer before he took 'orders' at the Abbey.

They still had 5 groats between them for some casual work that Peter had managed to find. They wanted to save as much as they could to give Mary when they returned.

Peter mused about Brother Andrew and spoke his thoughts saying "He was a lovely man"

"Who be that Peter?" asked Meg.

"Oh pardon Meg - I did think of Brother Andrew who did give me the sandals that I do wear to this day. They be old, like me Meg but they do serve me well."

"Did you like being in the Abbey" questered Meg.

"Aye and Nay Meg. For I was wrongly banished there by a lazy jealous man from Briarmeade."

"Is banished like beaten" she asked, her face the picture of fear and worry.

"Nay Meg, banished meaneth cast out or sent away from home. I was beaten by the brothers much in my early days there, but because I had done wrong in their eyes. There was nought that I could do to avoid it, as I had to make confession about my life and I had to suffer for it. Their rules were so very strict but I did learn much about mankind, the world and myself. For I did lose my wife when my last child, Peg, came into this world. Peg was the image of thee Meg. She was drowned in the moat at the manor when she had but three summers. Then I fell deeply in love with another man's wife. Her husband did bring about my banishment. Dost thou understand this?"

"Aye Peter, I do …….. most of what thou dost say."

"Had I not been sent to St. Benets Abbey I would not have learned to read and write, and worse still I would not have found thee my treasure. Thou has learnt well the letters I have shown thee. 'tis a great gift we are given."

She bent down and wrote with her finger in the mud on the road. 'Meg and Peter'. He coughed to hide his feelings that threatened to well up again.

"When shall we reach Briarmeade?" she asked.
"Maybe in 10 days - if it do not rain much."
"How shall it be when we get there?"

"I wish I knew Meg, 'tis in God's hands." They fell into silence. They walked and walked. Meg seemed so full of life. Now she would run off and hide and jump out on Peter like the imp she had become. Her fair hair was lovely, her face round and rosy, she was virtually tireless. When she did tire Peter sometimes took her upon his shoulders which she loved as she could see over hedges and into house windows which she would otherwise miss. He kept a tally of the days on his staff and at times he looked like St Christopher, for he too carried a child and had a ragged staff. He tried to walk a good distance each day and paced himself as he'd done for years.

Briarmeade came nearer with its mixture of hope and despair, anticipation and fear.

What had happened to his cottage?

Were his old friends still about?

What of the cook, the kitchen maids, the steward?

Would Tom the pot-boy still be there, whom he had taught to cut up onions without tears?

In such bad winters past several folk had died and some had left the manor. On the other hand most were from strong country stock and survived such ordeals. How many would be there to be at his homecoming?

His thoughts of Mary were ambiguous - could she still love him?

Would she be free to wed him if he asked her again?

Would she want to marry him?

Above all was she well enough to give birth to

a healthy son for him?

His own wife had died in childbirth and he did not think he could bear it if that happened to Mary as well. He wanted Adam to be born in wedlock unlike Peter himself who was cast aside at birth as stillborn and found in the 10 acre meadow at Briarmeade. But above all he wanted to be a real father to him and watch him grow up and teach him all he knew.

Often he found himself wondering who his real parents were, even more now as the time of his return was so near. Grace, the housekeeper, and William, the basket maker, had brought him up but when he was ten she told him that he was a foundling and not their own son. The shock of that news still stayed with him making him oftimes feel low and lonely.

Grace suspected who his real father was but had been sworn to secrecy as she assisted at Peter's birth all those 37 years ago. It went without saying that she also knew his mother, who died bringing him into the world.

Such a bad world, she always said. Anyone who lived past 40 was indeed old and a full set of teeth were unheard of, so, at nearly 60, Grace was past caring about her oath and was determined that Peter should know his origins before the secret died with her. She too longed for his return to the manor.

On March 11th Meg and Peter came to Briarmeade an hour or so after dark. Peter did not know what sort of reception they would get in Mary's cottage. So he decided to wait until daylight before going there. They walked through the small kissing gate at the side of the great gates that stood ghostly in the pale moonlight and went unseen past the saw pit and pottery. They found a couple of logs to sit on by the kiln fire and warmed themselves. There was a little pottage in the cauldron on the chain which they ate for their supper. The wood smoke made their eyes water, or was it the nostalgia of coming home? Tiredness and warmth lulled them into sleepiness and Meg fell backwards off her log into a mass of brambles. Peter dragged her out and licked her scratches clean, put her on his knee and cuddled her till her cries ceased. The fire went low and the night chill made them move on. They would not burn more of the potters' wood. He carried Meg up the path past the yeoman's cottage and the great barn to the comfort and seclusion of the woolshed.

This was a place that he knew well and where he knew that they could get a good night's sleep. It had wide stone steps leading up to an oak framed barn that stood over the byre. It was a large building and was used to store hay and straw when the great barn was full. But its main purpose was to store the fleeces and give space to house the great wheels and the looms so that the workers could work together on making cloth. It had three doors, one at the top of the stairs and the others, on the south side, for throwing hay down to the animals that were housed below. Each door was in half so that the top could be opened to let in the light whilst the bottom half could be left closed.

The pigs still lived beneath and murmured their welcome. The donkeys and the white mare came up to their fence to see who had come by and a few white doves in the roof cooed their lullaby.

Meg sat by the open half door looking up at the stars. She said one word 'fairies'. Peter heard her as he found two stuffed wool sacks, which he remembered from what seemed like a long time ago. He put them at the back of the barn in a quiet corner. He also found an old cloak that hung upon a beam. He smiled to himself remembering Alys, Tilly and Mary, all crowding in on his mind till he thought he'd go mad. He breathed deeply and all the phantoms left except for his Mary.

"Look up there." Meg said. "The stars that took us away from here have brought us back again." She pointed out the pole-star that Peter had taught her when he first spoke of star-wishes and fairies. She traced out the Plough too that she had seen so often these last months from St. Benets at Broadwells, to Briarmeade, to Ashingham priory and all the way back again. They looked out on that same scene that Peter and Mary had looked upon so long ago back in the glory of that August evening when they had conceived Adam. He reached out and pulled the upper half door shut and they lay down side by side on the wool sack with the sweet smell of the hay and the oily wool. He covered them with the cloak and they fell in to a deep sleep.

The dawn chorus and the little pigs below them, the doves and the donkeys all seemed to know that a friend had returned to them and murmured again as Meg and Peter began to waken.

The door latch snapped and made them fully awake. Tilly entered the woolshed to make ready for the day's spinning. Peter put his hand to Meg's lips. He knew that they should not be sleeping in there and he was not sure how they would be greeted. Someone was coming up the steps behind Tilly. He hoped that it was not Jonah.

His heart gave a jump.

Was that Mary entering the woolshed?

She looked so young and so pretty.

He shook his head and looked again. No, it was Kitty. She looked so much like her Mother and was wearing a blue gown as her mother had done all those months ago when he first talked to her. She was carrying a basket on her arm.

Tilly started to tidy up the skeins of wool and gave Kitty the broom to sweep the floor, then she came over to where they lay to open the half door. She tripped over Meg's legs and fell against the rough beams. She screamed as Peter rose and Kitty came to see what had befallen her. Peter threw back his hood and, when she saw who it was, they both hugged him and when Meg stood up to be noticed, she looked lost.

Peter turned to her, picked her up and they all began to talk at once. A great wheel was knocked over in the excitement and a leg came off its base. Meg was kissed and cuddled by all, as she was passed from one to another, like a baby that had just come into the world. Maria came into the woolshed wondering what the chatter was all about and joined in the celebrations of hugs and kisses all over again.

Maria said "I must run and tell Mary thou art come home Peter!"

Peter put his finger to his lips and placed his hand on her arm to stop her exuberance.

"How be Mary now?" he asked "Is she well? How are the childer and how doth Jonah fare?"

He had so much to ask, but in what order, and what right had he to demand it from these good women?

"Mary hath been ill of a great fever, Peter, and she did almost miscarry. It did throw her into a pit of despair from which she is now recovered." said Maria. "She did use the money thou didst leave for her and we did as much as we were able to keep them all warm and fed. Oh Peter, if only thou had been here to help, we would have fared better, but thou art here now among us. All the childer be well. They did all eat turnips from the fields for our hunger. They did fill us all and we be grateful. How has thou fared, Peter, and what of this little one thou hast in thy arms?"

Peter told them something of his journeys and how Meg found him and their trials and hardships.

"Cook hath been good to us, Peter, for she hath given food that she did save from the gentry and seen to it that Mother and all us childer were treated well in these hard cold times." said Kitty.

"Several workers have left the manor to go elsewhere for work so there be more food for pottage" said Tilly. "Would you have me go and tell Mary thou art here Peter?"

"First do tell me of my cottage and of Jonah for I cannot go further till I do know of this." Peter looked stern and anxious. Tilly and Kitty looked at each other blankly and Maria stared at the floor. All were loath to say a word.

"Must I guess?" said Peter feeling his anguish turn to temper, "or will someone tell me?" Meg was so startled by Peter's outburst. She had never seen him so earnest. She ran to him and hugged his legs for she felt that he would storm out of the woolshed and she would lose him. He bent low and picked her up and kissed her as he sat down on Tilly's stool. As he did so Rebecca came into the woolshed doorway.

"Father" she cried and seemed rooted to the spot. "Oh father 'tis so good to see thee - Mother hath been so ill we did all think she would die."

Mother! Peter said to himself. Oh what joy to return to. Becky had come to call Mary Mother. Meg had called him father at the Swan Inn had she not? He crossed the floor in two bounds with Meg close behind him. He fell to his knees and took Becky in his arms. Tears fell from them both and Meg came and held him from behind, her arms about his neck. They all looked a sorry sight. When the tears had subsided, Peter asked again about his cottage and of Jonah.

Becky said "The cottage that we lived in ere you left us, now has a new tenant. It be Samuel the saddler with his wife and two girls. We play with them and one will soon be old enough to work here with us, and the other will work in the great herb garden, with our little brother Rob."

Peter just sat in awe of her grown up command of language and worldly knowledge. When he went away she was just 9 and a half. She'd grown in stature and wisdom. She would pass for 12 now. Rob would be nearly 9 now. Becky cleared her throat and settled on Peter's left knee while Meg sat on the other one. He ran his fingers through their hair that tumbled out from underneath their coifs, as she began again.

"Our old Cottage had the roof fall in after the great storm, but a little while after they took thee away. The saddler had a bad time trying to find a roofer and a thatcher, but the steward found him one. His wife has plans to grow vegetables and herbs in the ground at the back of the cottage,"

All went quiet as Becky ended her talk.

In a low voice, Peter said "Who will tell me about Jonah the carpenter?"

Maria plucked up courage and said, "As he was Mary's man, the answer should come from her."

Peter heard the word 'was' in that sentence and hope returned to his heart. He would not question these good people further, he must see Mary.

"Where is Mary now?" he asked. "Does she spin at home? I have heard naught from her for so long, not since my fleeting visit 'ere I was sent to Ashingham priory."

"She be at home, for she is not yet strong and do spin by the cottage fire on these cold days." said Becky.

"Then I shall go straightway to see her. Come Meg. Let us to Mary for I do feel that she needs us and doth wait for us to return to her." He turned and walked down the steps and past the great barn. His heart raced at the thought of seeing Mary again. She must be near her time now.

How would he find her?

What would he say?

Would she reject him?

What was to be done about Jonah?

His feet crunched the gravel path and as he came to the stile he felt his habit snag on the post - or so he thought. But a post does not move, he mused as he looked down. The familiar tug on the gown was Meg attached to him as before. A few paces behind her came Becky, her face pale and her eyes cast down to the ground. He sat on the stile and called,

"Come Becky, take my hand and let us all

three go to see Mary together." She looked up, smiled, and ran to catch up. As he helped her over the stile she hugged him with great warmth. She had her father back, and she'd never let him go again. She thrust her hand in his like she did when she was little. On the way to Mary's cottage Peter told her all about how he came to find Meg. How Rags had passed away and where they had laid him to rest.

Becky loved Rags too - he was already a grown dog when she herself was born. He told her what he had to do in the Abbey as a brother and how he had learned how to read and write. He promised that all the childer would be given that gift. He would even try to teach Mary if she so desired.

The two girls grinned at each other. Peter could see that they would get along and felt their warmth growing. A bond was forming.

At the door of Mary's cottage they stopped while Peter plucked three sprigs of Rosemary. These were for remembrance. He knocked gently on the door and waited holding his breath unsure of what he would find. This time it opened almost immediately - not after ages like the last time.

Mary stood in the doorway with a clean white bonnet and white apron tied over a great bulge. Her face was rosy, her arms bare where she had rolled up her sleeves. She opened her arms and hugged him as best she could - Adam being so prominent. She was ready to kiss him this time and she did so with that long deep kiss that said "welcome home, never leave me again." She pulled them all into the cottage and shut the door against the cold. Her eyes had a twinkle about them. She looked so well because the last time he saw her she was the picture of misery. The cottage had been tidied and there was some wood in the pile beside the fire. There was the faint smell of lavender in the air that was coming from the open clothes box.

"I knew thou wouldst come soon Peter." said Mary " For I have had thy message three days since. Peter knew what she meant as he had thought and spoken to her with his mind like as if he was divining for water. The anxiety seemed to have deserted her and a radiance shone from her face. Peter said "Oh Mary it is so good to see thee and looking so well. A miracle must have come upon this manor these last few weeks."

Becky and Meg both hugged Mary at the same time and she bent as low as she could to Meg especially and kissed each of them in turn.

"Mary, tell me what has happened to Jonah, for no-one else will say ought." Peter needed to know the answer to the question that had been bothering him.

"Jonah was killed in an accident when he blundered before a cart. It were dreadful. I could in no wise save him. The fault were mine and I have been in deepest despair these last few weeks. It was thy last visit and Adam kicking me that did bring me back to thinking of the living instead of the dead. We did bury him in the churchyard and set an oaken cross on his grave." said Mary sitting down heavily.

A load was lifted off Peter's mind. Perhaps now she could marry him and Adam would be born as his own child. Was now the time to ask her again?

"Did I hear thee aright? He is dead and buried?"

"Aye, Peter. The priest saw to his burial these two months since and he is now with the Lord." Tears welled up in Mary's eyes.

"Who paid for his burial, Mary." asked Peter. Mary grew pale and silent. He had touched on a sensitive spot. She said no more and seemed to set a wall between them. Now was not the time to ask her to marry him. He had to find out what was wrong.

"What is it Mary - have I said ought to offend thee?" He gave her the rosemary and she took it but still looked as though she was despairing. The girls gave her their rosemary and Mary hugged both of them but said not a word. He felt he had reached an impasse. Mary stirred herself, reached to Meg, held her at arm's length and looked her up and down.

Then drew her to her and stroked her face as if she was her own child. She sighed deeply and began to regain her former composure.

"How didst thou fare at the Christmas time Mary?" Peter thought he would try another subject.

"Aye well enough" she replied, " I went up to the great house to help them to butcher the carcasses after the cows and some sheep were slaughtered. Bett the cook did give me a big piece of meat. I had not the wherewithall to savour it but she did tell me how to soak it 'ere I roasted it before the fire. She did even give me some spices that we had a feast at Christmastide. She hath been a good friend to me since thou wast sent from us. She do have a sharp tongue but there be a right goodly side to her. 'Twas she who did speak for thee and it be her words that did bring about thy pardon."

"I must seek her out and thank her." said Peter. "Thou hast not answered. Who paid for the burial?"

She turned her face from him and spoke quietly. "Master Robert De Vere Ashton hath need of thee Peter as soon as thou hast time."

She had turned off the subject as if she had not heard the question. Peter could feel his hopes of marriage and a happy homelife slipping away. Becky took Meg into the back room as she sensed that either an argument was about to start or perhaps the adults needed to be alone. She was a very sensitive and wise child for her age.

"Thou didst say that Jonah is dead and buried Mary - what dost thou have to tell me for thou hast a burden upon thee that perhaps I can share, but thou needs must tell me of it for I must help thee over this." Peter was in earnest.

"In our early days, Peter, Jonah and I loved each other greatly - I know thee well enough to know thou canst feel what I mean. He were good to me and ambitious but when the childer did come he could not share them with me and could not abide their crying. He took himself away to the tavern and the wenches. These last years he hath not slept in this cottage more than three nights. He wanted no more childer and he did not want to sleep with me lest he be tempted. He suffered a pox and was ashamed of it but did come home when he became very ill for me to nurse him."

The tears were rolling down Mary's cheeks unheeded.

"It was all my fault.

I should have been a better wife to him.

I could have kept the childer out of his way and I could have paid more attention to him.

I should have tried harder but 'tis too late now. At the end he was nigh to blind and blundered out to be run down by a cart.

Oh Peter I have been so alone without him and then without thee also after thou wast taken from us.

Please do forgive me."

"Forgive thee - for what must I forgive thee, Mary?" Peter frowned. He stood behind her and held her by the shoulders where she sat by the fire.

She stood up also and turned around. Large though she was and pressed herself to him. He felt the baby kick and whatever it was she craved forgiveness for, he would never reject her request. This was no trick but the craving of the one person he wanted so much to spend the rest of his life with.

"When Jonah was killed I had not a penny to bury him. None of mine nor thine. I saw the priest and he said the burial had to be paid for. All I had was the ring thou didst have in thy money pouch. That was all I had of value and he took this as payment as much in his sorrow as in mine. Wilt thou ever forgive me for this?" She put her head in her hands and sobbed as if the world had come to an end.

"Be not a-feared, Mary, for 'twas merely a morsel of metal after all. Thou didst what thou hadst - I forgive thee all."

"But it was thy wedding ring and I guarded it for so long. Oh Peter I did grieve much for Jonah these past weeks but thy coming hath brought me hope again. "

"I did give thee the ring to use, and thou didst use it wisely. Thou must not fret on this regard."

Was now the time to ask her?

Would she say yes?

It was hardly a romantic moment but it seemed to be the right moment. Peter went down on one knee and looked up. He could not see her face as Adam was in the way. He shuffled backwards and nearly tipped over the joint stool and saw a slow smile creeping across her face.

"I have come home and it is just the home that I could have wished for. I want our son to be born in wedlock and not a bastard as I was. I pray you marry me and let me live with you and all the childer. I have been promised work on the manor, though I know not yet what I am to do. I can help thee. We will have money to feed the childer and buy firewood. We can sleep together and keep each other warm at night."

Mary's smile widened and turned into a grin. She caught Peter's hand and helped him to his feet. It was more than she could have hoped for. A loving husband who cared for the children and most of all for her.

"If thou doest wish for this thou must marry me right soon or Adam will arrive before our wedding day."

"Mayhap we could wed on Mayday when all the manor will gather to celebrate the coming year?"

Mary thought a moment and then said, "That would be right well. Mayhap when thou dost see the priest, thou canst ask?"

"This I will do."

"Would thou eat with us for we do have bread

from this day's oven and a garlic cheese from the dairy?"

"Aye, I would Mary" said Peter sitting heavily on the earth floor.

Mary called to the childer.

Becky came first and found the stool and urged her father to sit upon it. He put his arm about her and from the back room came the other children one by one. Nem, Peter's youngest son stared at Meg. Peter knew not which to kiss and cuddle first and as the cuddles and love surged up, tension departed. The hard days and the cold were forgotten for a while. Peter had forgotten the names of Mary's children so she made each say their name as he cuddled them. Some hugged him that knew him and the others took delight in tugging his beard. He put his hand in his habit and took the phial of sacred water from about his neck. Mary took it from him and placed it on the highest shelf out of harm's way. He also took out his leather pouch and put the five groats he had left in Mary's hand. She looked straight into his eyes, smiled that warm smile that said so much without words and kissed him squeezing his hand.

Meg came to him and looked a little lost and sad among all this crowd of people. She was not used to having a family about her. Mary saw her distress and took her on her lap, but there was little room there. She held Mary tightly as she'd done so often with Peter when she felt low and the need for his love. She felt Adam kicking strongly now and was a little scared, but Mary said "What thou dost feel within me Meg will soon be thy new brother."

"How dost thou know that it will be a boy child?" Meg asked.

"I do know it in my heart for I did love Peter so much that I did want to give him a son. When I did ask the great oak tree, it did tell me that I would bear a strong son."

Peter shifted on his stool with tiredness and emotion only to dislodge one of the legs and he tumbled onto the floor. All the children burst into laughter as he picked himself up. He grinned and joined in their merriment. Mary too saw the funny side of it and joined in and chuckled. He forgot his hunger but Meg's moans for food reminded him that neither had eaten since waking.

'This is what home life should be,' he thought to himself. He looked around the cottage and wondered just how they had managed to eat and sleep. Three of her children and three of his children - where would he sleep and Meg too for that matter. Adam would have to be placed somewhere in a crib that had yet to be made. Somehow he would have to find some more space for them all.

He said "I must attend to many things that do trouble me Mary. First we must eat, then I must seek out mistress Bett in the kitchen to make my deep thanks for what she hath done to bring about my pardon. If Master Robert De Vere Ashton hath need to see me I must go soon."

Silence descended on the small cottage as Mary handed around the bread and cheese. Peter noticed that she made sure that the children had the largest portions and that he himself was only given a small slice and Mary finished up the crumbs that were left. Becky found the milk-jug that they had used to make a hot posset from the hearth.

"I will go to the bakery and the dairy and get thee some more milk, bread and cheese, for I do wish to see the folks there also." Peter was concerned that Mary was not getting enough to feed both herself and Adam. Now that he was home he could earn a wage and make sure that there was enough for all.

Meg ate hers as if she had not been fed for days. She choked on it. Peter thumped her on the back only to find her mouth bleeding. She had shed another front tooth. Mary consoled her and placed it in an old cup on the shelf and told her, "The tooth fairy will have need of that Meg, for in the night he will come and buy it from thee and give thee a gift."

"I have another tooth that I did lose on my birthday," she said producing it from her pouch. Mary put that too in the old cup. Peter rose and hugged and kissed them all before he pulled up his cowl. Mary came to him and clung to his hand but realised that he had much to do alone. She put two groats into his hand to pay for the milk and bread that he said he would buy and also handed him the phial of holy water which he hung back around his neck. Then she held him close with Adam between them. His heart pounded.

"I still love thee so much," she said.

"Aye, I know this Mary," he said - and feared he might hold her too tightly. Her face was flushed as when they had made love so long ago in the woolshed. She had a radiance about her that made her look so much younger than she did when first he had come home.

Meg called out "Hey, wait for me father," her rosy face a little above Mary's swollen waist, as she came up to them in the doorway.

"Meg, what I have to do and where I have to go I must attend to alone, and he held her close. He came down to her level, her gappy mouth made her speak with splashes and she began to cry and whimper.

"Meg," he said firmly, "I must see the Master about my work and position here, the cook, the baker and .... Oh! Come then." She took his hand again.

"Thou dost need a cloak, Meg." said Mary, turning, and taking her a donkey-coloured one from a nail on the wall. Meg wrapped it round her and, although it was a little large and dragged on the ground, she could walk in it. They both turned and waved to Mary as she watched them walk away up the lane.

"Where shall we go first?" Meg asked.

"First I must see the Master, Robert De Vere-Ashton about what I am to do here and where I may live. I must thank him for my pardon and to be able to be here at all. I must give the priest the phial of sacred water for the chapel. Then I would seek the cook, mistress Bett, for, though she be sharp of tongue, she hath ever been a friend to me. She will seem fearsome, but have no fear Meg; I bid thee, for she hath saved me much pain and anguish."

They passed the pottery and the warrener where Peter begged a brace of rabbit skins the which to make Meg some indoor shoes. The horses came to him and nuzzled their noses in Peter's hand as they went by their paddock. Over the door of the stable was the usual horseshoe. Peter told Meg the story of why the shoe was put above the door when the blacksmith had shod the devil's hooves in a bargain.

Perkin, the armourer called, "Good day" from the butts as they passed by.

When they came to the great hall, a steward made them wait in the porch sending a messenger to Master Robert De Vere-Ashton that Peter had come. They had not long to wait and soon were bidden to enter the solar.

Robert was a large man with white hair and the red face of a man who loved the outdoor life, hunting and good food. He wore a black doublet with many gold buttons down the front. His breeches were green as were his stockings and he had velvet slippers on his feet.

Peter bowed to him and made Meg curtsey. Then waited for him to speak. Robert seemed to be taken with Meg who was sniffing the bowl of pot pourri on the table like a cat.

"What is thy name little one." He asked, leaning forward. "Meg, sire," she said shyly, her head down on her chest. She was overawed by the great sunny room with all its rich tapestry hangings depicting hunting scenes, the carved wooden furniture and the woven wool mat on the wooden floor.

"Peter, I see thou art at last returned to us. I trust thy banishment did have no great ill?" Robert's voice was rich and full of authority. He ruled the manor with a strong hand but he always tried to be fair.

"At first it was most painful sire - but I was given two great gifts."

"Gifts?" questered Robert De Vere.

"Aye sire - one be that the brothers did teach me to write. The other be that this little waif was sent to me to replace the daughter who was drowned in the moat here. I did save her from death upon the streets."

"Peter, afore we speak further, hast thou the phial of holy water and hast thou seen the Priest at the new chapel?"

"Aye, I have the holy water but thou didst bid me to attend thee the earliest moment I did return to Briarmeade so I have not yet been to the chapel. When I have left thee, I shall go and seek the Priest to give him this phial."

He held it up and the sunlight passed through it making a rainbow on the floor beside them.

"Thou hast done well Peter, and I now pardon thee in person for good and all."

"Thou knowest the truth that do lie behind my banishment?" asked Peter.

"Aye I do, and I do regret everything that hath given thee grief - for had I known the truth much sooner, I would have banished those who did bear false witness against thee."

"What wouldst thou have me do on this manor now sire?" asked Peter.

"What skills dost thou have that we can put to the best use Peter?" They seemed to be getting along fine, now that the thorns of fear and bitterness had been blunted.

"I can cook, cut hay, keep bees and make their homes. I can shoot the bow, cut joints in house-building and turn wood in thy coppice."

"Thou hast a goodly list, and I would add to it the fact that thou canst read and write" said Robert. "Where wouldst thou live Peter, for the Estate Steward did re-let thy old cottage when thou wast taken away? The saddler do have it now with his family and I would not turn them out. It did cost me much to repair after that great storm."

"Might I be allowed to build on to the cottage that Mary and Jonah have, now he be dead and buried. She be but a month from the time that she would bring forth the child that she do carry, and I would wed her. She do already care for my childer. This-wise the baby would have two parents and be born in wedlock. Until I can build on to the cottage I would ask thy indulgence to sleep alone in the woolshed as there be not room for me in Mary's cottage with her childer and mine that be there at present." Peter ended and looked at the rainbow on the floor not knowing if any of this would come to pass.

"If thou wilt promise me that thou wilt not use candles to light thee in the woolshed, I will permit this, for I would not have my woolshed and byre burned down." said Robert.

"Sire, I do promise this and do give my word." replied Peter.

"Now..... Regarding Mary, the widow of Jonah, I see that thou art a good man and in earnest to see right by this thy chosen woman. I do wish thee well for thou hast done all and more that anyone hath asked of thee in the tasks I set thee, albeit after the falseness that did cause me to banish thee. Thou hast a great need to see thy family in larger housing." Robert lapsed into silence. He rubbed his head and was deep in thought.

Time seemed to hang and Meg became agitated. She had sat still for the longest Peter had ever seen her do so. He picked her up and put her on his knee. Robert stirred and shading his eyes from the sunshine began -

"Thou canst write now Peter and hast worked for me these 9 years and I do trust thee. I see thou art in earnest about this unborn child as if it were thine own, and I admire thy compassion for Mary. First I would that thou wouldst work in the kitchen and carve at high table. Second I would make thee prentice under-steward of the manor that thou canst learn a new trade and make use of thy reading and writing. Thou canst still work within the coppice if thou dost desire it. Lastly I bid thee a happy marriage and to this end I give - rent free - the vacant steward's cottage that hath three bedrooms and a garden. Thou needest not to consider all the laborious task of building to the widow's cottage. How say thee?"

Peter could not believe what he was hearing. It was more - far more than he had ever hoped for. He knew that the steward lived in the manor house and had no use for the old steward's cottage. It had been empty for some time but was of good solid construction and there was even some glass at the windows.

"Sire, what can I say? Thou doest me great honour. I give thee my grateful thanks and pledge my loyalty to thee. I shall serve thee as best I am able in all my tasks. I be overwhelmed with thy kindness."

"Thou hast been wronged in so many ways Peter that this wise I can make up to thee what do trouble me. There be secret reasons that I will not tell thee that cause me to make these offers to thee and thy kin."

Meg said, "All of my apple wishes have come true father." She hugged Peter as he bowed low before Robert De Vere Ashton.

"Go now Peter, see the Priest and give this good news to thy family, and once again I be most glad to see thee here again, with this thy new daughter."

Robert rose and shook Peter's hand warmly, the look in his eyes sorrowful.

"Can we take the pretty light with us?" Meg was bending down looking at the rainbow on the floor. She tried to pick it up and found that it had no substance. Peter showed her how to spread out her hand so that the light would fall upon it and she squealed with delight.

"The rainbow is not on the floor." explained Peter, "it is in the phial of holy water. We will take it to the chapel and put it on the altar that all may see the rainbow." They turned and left the solar riding on a cushion of hope and wonder.

Peter felt ten feet tall.

19 ~ RETURN

Peter bumped into mistress Bett the cook in the passageway to the great kitchen. They walked, talking fast and both at once, into the kitchen. The logs were burning in the great fireplace and a large joint of meat was roasting on a spit before it. The maids were busy cutting up vegetables and mixing spices and preparing all manner of food. Tom, the pot boy, was raking ashes out of the oven and all was bustle.

Eleanor, Phoebe, Rose and Ib came to Peter and thronged around him and Meg. Everyone talked at once, work was forgotten with such joy about. Tom had started talking to Meg, who went shy again.

Bett called for silence as usual with her great wooden ladle hitting the board. She welcomed Peter and Meg and gave her a small subtlety sheep made from an oddment of marchpane. Her gappy smile endeared her to the company as she took the sweetmeat which was made of almonds and sugar.

Tom boldly held her hand.

Peter took Bett into the root store. It was a small room off the kitchen and down some steps. The walls were lined with shelves on which were stored bags and bundles of food. The floor was partly covered with boxes in which the

roots were stored for winter. Each one had a
piece of sackcloth over it to keep the roots cool
and damp. There was one small window but as it
had some cloth hung over it to keep out the frost,
it shed very little light into the room.

Bett saw a look of peace on his face. It was
very different from the look he had given her
when she saw him arrested which was like that of
a scared animal.

"Bett," He began, "I have found that it was
thee that did the most to right the wrongs of my
banishment all those months ago, and I do give
thee my ever grateful thanks. Thanks can never
be enough to repay thee for my permission to
return and live here again. If there be ought I can
do for thee, please make it known to me. Without
thee I could not be here." She kissed him and
hugged him with such warmth he felt he was with
his own mother.

"I did see the great injustice that Jonah took
such delight in making for thee. I had to speak
out when dear Mary came to me. Nor would I
refuse when I could see that she did love thee so.
Some weeks after they took thee away from us, I
did see the Master, and, with the steward, he did
believe us."

He kissed her large hands and she grasped him
by the elbows at arm's length, then drew him to
her again and kissed him back. She always had a
soft spot for him despite her reputation as being
the dragon-cook. They returned to the kitchen.
He bade Meg stay in the kitchen while he went to
the dairy and the bakery.

He turned and left the kitchen passing the
great dovecote and found the baker, Dob and Eve
his wife kneading their second batch of dough of

the morning. The great table creaked beneath the weight of two people leaning their full weight upon it to mix the bread evenly. When they had finished kneading, they formed the dough into loaves. Then they set it by the warm fire under cloths, to keep out the draught. It was left to rise until the oven was heated.

Dob walked across to the oven, opened the metal door, and thrust his hand in to see if it was hot enough.

"No, not yet awhile" he thought to himself and shut the door.

The oven was built at chest height and had a chimney that was outside its door. Faggots were burning inside it and the flames were dancing on the brick walls. Then he scraped out the ashes and the dough was put in. The door was shut and in about three quarters of an hour the bread was cooked.

Next to the oven was a pile of faggots and some hot loaves were cooling on the basket-work trays. It smelled so good.

Peter walked in onto the stone flagged floor and nearly tripped over the barrel of flour and the wooden peck measure resting on top of it.

He embraced Dob and Eve. They talked over old times as Dob cast some fat upon the griddle in the large fireplace that dominated the other wall and followed it with three eggs. Eve sliced up a new loaf and toasted it before the fire as the eggs sizzled. Dob spooned up the cooked eggs from the griddle and laid them on pieces of new bread and all ate the bread with the hens' oysters on top.

Peter put the loaf that Dob gave him into his pouch and left the bakery and walked around the corner to the dairy. Mistress Rachel was standing at the sturdy central table straining whey from the curd. She used a scallop shell and scooped up a quantity of the milk that had been set with nettle juice and placed it gently into a muslin cloth in another large bowl. She gasped as she saw Peter standing in the doorway.

"Oh glory be" she cried and hastened to hug her old friend. Peter was always surprised how cool the dairy felt but on this cold March day the wind was blowing in through the window spaces and he marvelled, yet again, how Rachel could work in such temperatures.

There were several muslin cloths hanging up over bowls along the table and hand churns, like over-large jugs, standing on the side table. At this time of year there was not much milk and very little cream and only a little butter would be made. When the cows started to calve there would be a lot of work for the dairy maids. At the end of the dairy were four scrubbed wooden shelves on which the hard cheese was stored. Each week one of the dairy maids would turn the cheeses and any that had a sign of mould on them were rubbed with salt to keep them sweet. The sheep were just starting to lamb and shortly they would be making the sheep's milk cheese that the Manor was famous for.

Later in the year the ceiling of the dairy would be hung with elder leaves to keep the flies out. The walls were whitewashed and the flag floor scrubbed and the maids washed their aprons every day. The dairy was said to be the cleanest place on the manor.

They talked for a while and Rachel showed him the wall outside the dairy on which she had put a twig to cast a shadow. Where it fell, she had scratched lines into the red bricks to mark the hours, for 'twas her simple sundial by which she could tell how long the cheese had been straining. It said it was near the hour of ten in the morning.

"Thou art a sight for sore eyes Peter" said Rachel. She had a special place in her heart for him too as she had been the midwife that had delivered him and was also a close friend of Grace, the housekeeper. He begged a jug of milk. Bending with difficulty, she found a chipped jug from under the corner cupboard, and filled it for him. She put a muslin over it to keep out the dust.

"How be thy good husband?" he asked.

"He be nearly deaf now Peter but he still do love a joke and his ale."

"I do plan to wed on May-day, and I would hope that my marriage shall be as fine as thine. I would bid thee and thy good man to come. Thou art the first to be bidden since I did return to Briarmeade. I shall call upon ye both once I have attended to what I must."

Grace, Rachel and Bett were Peter's oldest friends and he had to ask them all to the wedding. He left with the jug thanking her for the milk. He was going to walk to the kitchen but something made him turn away past the dovecote and he found himself on the lane to the Great Hollow Oak tree. He knew not what made him walk that way but it was as if his feet had a will of their own. He turned off the lane and down the small track. It was not so overgrown at this time of year and the trees stood apart and dripped on him as he wended his way through them. He saw the wide trunk of the old tree and looked up at its tracery of branches against the grey sky. It seemed to be beckoning him. He slipped inside the trunk and sat on the damp earth.

What was it that Mary had said, "You cannot talk to trees with your mind but only with your heart." He grew quiet and emptied his mind of all positive thought. Wisdom, strength and warmth soaked into him like rain on an old cloak.

He did not feel sleepy but a profound peace took over his mind and he knew that he had come home.

The breeze stirred the branches above him and he came back into the world again. The muslin had come off the jug of milk and, as he replaced it, he peered in. The milk, normally so thin at this time of year had a golden crust of deep rich cream upon its surface. He shook it but it did not move, it had nearly all turned to cream. As Mary had told him, magical things happened when trees were involved with folk.

He left the tree and walked along with the jug in his hand and a spring in his step - It was a long time since he had felt like this. What a world he was re-entering. A new daughter, a new baby, a new cottage, new employment and above all a wonderful new wife. All of his friends were still about - he began to long for May-Day.

He came to the kitchen and all the maids were bustling about putting the final touches to the food that was to go to feed the gentry, Bett was shouting at an incompetent page but Meg was no-where to be seen. Bett beckoned to Peter with her chubby finger and he followed her into the root store. There she was upon the floor like a bundle of clothes.

Meg was fast asleep.

20 ~ WRAPPING

Bett tugged his sleeve and took him aside.

"Grace be ailing and in her room and would see thee soon." She said quietly.

"What ails her?" he asked.

"She do spit blood and the physic says there be little hope for her."

"Perhaps I might use some herbs as we did in the abbey of St. Benets. Horehound, hyssop and rosemary could be of effect. I will see her now, Bett, 'ere I do go to the chapel. Dost thou know that Master Robert hath bid me work with thee in the kitchen? He also hath told me to learn the trade of under-steward. I shall be pleased to work alongside thee again. I shall begin when I have attended to my affairs." He set down the jug and bade her farewell then turned along the passage to the house-keepers room.

He knocked gently. Then opened the door and entered a dark room. He could see little but heard well the cough and rattle of one very ill in a corner bed.

"Who's there" said the voice from the bed.

"Tis I, Peter Meade, returned to the manor. I hear thou art not well, Grace." Without an answer he crossed the room and drew aside the curtain to let in some light. It was made of a heavy brocade material which had become darkened with age and had an even darker mark on it where many hands had grasped it to pull it across the window. The floor was of wooden boards worn shiny by many feet walking paths across it. There was a table by the bed with drinking vessels and jugs upon it and a cupboard in the other corner with its doors tightly shut. The bed was large with four posts, one at each corner and a rail around the top so that a curtain could be drawn around for warmth and privacy. At the foot of the bed was a wooden linen chest. Under a patchwork quilt lay Grace. She was thin and pale and had a racking cough with much wheezing. In between coughs she spoke so quietly, Peter had to put his ear almost to her chapped lips.

She said but three of four words at a time, her breath was so shallow.

"Peter - I fear I- shall not see the - summer. But whether I do - or not - I must tell thee - a secret. First – thou must promise - me not to tell a soul - on the manor what I now - tell thee."

"If it be thy will, Grace, I do promise." She grasped his hand in her bony ones and held it tightly.

"Afore thou tellst me, I would tell thee that I have in mind to treat thee for thy illness, as I have learnt from the monks in the abbey.
Now speak and I shall listen."

Meg was still in the kitchen sleeping.

"Peter I must tell - thee what I have kept - secret about all these - years thou hast lived. - Thou knowest that Rachel - of the dairy - was at thy birth - and did deliver thee. I was there - also and took thee from her - and wrapped thee in the shawl that thy mother had made for thee."

"Thy mother was - a housemaid - named

Hannah. She - died soon after - thy birth. She had spent many long - evenings in the fading light spinning - the flax and weaving that shawl for - thee. When she was told that thou was stillborn, she said that I - must wrap thee up in the shawl and - bury thee in the ten - acre field where thou wast - conceived. I did as I - was bid but - as I was about to dig the hole - for thee thou didst - cry and I found that thou wast - alive. Thy mother - did not survive the birth. She died that very day - as I was nursing - my own child, Richard, and had - enough milk for two, I - decided that I would - raise thee as well."

"Thou knowest my Mother" said Peter "who then was my father?"

Grace went silent again for a while to gain her breath.

"I know not Peter. Thy Mother - did take that name - with her to the grave. I do know that - she was very much in love - with thy father and - there was much talk about the manor - concerning the gentry - but thy mother would never tell - the truth of it."

"Robert De Vere denied all knowledge - and he swore me to - silence and Rachel too. Thou must not tell a soul whilst Robert De Vere Ashton do live. Promise me - Peter promise Me." She pulled herself up to his face then fell back upon the pillows, rattling, coughing, and exhausted.

"I promise thee Grace until I be wed, for then I must share this with Mary."

"Thou art to be wed, Peter?" He could hear a lift in Grace's voice.

"Aye Grace, and on May-day - I shall have thee well enough to be present in the new chapel for which I did obtain the sacred water for its consecration."

"This do give me something - to live for Peter. I bid thee - find some herbs - and I shall do all - that thou wouldst - ask of me - that I might be there. But before thou dost go - look ye in the linen box - at the foot of my bed - and at the bottom thou wilt find - thy birthing shawl. I do wish thee to have it - in remembrance of thy Mother."

Peter lifted the lid of the box and underneath the blankets and linens he found a square of almost white linen cloth with a drawn thread pattern around the edge. It was stiff and slightly yellowed with age and smelt of old lavender. He unfolded it and took it near to the window and noticed that it had a pattern woven into the centre of it. It was not in colour but had been made by twisting the yarn differently so that the light caught it and gave it a sheen.

"I thank thee for this, Grace. I shall treasure it as it is the only thing I have of my mother's." Peter folded it and stuffed it into his pocket.

Her secret now told, Grace seemed already to gasp less.

"Peter, thou hast much to do - to put in order - to see me leave - this room. I shall be at thy handfasting - and Will too."

"Will must be at the wedding for he was my father when thou wast my mother as no others cared for me as ye both hath done."

"Thou hast - said thou art to marry, but who - shall thy wife be, – is she known to me?"

"She be called Mary Howe, the widow of Jonah, the carpenter. She will have me for I have asked her. We shall be wed as I did say, on May-day in the new chapel. There be one more surprise I must tell thee - it be that Mary do carry my child and not that of Jonah. Now this be a secret that I must hold thee to, Grace, for thou hast told me one about my parents and I do now impart this one to thee. There be not a living soul, save for Mary and me, who do know of this truth. We be so much in love that I must share my joy with thee. This child that we desire so much, be like to come into the world about the middle of May and it be my greatest desire that he be born in wedlock. Thou hast told me that I was born out of wedlock and I would not have any son of mine to suffer the pain of derision as I have."

"Peter, I be full of joy for thee. Also I can feel the love thou hast for thy wife-to-be. Would that thou will enjoy the same love that I have with my good man, Will. I shall desire him make, for thee both, a new wicker crib with rockers for thy new son. How dost thou know it will be a son Peter?"

"Mary would have such, Grace, and she did have the Great Oak to tell her what her child will be. She be in such earnest love for me that she is sure that she do give me a son. When I was in the Abbey church, she did come to me in a vision and did tell me that his name would be Adam, for as she did appear to me there, I was looking at the great rose window on the scene of the Garden of Eden."

"Peter, thou hast a wonderful love between thee and Mary. Thou art blessed."

He marvelled at her speed of speech now. She did not quake, nor gasp as she had done at first.

"I must go now Grace. Thou art already on the road to recovery".

With this he kissed her and left her with a

large lump in his throat. As he went out of the door he said. "I shall send someone to tend thee and I shall leave instruction for thy treatment."

21 ~ HERB GARDEN & THE FIRST NIGHT

As he left the house and he called in to the kitchen to collect Meg. He looked in the root store where he had last seen her and as the light fell on her from the open door she jumped up.

"Peter, wherefore went ye away and left me?" She was so angry with him that her face was as red as a hen's wattles.

"Oh, 'tis Peter now and not father!" said Peter picking her up and kissing her, "I did tell thee I was to go to the baker and the dairy. Thou wast so taken by Tom the pot-boy that ye did not hear me." His presence and his love soon calmed her down and she hugged him back.

"Where go we now father?"

"I must to the chapel and then shall we go home for I have bread and milk a-plenty for us all".

Together they walked to the herb garden to find it much overgrown. There were weeds where normally, at this time of year, there should be bare earth ready for the spring planting. The dead stems from last year had not been cleared away and the paths could only just be seen between the little box hedges.

Under the apple trees he found Grissell, wife of Silas the gardener. She was clearing some of the dead twigs that had been blown down in the spring gales and tidying them onto the compost heap. She was pleased to see him but told of how Silias had a bad ague of the bones and had not worked since October. He was mending but could not yet do a full day's work.

Peter saw that the herbs he needed were just beginning to show above the ground and he looked about for others he might need in the future. He showed Grissell that some herbs would be of help to Silas and was able to convince her to attend Grace in her room. He now had the authority to issue such orders but he made them seem requests.

The overgrown herb garden he would have put to rights by sending some fellows to clear last year's growth to allow the spring shoots to thrive. Poor Silas, he had been on the manor all his life from a lad. He knew every corner, every shrub and plant. Peter hoped he would soon be back to his usual tasks. Perhaps Silas should have an apprentice, someone he could train to do any of the jobs that he could not manage himself. Maybe the children of Samuel the saddler might be put to work in the herb garden - Oh and maybe Meg or some of his family too. He would keep it in mind.

He left Grissell and, on the way back, they approached the moat and saw the heron poised ready to take the fish and frogs that were collecting to lay their eggs. That tall grey fisherman was there each spring and was amply repaid for his patience. There were good carp and tench in the moat, some so large that ducklings were seen to be taken from below by them. They turned back to the house, went quickly to the kitchen and collected the jug.

"Come, we shall go home to Mary, Meg. She

be in need of this." They left the warm kitchen and he seemed to walk taller and with purpose. He had many good reasons. He had the challenge to restore Grace to health so she could be with Will, her husband, at the wedding. He would be under-cook and under-steward. Meg seemed to be calm and at home on the manor. When Mary and he were wed they would have the cottage to put in order. But it would have to be before they wed - Oh so much to do and so little time in which to do it. He felt the phial still about his neck.

"Meg I have still to go to the chapel ere we go home. I have to place this sacred water on the altar as I was bidden."

The chapel had been built by the moat bridge. As he approached the bridge, a chill went over his heart and he shuddered.

"What troubles thee father?" asked Meg as she felt Peter wince.

"This chapel stands near the place where my child Peg was drowned. She must have fallen from the bridge where it had been holed by a cart. She became stuck in the deep mud". He pointed to where the water was a hand's breadth deep but the grey mud was about two feet deep. He picked up a stone and tossed it into the moat. There was a small splash and then a gurgle of stinking mud as it sucked the pebble down. He bent down to Meg's level and, with a trembling voice said,

"Meg, promise me that thou wilt never come nigh to this moat for thou hast seen with thine own eyes what can become of pebbles or folk that do fall into it. If folk do fall in, they have no chance of escape - dost thou understand me?" He was stern and pale and almost beside himself with fear.

"Aye, father, I do understand thee. Have no fear for I shall not come here without thee. I do like to play with mud in the puddles but I would like not to be covered by it down there. The ducks do walk upon it but a dog or me could not." He put a protective arm about her and took her into the chapel. He put the phial on the altar between the two candlesticks.

Brother John, the scribe that Mary had used to write to Peter and to read Peter's letters to her, had been caring for the chapel. He had found a deconsecrated church in ruins and had taken the old altar and wooden cross and what else he could cart away to Robert De Vere Ashton's new chapel. Precious stained glass had been put into the windows that once were the old gatehouse mullions. The chapel held a feeling of peace, warmth and tranquillity. The font had been broken, but a good mason had repaired it ready for the service of consecration. Meg found a small joint stool and sat on it rocking it on the uneven floor. It echoed round the place.

Peter walked to the alter and knelt before it. He silently thanked the Lord for all the gifts he had been given. He took the file of holy water from round his neck unwrapped it and placed it on the altar. He knelt and prayed again for all the folk who worshipped in this place, that they would have happy healthy lives.

He stood up, turned round and looked about the place. The chapel door was still open and the sun streamed in across the floor. He jumped as he caught sight of a hangman's noose which cast its shadow upon the floor in his direction. Startled he knocked over a table with a clay vase on it that held some dried flowers. It smashed as it hit the chapel floor. He went cold as a feeling of doom came upon him. He traced the shadow up to the bell rope that Brother John had coiled up out to the way of children, lest they play with it.

He sighed with relief.

He mused that May-Day would be a double celebration, their union and the spring festival. He reckoned that Adam would be born about two weeks after May-Day but only God could decide when this would be.

He felt a cloaking feeling of warmth again but hunger stirred him. He collected up the shards of the pot and together they left the chapel. They walked home in silence down the lane to the cottage and there saw Mary picking tarragon and rosemary. They came up to her from behind as she bent with obvious difficulty. As she rose she placed her hands on her aching back. Her prominent bulge made Peter want to hold her close. There was something about a pregnant woman that Peter always loved. He liked to hold her from behind so that as she leaned her head backwards on his chest he could stroke her belly and feel the child within her moving. She turned round and saw him, he put down the jug and she took him into her arms.

"I do love thee so Peter" she said. He let go of Meg's hand and they kissed for what seemed like an eternity until they grew breathless. Meg tugged his sleeve and they looked down at her and both fondled her hair at the same time.

"At least thou shalt be at home among us." said Mary.

"And thou wilt marry me on Mayday and by

such time we can ask the priest and move to a better home. Time will fly apace." said Peter.

"What didst thou say of a better home Peter - what hast thou done?"

"I have seen Robert De Vere Ashton in person who hath made me under - cook alongside Bett. Also under - steward and hath, as a wedding gift, given us the stewards cottage that do lie vacant. It hath two bedrooms, an attic room and a garden and will be ours without rent." Mary went pale and he had to hold her from falling. He ushered her into the cottage where she sat heavily on the bed. Meg picked up the jug and followed. Mary soon brightened and smiled.

"I do have good news also Peter for we have been given a goat that will bring forth her kids at about the time that Adam will come to us, so I shall be able to feed us all. Thus I will give thee the strong son I did promise thee. All do seem to be pointing towards May-day. Aye 'tis good that thou hast chosen this day for our handfasting. Let us plan for the first matter of our move into the cottage. We shall have so much room that we shall lose each other in such space." said Mary.

Meg smiled the smile of such contentment that her final wish would come true on May-day. That wish was for the love of parents, but she had the additional joy of knowing that she would also have a new brother shortly afterwards.

The cottage was swept clean as a new pin. Mary had taken much more interest in her home with Peter coming and the new baby due.

"I have a posset on the fire Peter" said Mary. She rose slowly to take a small clay pot from the drawer and placed it with great care in the centre of the table.

"This be honey from Will's bees Peter. He did give it to me to give me strength and to help me to sleep." He took up the posset from the hearth and poured it into the cups. Mary picked up a knife and took a small portion of honey and added it to her drink.

"Tis for the both of us." She said - meaning herself and Adam. As he sipped the brew he watched Meg nosing around the room. She was like a partly tamed cat since she had not really known a stable home life that she could recall. Mary called Meg to come to her and she came and sat beside her. She took up a comb and proceeded to tease out the tangles from her golden tresses gently and soothingly. Meg laid her head on Mary's belly as she surrendered to this wonderful treatment, the like of which she had not had before. She put her hand to where Adam moved within.

"I can hear a tiny heartbeat mother" she said, 'tis not mine or thine but that of the baby." Mary bent and kissed her golden head and a small tear came from her eyes. She sniffed and sighed contentedly. Meg had called her 'mother'. All barriers to love had been demolished.

"Soon ye shall have a brother" said Peter. Patting her hand and holding it so that they could both feel the baby's tiny struggles within his mother's womb. The tyg was empty and Peter refilled it from the cauldron. This time Mary put honey in it for Meg and him as she had had enough. He remembered that he had bought the tyg at a fair. It had three handles on it, one for each of the three drinkers, as it was passed around.

He remembered also that he would have to

sleep in the woolshed until the move into the steward's cottage. He told Mary what he was going to do and that he would find some blankets ready for the nights to come. He could not sleep in the cottage with them, there was just not the room. Then an idea struck him. Why sleep in the woolshed when the new cottage was empty and waiting for occupation? Robert De Vere Ashton had given him permission to live there, so why not start as he was to go on? It was nearly the hour when the children would come home from work and with all that had happened he had not eaten since breakfast. Meg had stuffed herself silly in the kitchen chatting to Tom.

A hunger pain shot through him and Mary saw his need. She took a trencher and piled it with pottage that she had made earlier in the day. He was ravenous and devoured the food in silence. It was so good and satisfied him well. Mary took some in a bowl for herself but Meg shook her gold head as she was already full.

The pottage was made from red-roots, cauliworts, onions and beans. No meat was in the pot and had not been so for months. Meg changed her mind as she saw them eating and asked for some pottage. When she was given the bowl, she raised it to her lips. Mary said

"Watch me Meg, for I would show thee how to use a spoon." She showed her how to dip the wooden spoon into the bowl and raise it to her lips. After three attempts Meg got it right and finished the bowlful of food. She smiled, pleased that she had conquered this small task.

"The reason I did tell thee of this use Meg, was that oft-times the food be hot, and if thou didst drink from the bowl it might burn thy mouth.

If thou wouldst use the spoon, thou canst blow upon it to cool it."

"I can write me name now." she beamed with pride. Peter had mopped his trencher dry and Mary refilled it. Mary noticed the jug that Meg had brought into the cottage and put onto the table. She lifted the cloth and looked into it.

"Peter! From whence did you get this cream? 'Tis nigh impossible to have cream on the milk at this time of year."

"It is a present from the hollow oak. I did go to talk to the Great Spirit within the tree and the milk changed to cream." Mary took some of the thick yellow cream from the jug and put it on some bread, eating it with great contentment.

She leaned across and kissed Peter saying, "Thank thee my love. Now I know that all be well." The bond between them was as strong as ever. They sat together with their heads resting on each other. He felt love and peace with just the three of them sitting there by the fire.

He never wanted to leave.

"I must go to Grace and see if she would have any clothes that would fit me in her chest Mary, for I cannot go out in this habit to work, though I can use it to cover me at night."

Mary rose slowly and tried to lift the straw mattress from the truckle bed but found it too much for her, and let it fall back down. He came to her and did the task for her holding it up while she reached in under it. She took out a bundle and placed it on the table and proceeded to untie it. These were his livery clothes that he did not take with him when they arrested him and took him away. His shirts were mended and washed clean. His doublet with the livery badge upon it and his hose were creased but free of moth for she had stored them there with fresh autumn horse chestnuts to dispel the moths. This was a common country habit. His boots she also drew forth and though they were mouldy, were still supple from the neat's-foot oil he had rubbed into them.

How she must have loved him - still loved him and wanted him back with her so much. It showed in the care she took. He turned to her with tears in his eyes that he could no longer hold back. He could not speak but she saw that he was so grateful. He hugged her again fearing that he would harm her by hugging too tight but he hugged her all the same.

At that moment the children all came home and they tumbled into the cottage. It was immediately full of people all talking at once and everybody wanting to hug everybody again. It was time for Peter to leave the cottage for their new home. As he was gathering up his clothes he thought that he must give it a name. The name "Peace Cottage" came to him but he would not burden Mary with the name until he had thought it out more. He was now getting used to quelling his impetuous nature that often led him to make rash or instant decisions.

"Where art thou going father?" asked Meg as she and Becky saw Peter rise to go with his bundle.

"I must away to the new cottage for I cannot sleep here - there is but room herein for ye. Thou knowest that I would not be parted from ye, but it be for the best."

Mary said "I would not be parted from thee so soon, Peter. The childer can make room for Meg on the floor upstairs and thou canst sleep with me on the truckle bed. There is room for two if thou does not mind me close." Peter was not looking forward to a lonely night on his own and to sleep with Mary would be his idea of heaven.

"Hast thou a mattress for Meg? I would not have her lying on the cold boards." Peter was always concerned for others before himself.

"We have not a mattress for her but there be a spare blanket that can be folded to make a bed and a cloak for a coverlet." With this decided the children were bundled off to bed and Peter and Mary were on their own sitting by the fire and talking of all the things that had happened since they last met. Peter rose and put a couple of logs on the fire to last the night and returned to his place beside Mary. They felt mellowed by the fire, the posset and the successes of that day. The family seemed complete.

Mary moved closer to Peter and looked into his eyes. She could not read the expression there. He looked as though he was in a dream world. He was completely relaxed and at home. She put her head on his shoulder and picked up his hand and he looked at her. They sat in silence for a long time watching the fire dance on the burning logs. They savoured this long awaited togetherness after the seeming eternity of being driven apart. Mary reached under the mattress and pulled out a new shirt that she had made him.

"I did make this for our wedding day, Peter. But I do think that this is a better time to give it to thee." He took off his habit and she pulled off his old shirt over his head and put the new one on him. It smelled of lavender as did she herself. He felt the collar and touched a lump.

"What be this in the collar, Mary?"

"It is the traditional acorn for long life, strength and fertility for the bride-groom." He laughed.

"I have need of long life with thee my love and strength too, but I do believe that I have proven my fertility."

"Oh Peter I did wonder that we might not ever see thee again. After so much pain and the cruelty of parting. I do love thee more now than ever I did and do need thee with me." She fondled his hair and his neck. She nibbled his ear and made him groan and shudder. She smelled so good, but why did she and others all smell of lavender - was this some conspiracy he thought. Grace, Mary and Ruth all had that lovely air about them. It confused his feelings.

Then he kissed her very lightly and gently on the lips. It was the merest brush of his mouth against hers but Mary's body reacted with a warm rush of blood to the skin and a dampness between her legs that she was not ready for. This man had always had this effect on her. She did not understand it but she loved it. He looked at her and she knew what was in his mind. After so long without him, she burned a strong as ever with desire. She put her hands in his lap and found his manhood half erect. She stroked him tenderly and brought him to full extension. She took it and rolled it like dough between her hands.

"Mary I want thee so but I am afraid I may hurt thee or thine unborn child."

"Be not afraid my love. Just be gentle. I do want thee also." His hand rested lightly on her knee and he kissed her again. This time with more passion. They stood up and he took her into his arms but Adam came between them. He led her gently to the bed and sat her down. Kneeling between her legs he undid the lacing of the bodice of her gown, opened it and gently pushed it off her shoulders and slid her arms out of it. She stood up again and let the gown slide off her bulge and onto the floor. She sat down heavily with just her shift on. Peter took off his new shirt and folded it carefully and laid it aside. Then he picked up her gown and folded that also. He knew that he had all night to make love to Mary and he did not have to rush. Mary started to shiver. It was cold in spite of the fire. Peter picked up a blanket and laid Mary down on the straw mattress and covered her. Then he climbed in next to her and cuddled close. Indeed he had no choice the bed was only just wide enough for them both.

When she had warmed a little, he pulled up her shift and lifted it over her head so that underneath the blanket she was naked. He kissed her neck and her shoulders and ran his hands down her back. He knew that she had been having backache so he rubbed a little harder on the muscles that were being used to support the weight of Adam. He kneaded them and rolled them in his hands. Then slowly allowed himself the pleasure of cupping her breast. He felt the extra weight of it as nature was already preparing her for motherhood. He rolled her onto her back and made little circles of kisses on the pliable white mounds. Her nipples started to stand up for themselves and he sucked them playfully. His hands wandered down over her belly so swollen and full of promise. Adam was lying quiet for once and Peter put his ear against her to listen to the little heartbeat.

He reached down further and rubbed her centre of desire. He felt a rush of moisture on his hand and knew that she was ready for him. His own member sprang into life and throbbed at him with an insistence he had not known for a long time. Mary rolled over onto her side with her back to him and encouraged him to enter her vagina from behind. She could feel his need and as he moved slowly within her, she felt that this must be what heaven was like. He put his arm around her and relaxed; his manhood was rigid within her. She lay still not wanting to break the spell. Peter's breathing steadied and then fell into a regular, slow rhythm. Mary listened and realised that the grey blanket of tiredness had overtaken Peter's mind and that he had fallen asleep. It had been a long day full of ups and downs, full of emotional stress and after so many days on the road Peter needed sleep more than anything else. She reached down the bed and pulled another blanket over them to ward off the chill of the night to come and snuggled down into Peter's body warmth.

....

Mary opened her eyes. She need not have bothered.

It was dark. Very dark.

The sort of dark that is all around you and presses in on the senses. She could hear the wind moaning gently around the thatch. But she could not see the walls of the cottage. No starlight could get through the covering over the windows. She could hear a mouse scratching in the woodpile and the smell of wood smoke hung in the air but

the fire was out and not a glimmer came from
that side of the room. It was not just an absence
of light but a presence of dark. It must be early
morning but what had woken her. She felt Peter
still behind her blowing gently in her ear. He was
still in a deep sleep.

Adam moved. He was going to be a strong
baby and a strong man. She could feel his arms
and legs practising for when they would be
needed. She could also feel something else - a
tiny grating feeling. It didn't hurt. It was as if
someone was running a fingernail down a piece of
linen cloth. He must have grown his fingernails or
his toenails and be rubbing on the inside of her.
She put her hand on her belly and rubbed back to
show him that she cared. He lay quiet again.

She knew that it must be nearly time to get up
but she did not want to disturb Peter so she lay
still and thought about the day to come and what
it might bring. She was not sure if he was awake
or still asleep.

"Mary," he whispered, "do I dream?"

He snuggled up so close to Mary's back they
became like two spoons nestling in a drawer. His
left hand was under her neck and stroked her face
while his right slid beneath her right arm to cup a
breast.

"Mary - if ever I went away from thee again -
it would be in death only."

"Say not so" she began - "for I wish for many,
many years with thee and will not hear more of
parting. My heart is so full of love it doth hurt
me. Just thy touch upon my face, my lips, my
body - do cause me relief and desire both at once.
I pray thee never to talk again of parting, else I
would weep and never stop. I need thy presence

more now - I know that thou hast work to do on the manor and must go to it daily and we shall have a new cottage - but if we just had what we have now, I would be glad to suffer it - with thee among us."

This flood of words astonished Peter so that he just lay and listened and held her close. She spoke in a low voice but he felt sure that all upstairs heard every word said between them.

When she drew breath Peter said -

"God above hath given me so many things to give thanks for. My pardon and return, my place of work and our new home. Our new daughter and soon Adam. My gift of writing and, above all, the great tide of thy love that I would gladly drown in."

There was a rumble on the stairs. It was Aaron. He was usually the first one up in the morning. He pounded down the wooden stair and said;

"Art thou awake?

Why is the fire not lit?

Coo - tis dark."

Mary made as if to get up but Peter's arm tightened around her. Then Kitty came down and felt her way to the fireplace and re-kindled the fire and from it lighted a small rush wick to give them some light so that they could get started on the morning.

As soon as it was light outside they would be off to their employments.

Mary rolled out of Peter's arms and got up to make the breakfast. She cut the bread and put the cheese on the table for the children. There was a little pottage left from the day before so she warmed it up on the fire for anyone who wanted it. Peter sat up in bed with a hot drink that she made for him.

Meg came quietly down the stair. She got into bed with Peter and gave him a hug.

"What shall I do this day, father?"

"Me thought thou wouldst go with Alys to help Silas dig the earth and clear the herb garden so that the plants may grow unhindered. Wouldst thou like that, Meg?"

"Can I not be with thee?"

Peter knew that Meg was going to have to learn to work without him being next to her all the time. He was going to have to be firm with her. So he explained what he had to do and where he would be but told her very strictly that she must do her own work and leave him to do his.

Mary said, "Meg, dost thou remember the tooth fairies?"

"Aye, Mother. Have they taken my tooth?" Meg climbed out of bed and reached the old cup from the shelf where Mary had put it and peered into it. Her teeth were gone and in their place was a linen bag. She took it out of the cup and put it on the table. She had never had a fairy gift before and she was not sure what to do with it.

"Have a look inside, Meg." said Peter. "Carefully!" Meg pulled the bag open and looked at the contents.

"There be some little stones in here, father. What do I with them?" Meg was puzzled.

"Let me see them, Meg." Meg took the bag over to Peter and he looked into it.

"Why, they be seeds, Meg. If you do put them into the ground they will grow into plants. Ask your Mother what plants they will be for she do know such things." Peter was pleased with this gift for it would give Meg a good reason to go to the garden with Alys. Meg showed the bag to Mary and she told her that the white flat ones looked like the seeds from the herb angelica and the long black ones were sweet cecily. There were also some little round black ones that could not be identified because so many herbs had small seeds like that. Meg closed the bag and put it safely in her pouch.

"I shall ask Silas for some earth for to grow my fairy seeds."

Mary was sitting outside her cottage in the April sunshine. She was using her lucette to make a cord. The lacing in her gown was getting frayed and she knew that she would need a new lace soon. The lucette had a wooden handle and two horns made from the horn of an ox. She had one stitch on each and a hooked needle to weave them with.

Daniel passed leading the Master's horse. The horse danced when he saw Mary, and Daniel stopped to settle him down and show him that he had nothing to fear. He was a large well-built animal, mainly the colour of the chestnuts when they fall off the tree in autumn. He had two white feet and a lopsided white blaze on his roman nose.

"Good morrow, Mary" said Daniel.

"Good morrow to thee Daniel. Be the master's new horse settling down now?"

"He be missing his companion that he did have at the last place where he did live. I do not have another horse that I can put with him. I need some other animal to keep him company."

Mary had been trying to find a place to put her goat, but with no success. She was not sure that a goat and a horse would get on together but she could ask Daniel what he thought.

She asked if her goat would make a suitable companion for the horse and he told her that its last companion had been a goat and he would be very pleased to house her goat in the stable with the horse. Mary explained that it was ready to kid anytime and Daniel said he would make it a small stall area in the corner of the stable where the horse would not accidentally step on the kids.

This was a fine arrangement. Mary could now go to Ruth Weaver and tell her that she could take the animal home and that she had a place under cover where it would be warm and dry.

So when she had finished her cord, she put on her cloak and walked off the manor and through the village to Ruth's cottage. Ruth was sitting outside, watching the people go about their business. Her hands were resting uselessly in her lap and she was looking very unhappy.

Mary greeted her and she looked up, happy that someone had come to visit her. Mary told her about Daniel having trouble with the master's new horse and how it used to have a goat as a companion. Ruth had been concerned how Mary was going to find a place to put the animal overnight but this seemed a perfect arrangement. She got up from her stool and found a stout string for Mary to tie around the goat's collar so she could lead her home. The goat was called Imp because; when she was a kid, she was so naughty. She would leap on and off the piles of hay and even jump onto the back of the person who was

trying to milk her mother. She butted the ducks
and geese, and even chased the cats if they came
into the yard where she lived. She had a rich
brown coat and a large white triangle on her side.
She also had a dark stripe from the end of her long
nose to the tip of her tail and down the front of
her legs. Her hair was long and she had a dense
undercoat of wool to keep her warm in winter.

Mary thanked Ruth yet again for Imp and they
walked back through the village side by side.
They did make a funny sight. Mary waddled a
little with her great bulge and the weight of
Adam, and Imp also waddled with the weight of
her kids within her great belly.

When they got to the stables Daniel was
waiting for them. He had set up some hurdles in
the corner of the horse's stall, put down some
straw on the ground and made a very cosy place
for Imp. She nosed the straw. She was not used
to such luxuries. She lifted her ears and went
over and touched noses with the horse. They
blew at each other and then Imp pawed at the
straw and lay down next to the hurdle near the
horse. The horse sniffed her and then lay down
next to her.

"All is well." said Daniel, "they be friends
already." He threw a handful of hay into the
horse's hay rack and left a pile on the floor for Imp
and also made sure that she had a bucket of
water. Daniel turned to Mary and said, "I will give
the goat hay and water as she is helping me with
the horse but thou must find all her other food.
Dost thou know what she doth need?"

"Aye, Ruth had instructed me that I should
know how to keep her well." Mary had been
learning that Imp needed branches and leaves to

eat each day and that she must get some grain or stale bread from the baker for extra food when the kids were due and when she was milking.

Mary walked home across the yard knowing that the goat was in good hands. She would instruct one of the children to take the animal out on the common land the next day so that she could get her fill of green food.

One day, about a week later, Alys came running into the cottage where Mary was just preparing to go to the woolshed to work.

"Mother, Mother, Imp be not well. She will not get up and she doth lie and moan."

Alys had gone to take the goat out to the common to eat but she had come straight back and was most agitated. Mary went straight away to see what was wrong with Imp. They walked across the yard and Alys danced up and down and urged Mary to hurry. As they turned the corner to the stables they heard a bleat. It did not sound like Imp, it was too high pitched and the animal sounded as if it was in pain. Mary peered into the stall and instead of one goat there were three. Imp had had two kids and was licking them dry. One was all white with dark stripes like its mother and the other one looked black all over. They were lifting their heads from the straw and bleating and one was trying to get to its feet. It struggled and got two feet underneath its body and then fell again, its feet sliding out in all directions. Imp was lying down again and ignoring the kids whilst she moaned and pushed.

"Why doth Imp not care for her babies?" cried Alys.

"Hush," said Mary, "She doth have other work

at present."

The goat pushed out the after-birth and stood up with it trailing from her. She turned around and started to eat the red bloody mass. Alys turned away and Mary put an arm around her to comfort her.

"Tis nature's way, Alys."

The dogs had followed them to the stable and the smell of blood was just too much for them. A nose sneaked in under the rail and stole some of the meat from the goat. He clamped his jaw tightly onto it and ran away so that no-one could take it from him.

Mary and Alys stood and watched as the goat finished clearing up and went back to the kids, making sure that they were clean all over. They both eventually staggered to their feet and nuzzled at their mother's legs and gradually worked their way along her body until they found what they were looking for. There was an udder full of first milk for them and as they pushed at their mother the milk began to drip out. First one kid and then the other found a teat and began to suckle. Mary knew that they would now be all right on their own; indeed they had not needed any assistance at all. Imp had done it all by herself. Mary hoped that her birth would be as easy.

Alys was very excited and wanted to go and tell all the other children that the goat had kidded. Mary let her go.

The goats were going to get a lot of visitors that day.

22 ~ PEACE COTTAGE

One morning Peter was walking to work and he was met by the Steward, Richard Wood. They had been brought up together and he was often mistaken for Peter as they looked so like brothers. They even had the same shaped beards and walked the same. They had always got along so well together.

"I have good news for thee Peter and Mary too. Robert DeVere hath bidden me to tell thee that the cottage next to mine be ready for ye all to move into. The chapel also be finished and ready for consecration. On May-day thy wedding shall be the first to be conducted there and the Master hath declared a holiday on the manor to celebrate both thy handfasting and the May-day festival. Further he did say he would not charge thee for the use of the chapel."

"Then who will pay the priest's charge?" asked Peter. They both fell silent as Richard shuffled his feet in obvious embarrassment Peter sensed he had asked an awkward question, but how was he to know this.

"I would have told thee after thy wedding Peter, for it is I who will pay for it. When thou wast taken from us Grace did tell me that though we were brought up by her and Will as brothers, thou wast not their real son but an orphan taken in by Grace. Peter, I owe thee much for thy love as a brother these 37 years, that I insist that I pay for thy handfasting. How sayest thou to this. Thou willt accept it, I pray thee?" He was very serious for such a usually happy man. Peter crushed him in his arms. No words could he find for such love that had always existed between them.

"I accept and gladly on behalf of us both, Richard. After our wedding I have to tell Mary a great secret and thou shalt also be privy to it. I do feel a great charm hath been cast upon us both these past six months that I cannot understand but this I do know - whatever befalls us all, it seemeth to be a part of some great plan. I give thee my hearty thanks, for this do lift a burden from my mind and that of dear Mary's too. I shall still have in mind to have a ring for her, but I have not yet the coin for it. Mayhap I could borrow one." A lump came in his throat as he thought of Lydia's ring and of that fateful day when Peg was born and Lydia died.

"Hast thou been to see about a cart, Peter, for thy chattels?" asked Richard.

" Aye, I have and the use of two men but we have so little that I dare say that the children and I will be able to move what we own. As soon as we are bundled up we shall move into Peace cottage."

"Peace cottage!" exclaimed Richard with some surprise "do we speak of the same place?"

"Aye we are for I have named it thus before we go to it."

"I wish thee all good fortune Peter and all thy days there to be indeed peaceful."

Richard turned and with a wave of his hand,

he left Peter to continue on his way.

Later that day Peter, Becky, Meg and Kitty explored the new cottage from attic to garden and made mental notes of how they might all fit in for sleeping. They all seemed agreed that the boys should sleep in the attic as they thought it would be more their kind of domain.

The bright eyes of Meg spotted the legless figure of a wooden doll in a corner of the attic and, when she showed it to Peter, he said "I shall unto the carpenter to see if he can make thee some legs - see ye remind me."

Kitty found an old pair of children's shoes in the inglenook of the hearth. They were dried up but would be wearable after treatment with neat's-foot oil like Peter used for his boots.

"Who would they fit?" he mused. He stood up in the bedroom and hit his head on an old horn lantern that hung from the central beam. Becky heard him howl and rushed up the creaking stairs to see her father sitting on the floor nursing his head. He rubbed his head as he got up and took the lantern down to examine it more closely. It was square with a frame of metal, a metal base and a handle on the top so that it could be hung up or carried. Four panels of horn were put, one in each side, to protect the candle flame and make it burn straight. One panel was missing.

"Be dammed to it" he cursed still rubbing his sore head that had started to drip blood down his brow. He seemed more interested in the lacking pane of horn. Without it the lamp would not burn right. He cast about him searching for the missing item before he saw the blood on the floor.

"Father take this muckinder for thy head" said Becky pulling it from her pocket. He took it, not thanking her, as he was preoccupied with finding the missing horn panel. She searched with him and found it sticking up between two floorboards by the wall under the window. It was cracked but in one piece. He bent and kissed her and told her that she was a clever girl. The window had a hole in it and birds had flown in and made a nest in the roof. Under the window was a piece of sacking that a previous tenant had put in the hole to stop the wind and the birds. Peter replaced it, looking around first that he would not be trapping a bird in the cottage.

They left the cottage with hope and the feeling of a new page about to be written in all their lives. Meg clutched her legless wooden doll, Becky the old shoes and Peter the horn lantern so he could fix it later. He was convinced the name of 'Peace Cottage' was just right. They called at the bakery and dairy and begged a loaf and some milk with the promise to pay as soon as Peter took up his stewarding and cooking duties. He had arranged a haywain to carry their belongings, few as they were, from Mary's cottage. He had went to see Jon the carver for him to ask him to make a plaque to go above the door.

They called at the stable-yard and asked Kat for a cart.

"Aye I will have one for thee just after dawn. I will ask Roger or his brother Pip to prepare the plough-horse Conqueror to pull the wagon."

As they drew close to Mary's cottage, Peter stopped and put his head to one side listening.

"What is the matter father?" asked Becky.

"I do hear a rustling sound in my head, like autumn leaves" he explained. They all stood still and listened.

"So do I" said Becky.

"And me" said Meg. They walked on and the rustling grew much louder. As soon as they reached the door of the cottage it ceased. Mary answered Peter's knocking and beamed a smile as she took his hand and drew him in with the girls and kissed them all. Him especially.

Peter thought - how calm and serene she was as she took the bread and milk from the girls. The lines about her eyes were not there, the corners of her mouth turned upward and not downward in sadness. Her skin shone and was tight, not slack from underfeeding as it had been for too long.

Despite her shape and size, she moved with ease and stood tall with matronly pride. To him she was the dream he had seen in sleep so many times at the monastery. Each time he had reached out to touch and hold her in that cold abbey cell, she had dissolved into mists. So long she had been a phantom - a source of worry that he might never see her again and even worse never see the son she so wanted to give them.

Becky shook him as again he seemed in a trance - this was happening too often and it scared her. She feared that something was eating at his mind. He came to and found he was sitting by Mary at the table with a bowl of milk bread and oats, he looked pale and Mary could see that something was troubling him. He told her about the recurring bad dream he had in the abbey and she held him close like a frightened child that had just woken up from some nightmare. He rallied and began to eat the food she had made him. He forgot to tell her about the rustling they had heard outside.

"We shall move into the Cottage on the morrow my love. What little we have between us will fit easily on the wain I have ordered from Kit at the stable yard. Pip or Roger will help us."

Turning to the boys he said "We shall have the great chestnut plough-horse Conqueror to pull us there." He knew they loved the manor horses and donkeys. "We shall have to be ready as soon we have risen, eaten and bundled up on the morrow."

"Dost thou think of a name for our new home Mary? - I do have a mind and liking for the name "Peace Cottage".

She was silent for some moments then said - "Aye Peter - I like it well. What think'st thou Kitty?" turning to the girls beside them.

"Aye it do give me a feeling of love and comfort." she agreed.

"Then I shall seek out Jon, the woodcarver, and desire him make us a board for the door."

He rose and took up his boots doublet and hose and a fresh shirt and went into the upper room and changed. In his red hat with the broken pheasant feather and ordinary clothes, he came down as Peter, the cook and under-steward, leaving behind Peter the Friar.

Meg just stared at him not knowing what to do or say. He saw her dismay and picked her up and cuddled her before any tears started.

"Meg I am no different inside these garments. No different than when I did find thee in the streets of Binstead-in-Broadwells. I am still the same man who did care for thee. The same that thou didst travel with all those months in the cold and wet. I do love thee still, as all my children; even without thy front teeth, little lady."

She buried her face in his beard and hugged

him so hard he choked. She broke away a little -
far enough to kiss him and smile at him. Mary
came close and put her arms around them both as
far as she could and said "I love thee too Meg," and
ruffled her golden hair.

He set her down on her feet and said;

"My love, I have much to do on the manor, for
our move, and to see about the use of the chapel
for our marriage. I will see about the board for
our cottage door, the woodpile, and a water-butt.
I shall need a tinder-box and spills too."

His heart pounded with the joy of being home
and with the thrill and challenge of the future
over which he would now have control.

"My old boots feel stiff and hard but the dew
will soften them. I shall have to call on the
stillroom to fetch some neat's-foot oil. Be there
ought else thou wouldst have me do this day,
Mary?" he questered.

"Nay, unless thou canst find a pouch or pot of
money" she chuckled. "Why dost thou not take
Meg and Nem and Becky with thee for then Meg
will see the whole manor in thy day's business.

"Mary, thou canst indeed read my mind, for I
was about to bid them to come with me 'ere thou
didst say it."

Meg needed no persuasion and held out her
hand to him ready for the day ahead.

Nem said he would stay at home with Mary as
it was cold outside. Poor Nem - he really did feel
the cold and wanted his mother. He would often
stay with or near her. He was a mother's boy and
had nearly been lost at birth as he was so small
and early-born.

Becky said "I would love to be with thee
father, and Meg too, but I must be at the

woolshed as Tilly be abroad this day with her man." She giggled and said. "Tilly be smitten with Edmund the bowyer."

"Love doth indeed be free in the manor air these days" said Mary.

"My love is strong as ever Mary" said Peter. "Dost thou still remember the letter I did send to thee from the abbey. It did only take me in truth a few moments to make it in my head, but did take me all one night, in my slowness, to write it down for thee. I still love thee as I did all those months and dark days and nights ago. I have fallen to temptation only once since we were parted on the way home here, at the Swan Inn. I seek thy forgiveness if thou art willing." He bowed his head, his eyes shut, waiting.

"Peter, whatever thou hast done, thou hast suffered much these several months. I desire not to know what it was - but whatsoever - I do forgive thee. Thou art but a man. We all have need to explore the world the short time we be here - say no more of this." She kissed him and he sighed and rose to go out with Meg. She needed no persuasion and held her hand for him to take as Mary opened the door for them.

"I thank thee my love for thy blessing, I shall now go about the day's business and return this evening." He hugged her again and patted her belly gently as he would when Adam would be in his cradle.

"Wait here a moment Peter" Mary went back into the cottage and brought out two ring-dried apples she had kept since the autumn. She gave them one each. Meg sniffed at hers and wondered what she should do with it. The apple-rings were on a cord of flax like the beads of a necklace and rattled their biscuit-dryness at her.

"Do I eat this or wear it mother?" she asked in all honesty. Mary laughed loud and long. Her whole being wobbled in merriment. Meg felt silly and buried her face in Peter's hands.

"Why, thou canst eat it my pet. Shall I show thee what thou must do?" Meg turned to her and nodded. She added "Where are the stars and the wishes in my apple mother?" Mary was puzzled and asked Meg what she meant.

"Peter - father......" she corrected herself, though she need not have done .."Father did tell that each apple doth have star wishes in the pips and I had three given me by the fairies and that all did come true".

She told how it all happened when he had found her in the streets of Binstead-in-Broadwells. She splashed readily without her two front teeth and dribbled like a baby down her chin. Mary took a clean muckinder gave it her and she wiped her face with it. As she told the tale of the wishes she swelled with pride.

Mary smiled at Peter and then took an apple-ring, broke it in half off the cord and popped half into her mouth. Meg watched amazed and did the same with the other half. Mary showed that by sucking it she took flavour from it and eventually it softened and could be chewed and swallowed.

They looked a strange but funny sight. All three standing in the doorway sucking and chewing on apple-rings. They were very tasty.

Peter put Meg's cloak about her, as he took her hand. He hugged Mary warm and long not wanting to leave her again, but he must become used to it. At least he would see her every day and keep her warm every night. Oh how he loved this woman, how he missed her after he was taken from her. He roused himself and pulled away. Mary waved as the two travellers went off to Briarmeade manor.

As the door shut, the rustling sound began again, and they both stopped in the lane to determine from whence it seemed to came. Both Meg and Peter heard it but neither said a word. They stopped at the gates and were admitted by the keeper.

"Where shall we go father?" asked Meg. He did not reply. He was deep in thought and had not really heard her.

"Father" she yelled up at him, bewildered by his silence. Still he said nothing.

"Peter, Peter" she screamed, frightened by his strange change in character.

"Pardon Meg " he said. "I was miles away - what did ye say?"

"I just called thee, father, as thou wast in a trance again. Where go we this day?"

"I must go first to the great hollow oak tree and show thee where it is." he said. They passed the dovecote and went quickly down Harvest lane.

"Here is the source of much wisdom Meg - I bid thee come and feel it now as the leaves do appear and the sap is rising."
All around there was a canopy of light green oak leaves. They went inside the great wooden void. Peter sat on the rich dark brown earth and Meg did the same, feeling the earth with her small fingers and looking up through the branches at the blue sky above them.

The rustling began again and was so loud, it was frightening. They both heard it and covered their ears, then it ceased abruptly and all was cold silence. They both had a message thrusting into their minds which said - "Take my offspring from thy place and put it in thy new garden."

It meant nothing to them. Meg said "What does it mean father?"

"I know not Meg - but it may be that Mary might know as she doth commune with the trees at times for guidance".

He rose from the earth casting the message into the mists of his mind and together they left the tree. There was no more rustling and Meg walked along with a look of puzzlement on her young face. Peter set to thinking that he must remember to speak to Mary as soon as he was home.

They found Richard, the head steward, who told Peter what he should do when he encountered labourers, visitors and vagrants on the manor. Richard was a kindly man never seen to lose his temper and gracious in requests. Richard said that there was a spare tinder-box in the stillroom on the windowsill. He might have it but it needed a new striker. There were spare spills by the hearth in plenty. The smith would be able to fashion a new striker from an old horseshoe that would give multitudes of sparks.

Peter knew already where he could find tinder. Under the trees there grew the puffballs that if soaked in nitre and dried, would hold a spark for a fair time, to light a spill. He also knew how to heat scraps of linen cloth so that they turned black and made excellent tinder.

Meg and Peter arrived at the great kitchen, but Bett had no real need of him just then. She said that Sorrel was ill but she would not be missed.

"Would ye be about to carve at high-board at noon Peter?" she asked. "We have dressed peacock, pork and carp this day".

"Aye I will with pleasure Bett." he replied - feeling the warmth of being asked and wanted, as he was before he was banished.

"But I have not my knives".

"Ay Peter, Mary hath given them to me for safekeeping." She showed him the eight knives and his steel in their scabbards hanging behind the pantry door, oiled and sharp,

He took them down and examined each one and caressed each handle like meeting an old friend, then put each back in its proper place.

"I shall be back in good time to carve at noon" he said. The first flies of the year buzzed about the kitchen and the kitchen cat jumped about in vain attempts to catch them. Bett shoved it off the board where the maids were preparing food, and pushed it out of the door. Meg whined as she had been playing with it until then.

Peter took her aside and pacified her by showing her how Tom was turning the pork meat on the spit and basting it with a feather dipped in the dripping pan. He sprinkled chopped sage and onions on it now and then. The smell was wonderful.

Meg said "Can I stay here and do this with Tom father?" He turned to Bett who answered;

"Aye Meg, but thou must be aware of three things. They be fire, hot pots, and sharp knives. If thou dost hear a maid call, 'ware embers,' thou must give place and let her pass, for she will carry a shovel with burning embers from the hearth to charge the charcoal grids, or the bread ovens. Also have a care when thou wouldst touch a pot for though it do look dark or blackened thou shouldst best use a pot-clout or test its heat with a wet finger. The wool of thy clothes will not burn quickly from sparks but thou must dowse them as soon as thou dost smell it singeing".

Peter added to the conversation by showing her how to cut a red-root and an onion.

"Meg, thou must always use a sharp knife, for a blunt edge doth take more effort in cutting and can cause thee to cut wrongly, or worse, cut thyself." He showed her, using his own blade from his belt the small one he called his "prince" knife. He had another that he used for carving the great joints at high-board. It was fully 14 inches long and had its own scabbard. This one he called the "king of knives" for it was the biggest on the manor.

"Now if ye be cutting and would speak with a maid or cook, ye must not cut and look away at them. Many have cut and looked away and have lost their finger-tips. I would not have thy hands damaged at any price my little one. This be how to cut an onion."

He held the vegetable on a cutting board so as not to cut the great wooden table. He took off the top and nearly all of the root end.

"Why dost thou not take off all of the root end father?" she observed.

"Watch me and learn" he said. "I do cut the onion in half from top to bottom and then turn it to cut down again almost right through. I cut the round side across with this flat part on the board and......"

..............."It falls into little bits." she ended as he cut it.

"Peter did show young Tom how to do this

when he first came here." Bett said

"Tom! Come hither and show Meg what Peter taught thee." Tom proudly took out his own knife that Peter had handled and given him, and deftly peeled and chopped another onion. Meg peered closely at his actions and soon found the reason he used his blade at arm's length. As he wiped off the blackening juice on a cloth, Meg's eyes ran. The more she rubbed and wiped them, the worse they became. She cried both with pain and embarrassment and Peter let her bury her face in his doublet. He fondled her golden head as she sobbed but she soon stopped. Tom laughed at her which made her flush red. She rounded on him and glaring like a cat screamed -

"Horrid boy - I hate thee!" and she laid into him with her small fists. Tom held her at arm's length until she tired and quietened and gave up.

"Now Meg, dost thou see that Tom had been taught to stay as far as he could from the onions he did cut?" explained Peter.

Bett came and stroked her head as Peter consoled her. She picked her up and cuddled her, an action never seen before. She was thought to abhor childer, being, what all believed, a confirmed spinster and secondly a dragon cook.

Tom said "Meg, do forgive me - for I took the same chaffing and fun against me when Peter did teach me at first." She turned to him from Bett's clutches and grinned at him with her gappy mouth. She slid to the floor and Tom said "I shall show thee again if thou wilt let me Meg".

He took his knife and gave her another from the board similar to his own. These knives Peter had himself fashioned from old worn larger ones past their best. He had free use of the smith's water-stone, and made several for the maids and the baker.

Tom did each stage of preparing the onion slowly and Meg copied him - always at arm's length. She fumbled a little and dropped one half on the floor but picked it up and wiped it clean. Peter came behind her and placed his large hands upon hers to give her the strength she had not yet attained. She tried to turn and look up at him but he held her firmly and said "No Meg - what did Bett tell thee a moment ago? If thou wouldst look away thou must cease to cut." As she moved round she cut not her hand, but his finger.

She dropped the knife as if it had burned her. Bett came over and looked at the blood on the board and washed it off rapidly.

Peter tore off a strip from a pot-cloth, put a dab of fresh honey on a mint leaf and bound up the finger. Bett ripped the end and tied it round for him. Meg went pale, fainted and slid to the stone floor. Tom caught her just in time to stop her gold head hitting the ground.

He knelt beside her, patted her hands, splashed cold water on her face and blew on her closed eyes. She opened her eyes and came round in his arms. She looked up at him and smiled, realised who it was, she thanked him with a great hug.

Peter said to Bett "Love at 6 and 8 years old. It doth beat my first love at 10." Meg stood up feeling shy again and looked at the floor. The incident came back to her and she sat down on the bench.

"Father do please forgive me - I meant not to harm thee" She looked so pitiable.

"Have no fear Meg for I have done much worse myself. Tom doth care for thee, for 'twas he who did save thee from hitting the hard floor and brought thee back to us."

Tom sat on the bench beside her holding her hands stroking them. Worry left his face. She regained her rosy glow and ignoring all, who had moments before been all attention upon her, walked to the open kitchen door, and out into the sunshine, with Tom in tow. She found the cat.

Bett's ladle hit the board and work began again. Peter excused himself and went into the garden to find Tom and Meg playing with the cat. They were the best of friends.

Bett walked to the open door, leaned on the door post contemplating the scene, her arms folded across her ample bosom, ladle in hand. She smiled to herself with great comfort.

Peter called Meg to him and they walked home in comfortable silence.

As they came to Mary's cottage Meg tugged Peter's sleeve, "Dost thou remember the rustling. I hear it not!"

"I will ask Mary if she knows of it."

Inside the cottage all was quiet. The childer were busy eating and Mary nodded them towards the pottage pot on the fire and two bowls on the edge of the board.

When the meal was finished, Peter said, "Mary, I had a message which mayhap have come from the hollow oak. Methinks it did say:- 'Take my offspring from thy place and put it in thy new garden.' I know not what it doth mean. Canst thou understand?"

"Aye, I do know what we must do. I did take an acorn from that tree. It did wish that I plant it in our new garden that it may grow into a strong healthy new tree. As the tree do grow, so will our son."

The next morning Peter, Meg, Becky and Kitty, all woke to see a sunny spring morning. Trees had burst into life and the world seemed to rejoice for them. They had all slept well and were eager to get their breakfast and bundle up their few belongings ready to move out. Mary slept on as she'd had a restless night made from worry about those little things that women seem to concern themselves with.

Would there be any food cupboards? Would the cottage be noisy so near to the road and the gatehouse? Would the cottage carry any illness in its walls? She told herself not to be afraid, but in her present state she was easily troubled over the simplest thoughts.

Mary woke and looked pale but after she had a drink and some bread, she revived to her old self. She got the rest of the children up and made sure they all had a task to do so that Peter was given less to do when the cart came. The boys rolled all the straw mattresses and tied them up with some flax string that Mary kept for such times. Then they put the small amount of meal left in the barrel into a cloth bag. They packed the trenchers and other household utensils into the barrel for ease of carrying.

In far less than an hour, they were ready. Peter made several trips to the door to see if the cart was coming. At last it rumbled into view and the boys ran down the lane to walk alongside it. Daniel pulled it to a stop outside Mary's cottage and Peter and the boys loaded it. He lifted the children up onto the cart. Mary sat like a princess on the rolled-up mattresses and held the rail. She was midway between the two wheels so she was shaken less by the bumps in the road.

In a very short time they drew up before "Peace Cottage" where Jon the carver was nailing the wooden name over the door.

"Why do we have a bird and a twig on our cottage?" asked Nem.

Peter explained, "This bird is the dove of peace and the twig be an olive branch. When I was with the monks at St Benet's Abbey, Nem, I did learn about Noah and the ark. For the first creature to leave the ark and find land was a dove. The olive branch that the dove did drop upon the new land took root and grew into a tree that fed Noah and his family."

Nem looked at the bird again and said he liked the idea and the name "Peace Cottage". He hugged Peter about the legs.

They unloaded their belongings from the cart and it rumbled off back to the stables. They moved into Piece cottage and the children spent the rest of the day working out where they would sleep and where they would put their possessions.

The next day Mary went back to the cottage they had lived in to make sure that they had not left anything behind and clean up ready for the next occupant, whoever that may be.

She swept the floors and made sure the windows were covered to keep out the weather. The door creaked on its hinges as she shut it. Peter had never remembered to put oil on them. She heard a rustling and looked around – nothing to be seen –no wind – no people nearby. She shook her head, but it was not in her head but nearby. It seemed to be saying "take me

home....".
She had a feeling that there was something that
she had forgotten .....

She looked down and beside the door was the
broken pot. She recognised it as the one she had
planted the acorn into. The acorn that had been
given her by the hollow tree. She looked carefully
at it and she could see a small green shoot coming
up through the brown earth. She picked it up
carefully and carried it back to Piece Cottage.

As she walked home she was wondering where
to plant the tree. It night live for many years and
would need a place where it was not in anyone's
way and would not be cut down for its wood.

She put the pot down on the edge of her new
garden and looked around.

The garden was an odd shaped plot. It started
square up against the side of the cottage but long
and tapering along the side of the road. There
was a hedgerow along one side bordering the field
where the sheep were grazing. Along the roadside
was a wattle fence which did not go the whole
way along the side of the garden – it had seen
better days. She would have to ask the boys when
they go to the coppice if there were enough hazel
rods to make a new fence.

The oak tree -- where could she put it. She
wondered if it could be planted in the avenue
leading up to the manor – no that was not an oak
avenue and it would be out of place. Maybe
somewhere near the Master's greensward lawn --
no -- it would cast too much shade and the grass
would not grow underneath it. Maybe she could
put it in the cottage garden if it was right at the
end furthest away from the cottage. The garden
was very narrow there and not much would grow

and the land could not be used for much else.

So she carried the pot carefully down the garden and dug a hole and put the ball of soil in it so as not to damage any roots. Adam moved within her as she patted the soil back into place and she patted him also, it was his tree. It would need a stake and a tie to keep it upright next year but as for now it was in a good place, protected from the strong wind and the sun would shine on it almost all day.

23 ~ WRITING

The cottage became a place of constant visitors as the word got about the manor that Peter was back. He shared his time between the job of under-steward and cooking in the great kitchen. The news that there was to be a wedding, gave folk an event to look forward to.

Will made a wicker crib that could be rocked on oak runners made from the back leg frames of an old chair.

Each evening after supper was done and all washed and tidied away, Peter sat with the children round the large rough table. He showed them at first what he had learned from the monks at St Benet's abbey. He drew shapes like apples and twigs or spoons and knives, so that the familiar things of home led them into thinking that letters could be friendly and then come to mean something. He wrote the name of each article he drew beneath the picture in simple script. Sometimes he would say "Becky, come and draw a picture of a cat for us to see". She was clever at drawing and so was Aaron, Mary's son. The others watched and learned quickly how to hold a piece of charred wood or chalk to write with. Mary pretended to ignore what was going on but Peter caught her sneaking a glance at Alys when she drew her mother to look like a swollen ripe plum.

The more they learned, the faster they picked things up in other ways, and the whole newly combined family drew closer together. Love deepened and a calm came upon the house, now so aptly called "Peace Cottage".

Peter said one evening,

"I have found some old parchment and have discovered how to remove the old ink with wet wood ashes. Brother John hath lent me some ink, an ink-horn and quills. We shall now be able to form better letters."

The quill was a new thing to try and Meg was the first to accomplish the mastery of it having watched Peter at the abbey. The others were a little envious but soon picked it up despite the inky fingers. He was able to wash off the ink from the parchment after the evenings' efforts were over and re-used the skins the next day. Some writings he saved as the children had worked so hard at their letters and fixed them up on the cottage walls to display them. He praised them to the skies.

The night that all the children wrote their own names clearly, he prayed, as he had done at the abbey, and thanked God for the patience he had been given to see his task through. He never thought that he would have been able to do it.

Becky came a close second to Meg in writing her name copied from Peter's example page. Alys soon caught up. The boys played about too much to take it seriously enough even though Peter made it all fun for them. But they did not want to be outdone by the girls and eventually tried harder to catch up with them. They found it all much harder than the girls in any case.

One evening, Meg took an old nail and a roof-tile and drew the shape of her hand on it by tracing the nail around it. Then she wrote her name in the palm of it and sat back to admire it. This time Mary watched her from a distance while she sat using her drop-spindle.

Meg cocked her head towards Mary and said, "Shall I show thee how to do this Mother? Or wouldst thou like me to do it for thee?"

"I want not of this.. this.. writing things." she protested, "It be for those young folk who have much more life ahead of them than I do, I can count quickly enough and measure, so why do I need to write, or read for that matter?"

Mary said "If I wish to draw around my hand I shall do so and not thee." She was red in the face, not from temper but embarrassment. "I shall show thee and thee also Peter Meade."

Peter looked at the floor. She had never spoken so to him before - short and in haste. She strode across the room, sat at the table and turning the tile over to the unused face, drew round her hand and fingers. Meg held her father's hand tightly expecting an outburst from Mary. But she just sat at the table, looking at the shape she'd drawn as if awaiting instructions.

"There, I have done it as well as thee Meg" Mary pronounced.

Peter watched the act unfolding before him as the two of them argued over whose was the best tracing. Then he saw his chance.

He wanted three favours of Fate. He shut his eyes and silently prayed for them to happen. The first was to wed Mary on May-day. The second was to see Mary sign the parish register - with her own name. The third was to see Adam born in wedlock.

"Draw round thy hand again on this new tile for me Mary."

She started to protest, but when she saw that he was earnest about his request she obeyed him and took up the roofing nail again and slowly this time, drew round her other hand. She now had one tile for each hand traced out.

"Now, in the palm space draw around thy first two fingers." She did so and it formed an "m". "Now, next to that draw me an apple with a maggot coming from it." She did so and it formed "a".

"See my axe that do stand in the corner by the wood-pile Mary, I bid thee draw an axe with a short handle like I use with the lathe." This she wrote and she made an "r".

"Dost thou mind the twig I did use to divine for water in the days I did first come courting thee on the manor - then draw me that forked twig here now." She did that too for him and she wrote "y".

"Beloved, dost thou now see that thou hast writ thy own name. M A R Y."

She was holding it upside down and he turned it round for her. But she grinned as she already knew the way up that the first letter should be from seeing the M in Meg's name. She beamed all over her face and they all laughed together.

"With practice thou wilt be able to do it and write thy name at the wedding ceremony on May-day."

She flushed hotly, not in fury as Meg had feared, but from her shyness that Peter had used his wiles and wits to get her to do his bidding. She took up the two tiles and stood them against the wall by the fire.

"I shall do thy bidding Peter and try hard to write my name. I am pleased that thou dost teach the childer to write but where ever didst thou gain such patience?" Mary was eager to hear more of the life he had led.

"At St Benets I learned much about mankind, the world and myself. I wanted to escape and to return here and wed thee, and when I worked so long and hard to achieve all, thy refusal to learn set me a great challenge. Dost thou wish to learn to write more than just thy name?"

"Nay, Peter, I need not of such things. Do thou spend thy time teaching the boys for they have need of reading and writing."

He accepted her wishes and she kissed him so tenderly just before Adam made his presence known again with a great kick beneath her ribs. She sat down heavily feeling great discomfort. Meg came and held her and showed her love better than she had to Mary ever before. The baby had turned into his final position and settled. Peter held her hands as she overcame the disturbance within her. She regained her composure with several deep breaths and came back to her rosy colouring.

"Oh Peter I be so glad that thou art here now, for I need thee now more than ever before. So much is about to happen to us."

"Aye, I must go and see what can be done about the wedding at the chapel, though what we shall do for payment and the ring I know not"

"'Tis my fault that thou hast no ring to put on my hand my love, for I told thee I had to give it up for to bury Jonah." She fell silent, ashamed. Peter read the message in her mind and said.

"Thou hast been forgiven for this Mary, think no more upon it. We shall find a way, but how at present, I know not."

24 ~ VAGABONDS AND VISITORS

One Friday morning the gatekeeper sent his boy to the steward's room in the Hall telling of some wench who was at the gate and wished to gain entrance to find work. The poor lad was breathless from running the mile from the gate to the Hall. When he calmed, he told Richard that the woman was in some distress as she was bidden to come to Briarmeade manor but had no letter.

"Hath this wench said what she doth seek, or did she ask for anyone in particular?" asked Richard.

"Aye, she was told to ask for the head cook."

"Wherefore would she seek the head cook? 'Tis my place to see to the engagement of persons on this manor." Richard showed his displeasure and left the papers he was attending to, and taking his staff with the hound's head carved upon the handle, strode forth in haste in the direction of the main gate.

As he passed the clay pits, Peter was checking the fencing as a cart had run back into it the day before.

"Wither dost thou go Richard in such haste?" asked Peter.

Richard stopped in his tracks and said........

"I am bidden to the gate Peter as there is some wench there making some demands that she be admitted to the manor for work. I know not of anyone who is expected and this wench hath no papers with her. I must send her packing for we have but two places on the manor. One be in the brew house and the other in the great kitchen."

William, the gatekeepers lad shuffled his feet as he waited for the two men to decide what they were to do and who should go to the gatehouse.

A thought pressed into Peter's mind.

"Mayhap I could be of help in this matter, Richard?" He said it but knew not why he did so. He rubbed the hair on the back of his neck as a breeze blew upon him, but there was no wind that morning. Something strange was playing tricks with his mind. Ever since Adam's conception Peter had constant messages from an unknown source. Recently his sleep had been disturbed by a dog whimpering and the yelp of new-born puppies.

"Come William, we must go to the gate and sort this matter." said Richard. All three set off and in a while came to the gatehouse. Inside, Edgar the gatekeeper was talking to a young woman who was still weeping from the tongue-lashing she had been given. Each time she was asked she repeated that she was told a place might be here for her. Peter's blood ran cold......it was Ruth. Ruth from the Swan Inn. Her hair was all over her face as she shook with grief. Her gown...the green one he last saw her wearing...was muddied and her shoes were missing. Her feet were bruised, cut and bleeding.

"Calm thyself Ruth, 'tis I Peter. Dost thou not remember?"
Richard stared, amazed that his brother should speak in this fashion to one who appeared to be a stranger.

"Peter, who is this woman thou seemest to know so well?"

She stopped weeping and curtsied.

"But when I knew thee all those months ago, thou wast a friar with a little child thou didst call Meg. She called thee father. What hath become of thee since ye left the Swan Inn?"

She stood up and came to Peter, red in the face and looking nothing like the ravishing beauty she had been when he last saw her.

"Richard, I must crave thy indulgence, for this maid was the innkeeper's daughter I did tell thee of. Dost thou mind what I did tell thee of how she seemed to be sent to me in my night of need. How Meg had caught fleas from their dog?"

Ruth combed her hair back with her long slender fingers, those fingers that had charmed Peter that wondrous night at the Swan Inn.

"Oh sir, I have come here as thou didst bid me. I have left the inn as I could abide its confines no longer. My father began to drink so heavily that he beat me often. Then when he was sober, he demanded of me who had bruised me so. He threatened to kill the man who laid a finger on me thus." She pulled up her gown to show Peter her shins which told of her beatings. He held her close and her tears died away in his arms. Richard coughed with deep embarrassment and knew not what to say.

Edgar was restless too as he had given her much torment calling her a wayward whore and a wanton hussy. His reasons were that he had seen her when he had called at the Swan Inn on his way back to Briarmeade manor after visiting Winterbourne Latimer on an errand for Richard. Her smiling face with the drinking customers and her ability to attract the men folk there he mistook for whoreing. What he did not know was that she grew flowers in the inn garden and sold them to the wives of the carters who called and drank there too.

"Richard....Edgar... I must be held responsible for the trouble this woman hath innocently caused thee both. For I bade her come to this manor if ever she was in trouble and needed my help. She is a good woman and loyal. Any man who would be of a mind to wed her, could do far worse than to take her for his own. I tell thee both in truth, that if I were not promised to Mary, I would wed her the minute I could find a priest. Ruth be no vagabond or hussy but an honest hardworking woman."

They drew apart and Ruth smiled that smile that tugged the heart strings, a mixture of serenity and warmth with a lust for life lurking in the background. She sighed with relief that at last her hateful journey was nearing its end.

She started to say something to Richard but swayed sideways, wilted and fainted. She would have hit the floor had she not twisted and fallen against Peter who caught her. Despite the smell of stale sweat on her body from days of walking there, her hair still held the lingering hint of old lavender. Memories flooded back to him. Wood smoke, candlelight, feathers, a hairbrush and 'Chaser's' fleas. She roused as he bent over her and smiled up at him where he had laid her on the stone floor.

"Where am I?" she began....."Oh I remember....." she said as soon as she saw Edgar and William. Edgar gave her a mazer of cool water and she sat up.

"When didst thou last eat?" asked Richard, at last finding his voice and something to say. Peter stood aside and watched and listened to see what Richard would do or say in this situation. After his jilting how would he react. He knew his brother very well but as Grace had always told him......"ye can live with folk for years and still not know how they will be".

Where Peter would have pulled her to her feet, Richard stepped forth and taking her grubby hand, raised her up and sat her down on a small stool.

"Oh thank thee kindly Sir" she said as the colour came back to her cheeks......"I did eat upon the yester...I think".

"Then this mayhap be why thou hast suffered this weakness together with thy long journey to come here." said Richard looking concerned.

"If thou beest able we can take thee to my cot where we can tend thee and feed thee." said Peter feeling his friar days at St Benets calling him.

"Where be thy shoes Ruth, hast thou lost them or cast them away?"

The whimper of a hungry animal came from the bundle on the gatehouse floor. Ruth stooped and picked it up and untied the knots at the top.

She lifted out a white puppy with rusty ears and a rust patch on its rump. "This is the first and best of the litter that came from "Chaser." She had six pups two days after ye both left us. I trust that Meg was rid of the fleas soon. I am so sorry that she was so pained."

"I had suffered the same when I did live on a farm as a lad. I sometimes spent the night in our barn, but our dog had "visitors" too." said Peter.

She showed Peter her shoes. The left one had the strap broken and the other had a tear on the vamp.

"I could no longer wear these but I would not cast them aside lest I found a good cobbler for to mend them." She said looking straight into his eyes again as she had done at the Swan Inn.

"I shall take them to my neighbour Samuel, who will mend them at no cost to thee, Ruth."

Peter gazed at Ruth's feet, cut bleeding and sore. She limped but did not cry out nor did she complain. Her mind shut out pain as women can. Her whole objective had been to get to Briarmeade and to find Peter.

Inside the bundle Ruth took out two rabbit skins that had kept the pup warm. She put the pup on them on the floor but it refused to stay put. Peter picked them up and took out his knife. He made holes around the edges and took a strip off the longest sides of each skin. Then he took out his handkerchief and tore it in half and put one piece under each of Ruth's feet. Each skin he placed carefully beneath each foot and brought the strip up over and around her ankles. They formed a poor but serviceable pair of simple shoes.

She stood in them like a child on her birthday, looked sheepishly at Richard and came to Peter and kissed him so deeply he had to break free of her. He was once again, breathless. For the first time in his life he went red in the face. She beamed such joy that she forgot her soreness and collected up her few belongings as Richard picked up the puppy and Peter opened the gatehouse door.

Edgar turned away ashamed but Ruth turned

to him and thanked him for his kindness for the water. He smiled and felt better about it. He held forth another beaker of the cooling liquid which she took and drank in one draft. William patted the puppy which licked his hand in return. Peace had returned, and the feeling of discontent that had bothered all present, flew out of the open doorway and away.

As they walked slowly along the road to the manor, Ruth choose wisely to walk on the grass where it was softer to her damaged feet and surprisingly, Richard offered her his arm to steady her. He gave the pup to Peter who looked it over carefully, but found no visitors.

Richard asked "What would thou do for work on this manor? We do have but little work here 'til harvest-time. Mayhap thou couldst help in the brew house if thou hast served ales."

"I can make soap-balls sir, I have made them for years and sold them for to make some money should I ever come to be wed. I can show what be needed to make them for this manor if ye wish."

They walked at Ruth's pace, and in a while, came to Peace cottage. All workers were about their daily business save for the three men repairing the clay-pit fence. They doffed their hats to Peter and Richard as they passed.

At the door, Richard knocked with his free hand but answer was there none. He knocked again and louder - still no reply. Then Peter gave the pup to Ruth and banged hard on the door. He called..

"Mary, Becky...Kitty..." still no answer. Richard peered in at the window - he could see nothing and no-one. Peter grew anxious. He hammered on the closed door and the bolt gave way to his thrusts and partly opened, but something stopped it from within. He knelt down and put his hand around the door and felt a body - warm but unmoving save for breathing. It was Mary.

He gauged the gap the door and forced his body through it. His doublet tore on the bolt fixings as he fell inside. It seemed Mary had fallen for some reason and was against the door from inside. Her shoulders and upper back were against the bottom panels. He half pulled her, half rolled her away as Ruth and Richard gained enough space by which they could enter. She was a dead weight and an awkward shape to shift for two men, let alone Peter on his own.

She sighed as he had disturbed her, and opened her eyes as he blew on them.

"Mary - what has befallen thee - has some person been here and caused thee pain. What has happened?"

Richard looked about the cottage for signs of disturbance and Ruth picked up a broken clay flower pot and the flowers that lay in the shards. Foul play was suspected, but Mary smiled and then laughed, but went giddy when she sat up and sought the comfort of the floor again.

Twas as if she was bewitched. Each time she tried to rise, her head rolled to its left side and she fell to the floor.

"What task wast thou about afore we came to thy cottage and found thee?" questered Richard, as she lay in Peter's arms where he sat holding her. His face was creased with fear and worry.

"I was putting those flowers in a pot when I

did hear a storm and then a great scratching in my head. Then I found I could not stand but sit, then not sit but lie down.. I wast taken giddy and fallen down by the door in an effort to seek help. I must have slept for I heard not your knocking."

Peter sighed but still could not account for her giddiness and loss of balance.

"We had not any storms this day Mary" said Peter looking still puzzled. He felt Adam move beneath his hands as he held Mary - at least he appeared not to been harmed by her falling down. Ruth had remained in the background and had taken a stool by the hearth where she rubbed her bruised legs and took the weight off her feet. Meg came down the stairs to see who had come in and woken her from her sleep. She had been in a fever the last three days and nights, but was mending. She came straight to Peter and asked....

"Why doth mother lie upon the floor. Is the baby coming?" She felt hot still and he pulled her gown about her. Then she saw Ruth with the puppy, slid off Peter's knee and went and stroked the pup which licked her hand and face. Calmly she took it from Ruth and hugged it so tightly that it yelped and broke the silence that had developed.

Ruth drew Meg to her and took her upon her lap quite naturally as if she were her own child.

Peter said "Mary, I forget my manners. This is Ruth who hath come to seek work and a new life here."

From where she lay on the bed, Mary said, "I welcome thee to our cottage Ruth. Peter hath told me of thee. I wish thee well."
Ruth looked at the floor feeling lost and alone.

She ruffled Meg's lovely golden hair. Then after a deep breath of resignation, she raised her head and said,

"I thank thee. I seek work, as Peter hath said, on this manor since I have left the Inn and need a place to live. Dost thou have mind of a place I could stay?"

Richard took up the issue and said......."Upon this manor I have the management of the labour, and Peter the use and repair of all cottages and buildings, now he hath returned to us. He is a steward here also. Mayhap he do know of a.........."

Mary began....."I believe I know of a place. Thou couldst stay Ruth. It be with my neighbour M..........Oh there is the storm that cometh again and the mighty scratching in my head." She grasped Peter tightly who was horrified as she became agitated and strange with her head held over sideways. He felt she might have a fit and die on him as she rolled her eyes, wailed and began to vomit. She missed Peter but shot it over his boots where she lay in his arms. Ruth put Meg down again from her lap, and came over to Mary where she howled like one possessed as she put her hand to her left ear.

"Master, would ye light a candle" she said to Richard, "and bring it close that I may see. Meg, fetch me a willow wand from the bundle of kindling. Peter, give me thy knife." Ruth commanded all present with such authority, that all obeyed her instantly. Meanwhile, Mary still rolled about, and when she saw Ruth with the knife, looked at her in great fear.

"What will ye do Ruth. What be wrong with Mary?" Peter asked with fear that manifested itself in his strained voice. Mary stayed still while Ruth looked into her left ear....

"Oh Aye. I see what doth trouble thee Mary. She took up the slim whippy willow wand about nine inches long and an eighth of an inch thick. With the knife she split it half way down the centre and made it into a pair of tongs. She cut off the two ends across to blunt them and bade Mary to stay quite still.

Richard held the candle steady and Peter held Mary still. Meg sat holding the pup. All was silent save for Mary's rapid frightened breathing.

Ruth pulled aside Mary's hair from her ear and slowly inserted the willow tongs. Then pulled them out and away, and held up for all to see, a wriggling yellow moth.

"There be thy thunder storm Mistress." she said as she crushed it between her fingers.

Mary sat upright at last, but Peter still held her lest she fall down again.

"How did ye know of this?" asked Peter.

"I did have the same in the garden years ago at the Inn. Such a creature did plague me as I picked flowers in the spring after it had got in my hair. My mother took it out for me the same way."

"I thank thee greatly Ruth for thy care and trouble, for I do think I would have gone mad if it had remained much longer with me.. But it hath made me feel I have been soiled.....Peter I would wash my head now, for fear of other "visitors".

She sat upon the bed and became calmer and more of her usual self. Richard took some warm water from the hearth and Ruth found a scented soap-ball from her bundle. She soon had Mary washed and settled and able to rise and walk

about. Mary glowed with the pleasure of just the
simple act of walking. Richard never once took
his eyes off Ruth as she moved about and tended
to Mary.

Once the adults and Meg and the pup became
settled, Peter saw his tasks were not yet finished.
Ruth came and sat beside Mary on the bed and
they chatted about Ruth's life at the Swan Inn and
Mary and Peter's wedding and the imminent birth.
They talked about the move to Peace Cottage.
Peter got up and went outside where he
washed his boots and hands beside the rain-barrel.
Then he went inside to clean up the floor. The
cottage smelled better after he crushed some
herbs and strewed them about. There was still
warm water on the hearth and taking the rest of
the soap-ball he went on his knees before Ruth.
He washed and tended her tired cut feet. Mostly
the cuts were small, and what blisters she had
collected, had burst but were raw. He soaked off
the dried blood and dried them with a clean cloth.
Ruth fondled his head as he bent down and
attended to her, and showed her gratitude. He
had returned the same care and more that she
had shown to him when he was in a similar state
at the Swan Inn.
"Mary, be there we honey left or is it all
gone?" he asked.
"Aye we have a little at the bottom of the
pot, but it be just a morsel." she replied.
"Then I will have it for these cuts" He turned
to Meg and said "Meg would ye get me the pot?"
Meg was miles away still, with the pup the
centre of her attention, beside the hearth.
"Meg" he called sternly "fetch me the honey-

pot at once." She jumped out of her trance and took the pot from where Mary had kept it. She gave it to Peter who patted her hand and said "Thank thee Meg" and kissed her.

With clean fingers he dabbed the honey on Ruth's abrasions, then took the smoothest parts of clean cabbage leaves and covered the honeyed cuts with them.

"These will keep the honey lest it would be lost into the cloths." he explained. "Mary, dost thou still have my old shirt, for I have need of it now.?" He stood up and straightened an aching back after holding Mary so long and then from attending to Ruth.

"Aye Peter, but I would mend it. Forgive me for I have not done so." she replied, a little afraid he might be angered by her forgetfulness. She need not have worried. He loved her, oh! How he loved her. More now than ever he did.

"I have need of it as binders now Mary," he said as he took it from her. The body was still whole but the sleeves had holes at the elbows. Carefully he cut off the sleeves leaving enough at the shoulders to attach new ones when Mary would have time to attend to them. Then he ripped up one sleeve into strips and cut the other into two squares. He took each of Ruth's feet and set each on a cloth square with the leaf and honey coating inside. Then he bound each foot with the strips, and finally put the rabbit-skin shoes over the lot and tied them up.

Ruth put her hands over her face and burst into uncontrollable tears. Mary placed her arm around her where she sat beside her on the bed and said..... "Aye Ruth - let out thy sadness - I know thy feelings."

Ruth sobbed a while and then ceased. Mary handed her a handkerchief and she dried her eyes. Peter and Richard looked at each other very puzzled yet once more. They could neither of them see what was amiss. But nothing was wrong, just relief in its purest form. Mary looked up at Peter, smiled and nodded approvingly which told him, without words, that all was indeed, well. As her weeping ceased, Ruth looked up at Peter and took both of his hands in hers and kissed each of them in turn, rubbing her face against them.

"Oh Peter, I thank thee so much for thy kindness. 'Tis well after so much torment these last few days and weeks, to find friends again."

He ran his hands through her hair and tidied it. She sighed, stood upon her sore feet, and ignoring all about her, pulled him close to her and kissed him. Her arms were so tight about him like she wanted never to leave him. Richard looked away sadly but Mary gazed up at them standing there together. A sudden pang of jealousy ran though her mind but she was pleased and happy that her man had shown such kindness and compassion as she herself had experienced - and little Meg too for that matter. She knew that he loved all people and all creatures. She felt her own heart race a little.

They parted and Peter said,..."Now Ruth do thou keep thy feet thus bound for one whole week. Fear not, thou wilt find that as the ribs of the leaves do soften with walking and thy feet will ease. When thou dost take off these cloths, in a week ye will see new papery skin where were blisters and thy cuts healed with no scars."

Mary asked...." Peter, where did ye learn this skill?"

"The brothers of St Benets Abbey taught me Mary. I had a wound upon my left leg while sharpening my blade 'ere I made baskets from withys. Brother Joseph, who showed me how to read and write, did cleanse the gash and place upon it, a mint leaf with honey and did bind it up for me. In but two weeks, it had healed and left no scar. Without his care I could have lost my leg or yet worse. My old habit do bear witness of the injury to this day."

He turned and looked at Meg, asleep again, and thought of his former daughter Peg. She had suffered burns from the hearth a month before the poor little mite drowned. If only he had known the curative properties of honey then, he could have saved her from the ordeal and the pain of her scarred legs.

He roused himself from his thoughts and self-blame and said..."Mary 'twill be well for us to keep honey by the hearth, for it do heal burns and scalds also."

There came a knock at the door. Richard opened it and there in the doorway stood Maria as usual at that time day when she called to see how Mary fared. She was surprised to see a cottage so full of folk.

She came in and saw Peter cleaning up the floor.

"What has befallen thee Mary?" she asked, very concerned. She knew she had giddy spells at this late stage in her condition. She had not let on about them, as she herself had the same when she was pregnant at eight months.

Mary told her all about the storms and scratchings in her head and the giddiness, and how Ruth had rid her of the yellow moth.

"I've heard tell that folk call a person "cloth-ears" for not hearing so well. Should we then call thee "moth-ears" Mary?"

The cottage echoed with laughter and Mary felt foolish, but saw the funny side of it all. Maria could hit the nail on its head with maximum embarrassment at times. She was known to have a mouth as big as a bucket, but likewise she had a heart that size too and full of care, compassion and humanity.

"This be Ruth," said Mary to Maria nodding in her direction as she had the sleeping Meg on her knees now. As Ruth's name was mentioned, Meg awoke. She seemed to be a little cooler. Peter had finished cleaning up and went out again to wash his hands by the water-butt. He felt so tired he could have slept by the barrel if he had sat down. When he returned, Meg said:

"She that hath the rabbits' feet hath said the puppy be for us, father. May we keep it? Pray father? Methinks I have seen her before." Peter realised that her memory had been jarred by her recent illness. He fondled her head and picked her up in his arms. He buried his face in her hair. Just her calling him 'father' brought a lump to his throat, even now.

The days of torment for them both on the streets of Binstead came flooding back to him now she had been ill again. But this time she was older, she had been better fed and had slept for long periods so that she overcame the agues sooner. Peter had hesitated both from deep felt emotion as well as remembered moments of past depressions.

"Father, I pray thee," she implored "may we

keep this puppy. I do promise to look to her just like a person."

Peter answered her, saying quietly... "What name would ye give her then my sweet one?"

"She is just dog, father." He fondled both Meg and the pup and his arm grew tired from holding them. Ruth had rested well and stood up and came to be beside Richard who leaned with his left arm on the hearth lintel. They both felt a little out of place. He put his right hand lightly on her shoulder and she turned and smiled sweetly at him. Peter looked at them and saw the seeds of love being sown. Peter sat down beside Mary where Ruth had been.

Oh if only it could be for them as it was for him and Mary; he wished with all his heart.

Mary had read the same message written on their faces and held Peter's hand and kissed it on the palm. She reached across to him and said, close to his ear:

"I love thee Peter".

Ruth stirred herself and said:

"Mary, I began to ask of thee if there be a place upon the manor where I might stay, but we were interrupted by the storm and bother with thine ear. What sayest thou?"

Maria spoke before Mary could answer.....

"I have room enough for you and more, if you would care to stay with me. I be widowed these past five years. You would be company for me. What say you to this?" Maria looked at Ruth and smiled.

"I accept your offer good Mistress and would make you agreeable payment for my bed and board and I will help you with the labours of your house. I can cook sew and spin a little. I thank you indeed - for so much hath been my good fortune this day - I fear it could end all too soon."

Meg perked up and from Peter's lap declared.....

"If I can choose a name for our dog, then I shall call her 'Dog' - for that is what she is, and will always be."

Peter said

"Thou wilt always be Meg; but I would not call thee girl or child or some such. If that be thy wish, then let it be so." Mary looked at him, sternly at first, thinking that he would be put out by this wilful choice by one so young. But he was not at all - more glad that the decision was final. Mary grinned up at him, reading his mind. They both agreed that Meg had a will of her own.

From that day on, for many years, 'Dog' and Meg were never without each other, day or night, indoors or out.

She kept her promise and cared for "Dog" just like a person. They seemed to have a complete mutual understanding, each for the other right from the start.

Maria had brought a pot of Will's honey and six eggs from her own fowls for Mary.

"He hath set three skeps of bees in the orchard now the apple trees are nigh to blossom, but the honey I bring hath set hard as it be from yesteryear. If ye would have it softer, ye need warm it."

Mary smiled and thanked Maria. "I know not what I would do if thou didst not come to me daily."

They were very good friends - had been for

twelve years - through all of each-other's trials, joys and troubles. Mary said:

"I feel much mended, now that I have all here with me. I cannot thank thee enough, Ruth, for thy attention with that cursed moth and I wish thee a settled life here at Briarmeade Manor. 'Tis not the best place in the world, but it be a good manor and the Master be firm but fair to us. Richard be a good steward and thou canst trust him in all respects. Thou knowest that Peter is his brother."

Ruth moved a half pace to her left and made contact with Richard's side. His right hand gripped her shoulder more firmly where it had remained ever since Maria entered Mary's cottage. She blushed and once again looked at the floor.

"Dost thou like the puppy Meg?" she asked, diverting the attention from herself, but once again both Meg and 'Dog' were curled up on Peter's lap, sound asleep.

She murmured in her sleep but the only words that anyone could make out were "Star-wishes... Rags.... Dog.... and Mother."

Mary sighed and rested her head on Peter's shoulder. She looked down at the sleeping child and her companion and said:

"Peter, what hast thou done to thy doublet?" fearing that he had been in a fight on the manor. A black vision of Jonah and his fights and injuries came before her and she looked pale and shuddered. Maria saw her anguish and said:

"Peter would never have been in a fight on this manor, everyone knowest him as a friend. He has no enemies Mary."

"Nay my love, 'twas when I had to force my way into this cottage, for thou wast lying hard up against the door. I tore it on the nails that held the door bolt."

Ruth and Richard became restless and Maria saw their need to leave, now that all was settled with Mary.

"Come and see my cottage Ruth. It was named 'Dove Cottage' by my late husband Benjamin just after we were wed. It was because the white doves from the manor roosted in our eaves each night. There be room aplenty for us both ye shall see. I shall carry thy bundle - thou hast but few possessions in this Ruth." she said hefting it in her hand. She put her arm round Ruth in a caring motherly way but Ruth flinched in pain. Maria was taken aback and feared she had been too bold, as she was known to be with her tongue. Ruth was in obvious pain where Maria had touched her back.

Mary looked up at Ruth and saw the incident.

"What ails thee, thou hast pain in thy back" she questered. Maria knew nought of Ruth's life at the Swan Inn or indeed anything of her past or how she came to leave the Inn.

"'Tis but little" she replied "I would go to thy cottage now with thee Maria and talk to thee of it." She was in quite some pain but anxious not to bother Mary any further with her troubles. Peter moved and Meg stirred. He got up and put her back on the bed beside Mary with 'Dog' where she slept on. He thought she would take a couple more days to mend fully. She just needed food, sleep and many drinks.

Maria carried the bundle as Ruth said farewell to Mary and Peter.

Surprisingly she said to him:

"I pray thee dear Peter, wouldst thou come with me to Maria's? I have great need of thee." Her face spoke a thousand pleadings. He just could not refuse her, no matter what it was for.

"Just be with me a while, that I may settle." Mary nodded her approval as Richard opened the door. The four of them set out and Peter pulled the door shut behind them.

Maria led the way with Richard and Peter hovered near Ruth. She still had taken no food and was becoming weak from the lack of it. She took slow painful steps. Richard looked back frequently to see that they were not too far in front. They reached Maria's, went in, and Ruth sat on the nearest stool and sighed deeply. Her face was very pale and creased.

Maria said, "Would ye have some food Ruth? I have eggs from my three fowls and a cheese?"

"I would gladly eat whatever thou dost offer - if thou hast enough."

As she rested her back against Richard who stood behind her, she flinched again and bit her lips. He asked:

"What ails thee Ruth for I touched thee but gently?" fearing that his large hands had harmed her in some way.

She pulled Peter's head down to her level where she sat and said

"I pray thee look at my back for me - but away from Richard."
Peter said:

"Richard, pray fill the bucket from the butt in the backyard for me and set some to heat upon the hearth?" Peter had a feeling that he would be needing some warmed water.

Richard went outside without question. As soon as he had gone, Ruth pulled off her shawl and Maria helped her to remove the gown from her graceful shoulders. Maria gasped as she exposed Ruth's bare back to the waist. Her leather pouch, that carried her meagre savings hung beneath her armpit for safety. Her back had great blue and black wheals across it with weeping blisters that had stuck to her shift, with patches of dried blood.

Peter could not believe his eyes - he was horrified. No wonder she flinched and looked so pale and felt so weak. He felt rage well up in him and wanted to beat the swine that had made such injuries.

"In God's name - who hath done this to thee Ruth?" he asked, his voice trembling with emotion mixed with an inward hate. His fists clenched so that the knuckles turned white. He took her gently in his arms and fondled her head as she let yet more tears fall on his arms. He kissed her bare shoulders and Maria held her hands in sympathy.

He settled her and asked:

"Tell me Ruth, who hath caused these wounds to thy body".

"The night I told him I would leave the Swan Inn, my father came to me, drunk as usual. He still had wits enough to hold me as he tied me to my bed and tore off my clothes. He took off his belt and beat me across the legs and back with it. Because I did not cry out, he beat me more until I did at last weep loudly. He left me, and one of the carters' wives heard me and untied me. I made her promise silence about my beating, and she did help me dress and escape from the back of the Inn. That was three days since and ye now see what I suffered at my father's hands. I would have brought thee another pup for thy family Peter, but I had not the time - forgive me."

Richard had come back into Dove Cottage, unheard, and had stood and listened to the whole story. He stood aghast with an ashen face. Maria found an old but clean shift and tore off the arms to make strips. Then she laid Ruth gently face down on the bed by the hearth. She carefully washed the wheals and soon soaked off the blood. Then she applied honey and goose grease to the wounds. Finally she covered Ruth's back with the shift and secured it with the strips about the neck armpits and waist.

Peter said:

"This treatment be so fast to heal thee Ruth, 'tis a wonder she do not catch her fingers in the cuts." Ruth smiled at his attempt to cheer her. Richard was by now as white with rage and anger as Peter had ever seen him. He said:

"If ever thy father do come nigh to this manor, I shall arrest him and put him in the whipping post and stocks. He will be beaten to within an inch of his evil life." Once again Ruth smiled with some relief that she was now safe from harm and among friends.

She put out an arm towards Peter and Richard. Richard stepped up, took her hand and held it gently. She squeezed his hand in return.

Peter saw the griddle by the hearth and placed it on the embers. Then Maria went to her cupboard and fetched four eggs, a dab of fat and some flour and milk. She broke the eggs into a wooden bowl, added some flour and milk and beat them into a cream. As soon as the fat sizzled on the griddle, she dropped spoonfuls on to the iron plate. She flipped them over put them on a trencher and dribbled some honey on them. She set them before Ruth with a tyg of milk. Ruth gave one to Richard who still held her hand and they ate in silence. Richard at last sat down beside her. Peter sat the other side of her.

Maria smiled and said:

"I see a flower set between two briars before me". Meaning the trio sat on the bed. When she had eaten her fill, Ruth said:

"I can never thank ye enough for the love and care from all of ye. 'Tis well to be among goodly folk - I feel a little mended and rested. Permit me a short time for resting further and in a few days I shall attend the brew house or the great kitchen or herb garden to earn a living wherever ye will have me to work."

Richard swelled with pride, all anger abated. He could fill one of the vacancies on the manor and do a good deed into the bargain for such an attractive wench.

"Where dost thou wish most to work Ruth?" asked Richard.

"Methinks I would to the brew house first as I do know the trade." Richard smiled in contentment and replied:

"'Tis well. Come unto me when thou art mended."

Maria went to the upper room to prepare the other bed and could be heard dragging the bed away from the wall to tuck in the coverlet. Peter joined her and helped her to shift the furniture about. He bent and helped to shift the bed frame back to the wall once she had finished to her satisfaction. She thanked him and stood still as they heard Ruth and Richard talking below. Peter would not eavesdrop on his own brother, so he went back down the creaking stairs only to see the couple looking into each other's eyes and holding hands.

Peter began - "Pray tell me Ruth, how dost thou make soap-balls, I feel the master would encourage their making and use. Are there many costly ingredients to buy?"

"There be but few things, Peter, but I can tell thee what to do, I have oft done it over the years."

Maria said, "I do think that Ruth hath need of rest now. There be much talk to do but mayhap upon the morrow."

Richard nodded his appreciation and the two men left the cottage deep in thought. They wended their way back to their labours.

25 ~ ACCIDENT

It was a fine sunny morning and the family were all eating their breakfast. The children were sitting on benches on either side of the scrubbed wooden table. On the table were some bowls and trenchers with slices of bread and cheese on them. Aaron had his hands in the food first as usual and Mary had to tell him to wait for them to say grace before he started to eat. Meg sat at the end of the table next to Becky who was feeling quite grown up. Rob brandished his new knife and cut his cheese into small pieces

When they had finished eating Becky and Kitty got ready to go to the woolshed. Becky got Nem ready so that she could take him to the Manor cottage and Kitty managed to pin down Aaron just long enough to put a cloak on him. Rob was going to the coppice to help Kit. Alys and Meg were going to the garden to help with the planting of the new herbs.

Peter was off to the kitchen to help cook the gentry dinner and he was looking forward to a morning working with Bet. She had a new idea for a way of cooking the large carp fish that had been caught in the moat the day before. They had been hung up in the large kitchen chimney for the smoke to flavour them overnight and Bet was going to show Peter what she had in mind. Peter finished his food in a rush and, not bothering to wear his cloak, he swept out of the door. He always seemed to be in a hurry to get to work these days. Mary hardly had time to give him a quick kiss.

She was going to the woolshed today to spin on the great wheel. There was a lot to do for the weaver needed some thick wool for a special piece of cloth that Master Robert had asked to be made. After all the others had left she pulled her sunshine-coloured cloak about her and shut the cottage door.

The old wooden door creaked on it's hinges and swung shut reluctantly. Peter had been so busy that he had neglected to grease the hinges as he had said he would. She left the place in a cross mood. She did not like these new jobs that he was doing. He seemed to have so little time for her and the family now. She knew that he had to earn enough to feed them and buy wood for the fire, but with her wages and the little that the girls were earning they had an adequate income and she was sure that he did not need to work quite such long hours.

She trudged to work and the sky clouded over and a light drizzle began to fall. She climbed the steps into the woolshed and said a cursory hello to Tilly and started working. She was spinning too fast and had to check herself when she found that the wool was not making a good thread. She slowed down and dropped into the steady rhythm that would allow her to spin all day without getting tired.

An hour later she felt a prickle down her spine. An uneasy feeling came over her. She could not explain it and she could not shake it off.

Something was wrong. She looked about her. All
the maids seemed happy and the work was
progressing apace. She shook her head to clear
her mind and got back to work. An hour later she
still had not shaken off the feeling of doom.

What could it mean?

There was nothing amiss in the woolshed.

Perhaps there was something wrong with
Peter - he had spoken to her before with his mind
- was he doing the same thing again?

No, it could not be so.

But halfway through the morning the feeling
was still there. It was dragging her down. She
asked Tilly if she could feel anything but Tilly said
that everything was normal.

Mary had to go and find Peter to ask him if he
could feel it too. She left her work and hurried
across the Manor to the kitchen to talk to him.
She pushed open the heavy door looked around
the large room but he was nowhere to be seen and
she asked Bet where he was. Bet said that Peter
had to go to do some errands for the master and
he had said that he would be back to help her
with the food halfway through the morning. She
was expecting him back at any minute.

Mary went back to work content that
everything was as it should be, but the feeling
followed her. She could not shake it off.

By dinner time she was certain that something
dreadful was about to happen or already had
happened. She could not eat and she could not
settle to her work. She felt that she must go
round to the children to make sure that they were
alright.

The two older girls were working with her in
the woolshed so she could see that they were not

troubled.

She went to the Manor Cottage to ask Alys how the two youngest of her family were. She was met at the doorway by Alys with her finger on her lips. She beckoned Mary in and on the corner bed lay a heap of children and among them were both of her boys fast asleep. Alys drew her outside and said that Kit had made a new set of wooden skittles pegs and a wooden ball for them and they were enjoying using them. They had tired themselves out that morning.

The other two girls were in the herb garden which was next to the moat. She hurried through the paddocks and past the butts where there were but two men practising their archery. She went through the gate in the wall but she could not see anybody.

Where were they all?

Had something happened to her girls?

She hoped that they had heeded the warnings to keep away from the moat. The ground had been dug and the plants were lying there ready to be planted but no gardener and no children. She hastened across the grass and there, under the apple trees, were Silas, the gardener and the children. They were lying on the ground. Mary rushed over to them. Meg opened one eye and said

"Hello Mother. Dost thou come to see how we do? Grissell said that we had worked so hard that we could have a rest."

Mary was relieved that her fears were unfounded.

Rob should be in the coppice so she went to look. He greeted her with his usual eagerness and showed her what he had been doing that morning.

Kit was making a new pole lathe and several boys
had been helping him. They proudly showed Mary
the bits of wood that they had shaped and where
they were to go. She questioned Kit but he felt
nothing wrong and Mary began to question her
sanity.

She felt foolish worrying so much about the
children when she knew that they were in good
hands.

She plodded back to the woolshed and went
back to her spinning but the thread kept on
breaking. It would come out thick and slubby and
then thin. This was not like her, she normally had
no trouble with the work. The heavy cloud was
hanging over her and she could not shake it off.
The prickle in her spine had gone but it had been
replaced by a feeling that her mind was closing in
on itself the world was going black.

She realised that she had not actually seen
Peter since breakfast.

Fear clutched her heart.

Was it he that was in trouble after all?

She dropped her wool for the second time
and, in her hurry to go and find him, she knocked
over the great wheel. It lay where it fell on the
floor as she rushed out and ran across the sward
towards the kitchen. It was the first place to look
as that was where he should have been working
that day.

The place was nearly deserted. The food had
been served and the cooks were just clearing up
the last remains of the washing up and putting
away everything. Bet met her at the door.

"Hast thou seen Peter, Mary? He was to have
returned and helped us this day." Bet seemed
worried.

This was the last straw. It had been a harrowing day for Mary and she could no longer hold back the tears. She clung to Bet sobbing and calling out Peter's name. She knew now that something dreadful had happened to him. But what? Through her tears she blurted out

"Where is he? Where is he?"

Ib pushed herself forward and said:

"He did say that he must go and see the fence about the clay pits. He thought not that it would take long."

If anyone else said anything Mary did not hear it. She picked up her skirts and ran out of the kitchen and down the manor drive. Her breath came in quick gasps and her throat was sore but she kept on running. She knew now that Peter had been calling to her for help. She ran out through the manor gates and round to where the new fence was. Everyone knew that the clay pits were dangerous and Peter had only recently had the fence around them mended so that no animal or unwary human would slip down the sides and into the sticky slime at the bottom. Once down there it was impossible to climb out and the farmer had recently lost two sheep that way.

Mary saw that the fence was intact but she could feel herself being pulled towards the edge. She stopped at the fence, gasping to get her breath back after so much indecent haste. She was terrified to look into the pit afraid of what she might see but she was drawn to it like a fly to a candle flame. She looked down. All was grey clay but one lump was larger than the others.

It was man shaped.

She screamed and screamed again, the sound tearing at her already sore throat and only just managed to stop herself sliding down into the pit. The news that someone might be in trouble spread around the manor like wildfire and within minutes, Kit came striding up to Mary carrying a rope. He was followed by his brother. Mary could only watch as Kit roped himself to a fence post and his brother tied the other end of the rope around his waist and started slipping down the side of the pit towards the still and silent figure.

When Mark got to the bottom he was nearly the same colour as the clay himself. He untied the rope from around his waist and tied it around the unmoving man. Kit started to pull him up and several willing hands helped him. A crowd gathered and, as they got him to the top of the slope, Richard, the steward, told everyone to stay back and away from the edge of the pit. They lifted him over the fence and Mary could see that he was still alive but barely. His face was covered in clay as were his clothes but she could see that he was still breathing. He opened his eyes and looked at her and then closed them again as if it was too much effort to keep them open.

Kit threw the rope back down and pulled his brother to safety.

They carried Peter, for it was he, to his cottage and put him on the floor. Mary and Becky took off his wet and slimy clothes and washed his skin with hot water to get off the clay. He said not a word as they laid him on the bed. His skin was grey and cold. His breathing was shallow and his eyes were shut. Mary knew that some way she had to get him warm. She covered him with several blankets but she had to get some more warmth into him. Somehow she had to warm him up inside.

She took her clothes off and told Becky to do the same. Then, wearing just her thin shift undergarment, she got into bed with Peter and lay next to his back with her body as close as possible. Becky got in on the other side and lay next to the front of his body. They both radiated heat and after a while Peter started to shiver.

He was making his own heat.

Peter was beginning to stir.

His wife and daughter cuddled as close as they could and slowly he came back to life. He put an arm around Becky and pulled her closer to him and mumbled something incoherent.

. . . .

Peter saw a finger of light pushing into his mind. He felt the warmth of the two women each side of him and tried to figure out where he was.

He remembered going to the clay pits to check the fences. When he got there, he had looked into the pit and he saw something flapping in the bottom. He could not make out what it was. He moved closer to get a better look and climbed over the fence. Could it be a small child struggling in the cold grey mud? Suddenly the edge gave way beneath his feet and he found himself sliding down the side. He clawed at the sticky mud with his hands but to no avail. He landed in the slime at the bottom which was three inches deep but solid underneath.

He ploughed through the sticky clay and it clawed at his feet on every step. The object that he had seen was a piece of linen cloth. It must have been blown in by the wind. It was of little value and he left it where it was.

It was only then that the seriousness of his situation dawned on him. How would he get out of the pit? He tried to climb the side but he knew that it was hopeless. It had been raining and the clay was extra slippery. He shouted, but he did not think that anyone would hear. He knew that no one was working nearby on this day. He shouted again and again. What else could he do? His throat got dry and his voice was hoarse but no one came.

Had he told anyone where he was going? He could not remember. Would Bet send someone to look for him when he did not return to work? Where would they look?

He was already wet from the drizzle and the water was beginning to seep through to his skin. He was beginning to get cold. He moved around and beat his arms against his body to try to make some heat. He tried to stamp his feet but only succeeded in falling over and getting covered in wet sticky clay. He rose to his feet and started to shiver.

He thought of how he and Mary had communicated in the past through contact in their minds. Had they really been in contact or was it just his imagination at a time when he had felt in great need?

Could he do it again?

He had never deliberately tried to talk to her this way. In the past it had just happened. Whether it was real or not he had to try and hope that she would understand.

He sat down on a lump of clay and thought of Mary.

No. This was no good.

If he could just talk to her by thinking about her

then everyone would be doing it. It just could not happen that way.

He thought of the old hollow oak tree and how it had spoken to him and suddenly knew that was the way to communicate. He had to empty his mind and feel his way to Mary's thoughts.

Time passed and still no-one came. It was a silly idea. People just could not speak to each other that way. It was just his imagination that he and Mary could contact each other like this.

All he wanted to do was sleep. He lay back against the side of the pit. A blackness started invading his mind. He had stopped shivering. He was too cold to move.

He knew that he was going to die and the world was slipping away from him.

. . . .

But now he had the warmth of someone next to him. He was grateful. He put out an arm and hugged the warmth closer and drifted off into the sleep of exhaustion.

When Peter drifted off into sleep, Mary and Becky quietly slid out of the bed and left him to rest.

26 ~ PETER'S SADNESS

Grace grew in strength daily and two weeks after Mary, Peter and the children took up residence in Peace Cottage, he called to see Bett in the kitchen. She gave him a honey cake all sticky and full of flavour with candied angelica in the top in the shape of a flower. He took it with him in a cloth along to Grace's room and put her shawl about her ready to take her for a walk promised earlier.

"The sun feels good to my old bones Peter, where shall we go?"

"I had a mind to go about the walled garden and feed the fish if it would please thee mother." He had not called her mother for years and years - it seemed fitting to him on this occasion and did not realise what he had said until Grace said "Thou hast not called me mother for a long time Peter - it do sound strange now specially as thou hast little ones of thine own."

"Aye Grace - I know - it just seemed mete to me to do so. Thou hast a grand-daughter in Meg now and soon thou wilt have another grand-son."

They walked slowly but Grace was full of energy and tended to pull Peter's arm as she was anxious to get to the garden as soon as she could. Her renewed strength amazed him.

Over the back-bridge they turned and tossed a

little stale bread to the fish in the moat but saved
some for those in the fishpond. Together they sat
on the low wall and watched as the creatures
swam lazily about and then dashed hither and
thither as Grace crumbled the bread and sprinkled
it on the water. It was from her that Peter got his
love of all living creatures, she loved anything
that she could stroke or pick up and love. Water
fowl were her favourites and she would never eat
duck or goose.

Peter remembered that she once refused to
eat such birds and stood by her feelings so
staunchly that she ate plain bread and cheese.
Will had been upset that he had obtained a duck
especially for their meal from Silas. But he loved
her and saw that she meant what she said.
Peter and Richard both had had more than
they had eaten for years at one meal so the cold
duck was kept and eaten over several days.

"Wouldst thou have a piece of this cake that I
was given by Bett - 'tis honey and angelica." said
Peter.
"That will be a pleasant change from hard
sweet biscuits."
They rose and walked to the end of the yew-
walk and sat in the arbour. The spring flowers
had started to come out. The last few sunny days
had brought them on. The bees buzzed about the
new flowers and the air was like wine as it
refreshed the senses.
They sat watching the laundry-maids by the
pond washing the aprons and shirts for the dairy-
maids and bakers. White cheese cloths and
muslins were being rinsed and hung on the bushes

in the sunshine for the dairy.

"How be Mary and the childer Peter - are they well? I would love to see them soon if thou canst bring them to me, for I fear that at present I be not yet strong enough to go far."

Peter told Grace the names and ages and she nodded as she took in as much as she could.

She waved at the laundry maids as they came by the arbour and curtsied to such an amiable old lady. She was well loved by all who knew her.

"Silas hath worked well after his ague was gone, and the herbs that thou hast taken to aid thy chest and breathing do come from his plots."

"Give him my thanks and to Grissell, for together they have aided me much." Grace smiled up at Peter as he had stood up and turned to look towards the high red brick garden wall.

"I bid thee stay at this arbour a while I go and see what bees are here and what they do carry to the skeps."

He left Grace sitting against the arbour wall watching the movements of the fish in the pond. He went and stood to one side of the row of skeps and saw that the bees brought several colours of pollen on their back legs as they crawled into their homes. He moved his hand so that it cast a shadow over the entrance and made the guard bees to be defensive.

All was calm.

He remembered how his father Will, had taught him to husband these creatures with safety so long ago. But he also mused on how his skill had not been forgotten when he tended the skeps at St Benets abbey.

He turned to Grace and called "They collect pollen of wondrous colours, but I know not from whence they do fetch it."

She had watched as Will calmed his bees most of their married life but she had always had a fear of them. Peter was sure she would be safe just sitting in the arbour where she waited for him. To his great surprise, she came to him and made him jump as she grasped his arm to steady herself.

She watched the bees and as he turned to speak to her, she caught a bee in her hair. As she put her hand to her head she crushed the insect accidentally between her fingers and was painfully stung. Immediately she was assailed by three more of the creatures brothers to replace their fellow who had died. 'Twas as if someone had summoned them by a bell that had been rung.

She lunged feebly at the bees on her face so Peter grabbed her and pulled her from the skeps and into the orchard through the door in the high wall. With his thumbnail, he scraped off the stings from her hand and face and laid her in the shade upon the wet grass.

It was over in seconds, from calmness, to the fury and anger of the venomous insects. She wailed and shook with pain. Peter soaked up as much moisture from the grass in his muckinder as he was able to wet her poor face that grew redder by the minute. He put his mouth upon the livid stinging points and tried desperately to suck out the poison that made Grace swell up so rapidly - but to no avail.

Her rattling cough returned and she gasped for breath and air. She clutched at the air as if she would pluck it and devour it to live.

"All the work of the herbs had come to nought" Peter thought to himself. "That is not true" - he argued, for Grace had come through her consumption in spite of what the physic had said with all his wisdom.

"Grace - speak to me, Grace - GRACE." She gurgled and rattled and went purple in the face.........

"For pity sake speak to me." Peter was in desperation, he knew not what else he could do.

What he had not seen was that she had been stung on her tongue, and that it had swollen so that it did cram her mouth. 'Twas the honey cake that a bee had taken a taste at as well as the attack of the others. She could say nothing save for the odd word which was not audible.

"Oh God no - please - No....." he cried "Not to Grace - please".

A hand fell on his shoulder. It was Silas who had seen all from his cottage in the herb garden. Grace put her arms up to Peter and hauled herself up to his ear. She murmured just.......

"Peter... my.. Son..... "

She went limp as life left her frail body. Peter crushed her to him like some rag-doll. His back ached from his knotted muscles but he cared not, for if it meant that Grace could be made to live, he would have stayed there for a week.

Grissell had joined her husband and put her hand on Peter's shoulder to comfort him. She stroked his head - wet with sweat from his exertions.

None of them had noticed that the sun had rapidly been covered by storm clouds. As one who keeps bees knows, bees turn sour of temper and wilder, as soon as rain clouds form above.

Peter stood up slowly, with the body of his beloved foster-mother in his arms. Silas led him to the housekeeper's room where they laid her down with great care and reverence, till she could be taken and laid out in the chapel.

He started for home not noticing that it was pouring with rain.

A thought pressed like a knife into his mind. All of the first uses of the new chapel would be connected with him. Grace's funeral. His wedding with Mary. The christening of their child - Adam.

He came to the door of "Peace Cottage" and rapped on the door. The rain on his face blinded him so he could not see the latch.

He knocked again and as Mary opened the door he stumbled in and sank down on the bed, his head in his hands and the tears mixing with the rain on his face. It was quite a long time before he could answer Mary's earnest questions as to what was wrong and what had caused this misery.

"Grace is dead." Was all he said and then he curled up on the bed and lay still.

Mary sent the children to bed and lay down next to Peter and eventually drifted off into fitful sleep.

27 ~ THE WEDDING ON MAY DAY

May-Day dawned.

Aaron Nem and Rob bumbled down the stairs and Nem said:

"Where is everyone, it's May-Day, and I've been awake since the sun came up." He prodded Peter who huffed at him in mock temper, then grabbed him and bundled him into the bed making him go into peals of laughter. There was little room in the bed but Nem was little too and they woke Mary with their antics.

Peter loved him, loved all of them so much each thought they were his favourites. Becky was wise and a planner and was getting to look so much like Lydia. Rob was agile and cheeky, he was the first to be able to count in tens and dozens which he learned from Peter when he showed him how he counted beams in a house. He loved animals, especially horses. Nem was bright and could recite stories at bedtime that Lydia had told him when he was ill and songs that she sang to him well after he was teething.

Mary turned over heavily and sat up. She cuddled Nem, then Aaron and Rob. Peter got up and stirred the fire putting on some wood and swung the pan of water over it. Then girls came down. They all sat on the bed where Peter had lain like birds on the branch of a tree.

Meg, Aaron, Nem, Kitty, Rob, Alys and Becky. Peter began - "Today is May-Day and is also our wedding day. Thy mother and I shall be wed in the chapel after we all have eaten, washed, and dressed in our best. Then we shall all join in the May-Day festival and there will be great merriment for all on the manor." He stopped and said:

"Mary------- " He paused and put his hands to his mouth in anguish. "-----what shall I do for a ring --- in our move here, and all my work on the manor, I did forget that I do wish to give thee a ring." He sat heavily down on the edge of the bed. Mary came around the bed and putting her hands on his shoulders said:

"Be not troubled Peter I can make us one".

"But I would have desired the blacksmith to fashion one from iron or pewter. Oh Mary I feel so bad in this------"

She butted in - "I said I can make us one," she repeated commandingly.

"But how can ye do this for we have not metal here, not even an old nail we could bend." She pulled out a skein of golden coloured flax and plaited it into a circle that had no end and no beginning.

The whole household watched how their clever mother solved yet another problem for them. Peter felt very foolish and looked at the fire sadly, but Mary saw his dismay and came and kissed him as she showed what a good fit it was on his little finger which was the same size as her ring finger.

"Look, see now we have a golden ring and all the world shall see that love does not depend on precious metal and that it has no beginning and no end."

Peter felt so proud that she had put things right - he forgot the pot over the fire and it boiled over and splashed on his foot and scalded him. A little of the hot liquid also splashed poor Aaron's foot too. He wailed as the pain took hold of him, but Mary put cold water on their scalds then a dab of honey on a mint leaf and bound it up. She cuddled Aaron and Peter said,

"'Twas my fault Aaron - do forgive me son". He soon stopped crying and went to play with Rob in the garden.

Peter had made them a swing with rope hung from the apple tree. The tree was quite old but still gave a goodly crop of sweet apples each year.

They had all brought out their trenchers, bowls and mugs ready for breakfast. Kitty made the oats and milk mixture with a little honey that was still left. Peter called the boys in. When they all finished and cleared away, Peter sat by the fire feeling the flaxen ring on his little finger - wondering. He thought to himself - "What a woman" then turned about, stopped Mary from what she was doing and held her close and kissed her deeply and long. No words were said but that kiss spoke a hundred words. She saw again how much he loved her and she took both of his hands in hers and kissed them tenderly.

She stayed seated to save as much energy as she could, to meet the day ahead. She was uncomfortable and found it difficult to find a way to sit. She was eight and a half months with child now and Adam was quiet but still told her that he was alive within her. Her breasts ached with their weight, she had made a binder to support them now and when she would be feeding. Kitty and Becky, who seemed to be doing the bulk of all the work of late, cleared away and washed the vessels with the boys helping. Peter had asked that they give a hand to make lighter work in order that all could enjoy their special day and the May-Day celebrations.

Mary took some warm water left over from breakfast and washed. Peter helped her where she could not reach and then she washed him. She took out her clean clothes and his new shirt. He put it on and she admired her husband-to-be standing in front of the hearth in just his shirt. She struggled into her white shift, her gown, and donned a crisp clean white bonnet. A large white apron she put on last of all and smoothed it over her great belly.

Peter just gazed at her and admired this woman that he would wed in just a few hours. She was still as pretty and comely to him, even though so full of child, as she was when he made her this way. He drew her to him, leaned forward and kissed her tenderly and deeply. She shuddered as her belly hardened and Adam moved as if to say "I know that ye love each other, and made me - I wish soon to see thee both too".

They stood together for just a short while, then Peter put on his breeches, doublet, hat, pouch-belt and boots. He still had the flaxen ring to give to Mary in the chapel and toyed with it absently on his finger.

There came a knock at the door - it was Richard with Daniel.

"'Tis time for ye to wed, Peter. We are here to see thou dost not fail this wench and run away." They laughed and Mary and Peter joined in their merriment.

"Will thou be at my side this day Richard?"
Peter asked "Thou hast been my brother all these
years and I deem it thy rightful place now".

"Aye, I will and right gladly " said Richard.

"Daniel, would thee also be with us to give aid
to Mary as if she were being given away by her
father?"

"Aye, I will Peter and be honoured also."

The three men went inside Peace Cottage and
led the childer out to the waiting blue hay cart.
They had brought it as a favour to Peter and Mary,
especially as Mary should not walk too far and tax
her strength. They put her up by the side with a
good handhold and the childer were put aboard
and sat about the cart-floor peering over the
sides.

Peter and Richard sat up with Daniel as he
took up the reins and stirred Conqueror to pull
them slowly up the lane towards Briarmeade
Manor. They stopped at the doors of the chapel
where Mr Medlock and Brother John were waiting
to welcome them with embraces for all.

From the gathering crowd, the first to step
forth was Will, who carried the wicker crib he had
made under his arm. He set it down and put his
arms about Peter, as he always did to his foster-
son. Then he hugged Mary. He looked well but so
sad as he was still grieving the loss of Grace.
Behind him came Maria, Tilly, Bett, Grissell and
Silas. Richard took a few paces behind the chapel
and brought forth Ruth in a lovely blue gown. She
blushed when she met Peter - their memories of
the night at the Swan tavern still fresh for both of
them. She embraced him tenderly as an old
friend and whispered in his ear, "I am to marry

Richard."

"It gladdens my heart to hear thus, Ruth," he said quietly, then kissed her on the cheek. He turned to Richard and said, "'Tis bravely done, ye lost no time. Thou hast made a goodly choice, Richard. I wish ye both as much happiness as mine, and for many years to come."

"Mary, I must tell thee - Richard and Ruth are also to be wed. I am so glad for him after the trials he endured with his last love."

Mr Medlock motioned them to enter the chapel, already filled with folk from all over the manor. Some had come from as far as Winterbourne Latimer, a good two days walking. The few benches and stools were taken so most folks stood, or leaned on the walls.

Brother John had kept a stool free beside the altar for Mary to sit on. He brought it forth and Mary sat down. Peter stood on her right and Daniel on her left. Richard stood beside Peter and Ruth, Maria and Tilly stood behind the bride and groom shepherding the childer. Maria spoke quietly and told them what was happening.

Peter looked behind him and was just in time to catch sight of Robert de Vere Ashton entering the chapel. He slipped into a space near to the wall just inside the door.

Mr Medlock held up his hands to the gathering. Everyone ceased talking and a hush came upon the assembled throng. The odd cough and child's chatter now and then disturbed the peace.

"We are all gathered this day for this the first wedding in Briarmeade Manor chapel. Ye all are bidden to witness the marriage of two of our dear friends on this manor - Mary Howe and Peter

Meade. Ye all know them and their childer here present".

He bent forward spoke quietly - "I bid each of ye, Mary and Peter, to answer Aye or Nay to the questions I must put to ye both. Be ye desirous to wed each other before this company?"

"Aye" said Peter and Mary as one voice.

"Be there anyone here who knoweth of any reason why these persons should not be joined together in holy wedlock?"

Mr Medlock looked about the chapel, but answer was there none. Some folk coughed and others shuffled their feet while those seated looked about.

Turning to Peter he said "Peter Meade, dost thou take this good woman to be thy wedded wife?"

In a loud clear voice Peter said "Aye I do"

"Mary, dost thou take this man to be thy husband?"

"Aye I do" said Mary softly - now standing up and holding onto Peter's left arm. She was uncomfortable both standing and sitting and held his arm tightly as she felt a little faint.

"Wouldst thou wish to sit for the remainder of the proceedings Mary?" asked Mr Medlock. She shook her head, biting her lips and feeling hot. She stood proudly and as erect as she could and took a few deep breaths. She calmed and nodded for him to continue.

"We have heard the desire to wed of these two people to each other and there be no impediment expressed why they should not be joined together." Peter played with the flaxen ring on his finger and guessed that at any moment it would be needed. Mary jerked his arm to stop him fidgeting like a naughty child and he stood still.

"We do have now two things to ask of thee Peter. It hath been ordered that all who are born, wed or buried in this parish, must be recorded or registered in a book. Canst thou write thine own name?"

"Aye, that I can." said Peter.
"The other be that a token of thy desire to wed must be exchanged between thee and Mary.?"

Peter fumbled with the flaxen ring, took it off his hand and placed it on the open bible but it rolled off onto the floor. He bent down and found it. When he stood up and placed it again on the bible for it to be blessed, he could not believe his eyes. For on the book shone a silver ring beside the flaxen one. Mr Medlock had kept it safe from the day of Jonah' burial for just such a day as this. Mary sat down heavily on the stool. She had thought never to see that ring again. She had felt very bad about having to part with it but Peter had been so understanding when she had told him. Peter took it, and trembling, put in on Mary's hand. She felt very proud to be wearing the little band of silver again and silently vowed to herself that she would never part with it again unless it was a matter of life or death. Peter kissed her on the cheek. Mr Medlock gave the flaxen ring to Mary and she put it on Peter's finger, and she kissed him back.

"Brothers and sisters, we have now witnessed the wedding of Mary and Peter Meade and I declare they now be man and wife. We pray for a blessing on their union and a long and happy life together." He turned aside and took up the newly bound parchment register that Robert de Vere

Ashton had ordered to made and had paid for. A
quill and ink were brought by Brother John and he
held the book as Mr Medlock pointed to the spaces
for their signatures. Peter took up the quill and
signed his name clearly and boldly. Not to be
outdone, Mary took the quill from Peter and wrote
her name in the proper place.

He felt so proud. She saw his lips tremble as
he sighed and sniffed. She smiled up at him - her
eyes alone saying, "I love thee so much."

Mr Medlock looked amazed, cleared his throat
and took Mary's right hand and Peter's left. He
turned them round slowly to face the chapel full
of folk, held up their hands and said -

"Behold, the first couple to be married in this
chapel." He led them forward through the throng
towards the chapel door and everyone pressed
forward behind them as they walked out into the
May Day sunshine. Everyone talked at once and a
cheer went up as Mary and Peter stood together
against the chapel walls to greet their friends.

Tilly and Maria led the childer out to be with
their parents. Mary beamed and looked calm
again but hot and blushing a little. Peter looked
and felt like a king at his coronation.

Mr Medlock stood aside trying to be
insignificant, but Peter beckoned him to come
close so he could speak with him.

"I thank thee Mr Medlock for thy gift and
kindness. I shall be ever in thy debt for this."

"Peter, when Mary did use it as payment as
thou knowest, her sorrow was deep as was mine,
and I vowed that if ever I could restore it to thee I
would do so. It be now in the proper place. I do
wish thee lifelong happiness together."

The crowd parted, as if the wind had blown

upon a cornfield, as Robert de Vere Ashton walked slowly and deliberately towards Mary and Peter. All the childer were round them in a ring and were still tended by Tilly and Maria with Daniel close by. He put forth his hand and Peter took it and they grasped hands warmly then he turned to Mary and embraced her too.

"I see that thou hast made a goodly choice in thy new wife Peter and I wish thee both much happiness. How goes it with you in your new cottage Mary?" She was taken by surprise that she should be spoken to and indeed asked a question. She was a bit taken aback.

"Oh good Master, it hath been the answer to so many troubles that would have vexed us, most especially the space we did badly need." She fell silent as Robert de Vere Ashton turned to the ring of childer and with great surprise to all assembled, bent and picked up Meg and said:

"Thou must be Meg with the golden hair that I do remember when thee and Peter did return to the manor."

She held on to him with one arm about his red bull-neck. Compared to him, she was like a brooch on his coat.

"Now little one, pray tell me the names of thy brothers and sisters here present."

Proudly Meg called to each in turn by name and they came to him and bowed or curtsied as Mary had taught them. He smiled at them and nodded to each one. Mary stood aside and looked at Peter's reactions. They both flashed a thought to each other that said,

"'Tis like unto a man meeting and greeting his own grandchildren."

His greetings seemed natural and warm.

Robert, Peter, Richard and Mary wondered why this could be.

28 ~ MAY-DAY MERRIMENT

Peterkin the brewer had been very busy making a special brew for May-Day. Peter had found that Will had enough honey to make a good mead. He had been given a special mead recipe by the monks and had told the brewers how to make it. The proportion of honey to water would be right when a fresh hen's egg floated in the mixture. With the warmer weather it fermented and was done in three weeks. Flavoured with rosemary and juniper berries, it was exceedingly strong.

The cart with the Meade family drew up before the great barn on the greensward where already there was a goodly company of folk waiting for the May tree to arrive. As Peter helped the children down off the cart, Daniel held Conqueror's head lest he move and make them fall.

Mary took a long time to descend to the ground and rested on a sack of sheep's fleece that had been brought down from the woolshed for her. Many folk had walked behind them from the chapel and thronged around the newlyweds. Richard took charge of the situation and bade Peter sit beside Mary so that folk could talk to them.

The day before, the last day of the 'old' year, last year's May-Tree had been cut down and burnt. The old year was now finished and the work of planting and harvest would begin all over again. In the morning of the first day of May, the lads had taken the cart into the wood and with great care they had chosen a new tree.

They had said a quiet prayer to the spirit of the tree, thanking it for letting them cut it down and use it as a symbol of the birth of the new year. It had been cut down with great gusto as they swung the long handled axes and chips of wood flying in all directions. As it fell they had run out of the way of the crashing branches and all cheered. An acorn had been planted next to the stump of the tree to replace it. Then they had dragged the tree out of the wood and loaded it on the cart. The maids and children who had come to watch had climbed onto the cart also and the piper played a merry tune as they trundled back along the lane to the greensward by the barns.

A buzz of conversation went round the assembled company as the procession came into view and everyone brought out of their pouches and pockets strips of cloth with which to decorate the tree. Each ribbon tied to the tree would bring good luck. When all the ribbons and braids were tied onto the tree it was taken off the cart and set upright in the same hole as last year's. The piper started another merry tune and all present formed large circles around the tree and did a traditional dance. It grew faster and faster until only the youngest and fittest were still dancing. The piper stopped playing and everyone flopped down exhausted.

A barrel was lying on its bilge ready for the lads who did the balancing acts to pit their skills and amuse the crowd. Stilts were standing up against the barn walls and a batch of clubs and sickles lay beside them ready to be thrown about by the jugglers.

Kitty pointed to the trestle tables that lay inside the barn, these would be used to set out the food and drink. A good way from the barn a pit had been dug and iron cross-pieces driven into the corners of it to take the spit where the pig was already roasting. The fire was burning brightly and pans placed to catch the dripping lard.

Gera came out of the barn and shyly came up to Mary. She took out of her hanging pocket, a horn spoon, small enough for a child, with the handle made in the shape of an oak-leaf. She handed it to Mary who thanked her warmly. She showed it to Peter who also thanked Gera very much. Mary held it, turning it in her hands. Peter looked at Mary. They both had much to tell the great oak tree.

Samuel came to them next with a bundle in his hand. He unwrapped it and showed them two exquisite leather pouches. They were made with scraps of leather joined together with neat stitches and with an oak leaf tooled into each one. He said:

"I made these for ye both that ye may never be short of money. 'Tis not much but if ye ever need saddlery done for thee, do come to me."

Eve and Emma, Samuel's girls, had made some plaited figures from grasses and gave them to Mary and Meg as May dolls.

Richard had no need to do anything save stand by and admire the queue of well-wishers. Ruth stood beside him and they held hands which made Peter feel so very glad that at last his brother had found love after the jilting that had knocked him sideways.

Bett had made a sweetmeat of the bride and groom from marchpane but she had made the bride very slim. She looked pleased to be present and talked for a long time with Mary and Meg. Meg asked,

"Where is Tom the pot boy? Will he be here with us this day Bett?"

"'Twould seem that Tom hath made a conquest " said Bett to Mary aside.

"Aye" said Mary "I shall have to keep my eye on things" she chuckled and Peter laughed.

Kit came to the little group that was growing by the minute and said

"Peter, if ye will come to the coppice with a sack or two on the morrow, I have singled out a cockerel and three laying hens for thee. They be good fowls that I did breed myself. I will come to thy cottage and make a pen for them if ye wish."

Peter said, "With all I have to do, I will gladly ask thee to make the pen for them, Kit. We both give thee our hearty thanks."

Josiah the blacksmith, came across the sward with a great iron bar with a basket in the centre, all made at the forge. His lad carried two fire-dogs to be driven into the floor of the Meade's cottage hearth. Peter just could not believe his eyes. This was what he always wanted, a cottage of his own with a goodly hearth and a basket spit to roast meat and poultry upon. He rose and shook Josiah's hand.

"My good friend this is far more than I could have wildly dreamt of owning. We thank thee so much, and welcome thee to our cottage, when we are settled, to eat with us. I shall be ever grateful for this." For a man of his great size, Josiah looked embarrassed but was pleased that his work was appreciated.

Edmund, the coppicer, stepped up to Mary and held up a rattle that he had made on his pole lathe. Two thick candlesticks also he pulled from a sack over his shoulder. Mary thanked him for the baby's rattle and wondered if it was an omen. Peter thanked him for the candlesticks and as he was doing so, Tilly came along right behind Edmund and gave them two candles that she and Gera had made. The middles were of tallow but the outsides were made from beeswax given by Will after he took the honey crop. Mary looked at Peter and they both saw another romance in progress with that last pair of visitors.

Those folk who had no money to buy gifts or had no skills to make any, brought much sought-after logs for the Meade's family woodpile. These they put aboard the cart along with all the other gifts that had been lovingly given.

Soon the place was all a-bustle with folk fetching and carrying food, drink, and implements for cooking and carving. Bett supervised the roasting of the pig given by Robert de Vere Ashton. It had to be basted all the while lest it burn.

Tom was basting the meat with a bunch of herbs that he dipped in the dripping pan. Not to be outdone, Meg insisted on joining him and together they did a grand job. Bett came to them and said:

"Thou art making a good cook Tom, I shall have to watch out or mayhap I could well be out of work." She was seldom known to be so cheerful, but it seemed that these two youngsters had made a great impression on her. It might have been when Meg cut Peter's finger and fainted, that she had had a change of heart.

Meg looked at Bett and asked, "Dost thou have a mind to have me to work in the kitchen. I promise not cut anyone and I will work very hard." She looked up at Bett with pleading eyes and her father heard her. She still talked with splashes having lost two more front teeth - this time from the upper jaw, a few days ago. She had also more seeds from the fairies to sow in the garden at Peace Cottage.

Peter said, "Dost thou really wish to do such hard labour at thy young years Meg? If thou wouldst try it for a week or twain and Bett would have thee, I will allow it."

"Why bless thee child, I would have the use of another kitchen maid. I will sort out some tasks for thee to do." Bett really had turned over a new leaf of kindliness. Peter felt so proud that Meg had settled in, both in his home and family as well as on the manor. Tom beamed and smiled at her.

Rob, Nem, Aaron and Kitty found the men had set up the trap-ball and were the first to start knocking the wooden ball into the air and clouting it all over the sward. Mary was so pleased to see them playing together. She pushed her hand under Peter's and laid her head on his shoulder.

"Oh Peter I feel so happy at this moment just watching the childer at play. When thou wast away at St Benets, I did wonder if ever we would see such events together."

Becky sat next to Peter, and Alys sat the other side, next to Mary, all on the wool sacks. Becky looked a little sad until Peter saw her looking down-hearted and fondled her hair. She cuddled close to him as she felt the same as Mary. He loved her so much, but he could not show too much, lest the others became envious. Alys left them and went to join the others who had tired of trap-ball and were tossing the hay ball about.

Jacob came out of the barn with Dick the bowyer's lad. Together they jumped up on to the large barrel and walked it along the sward until one fell off because he was trying to juggle at the same time. Dick went to the barn wall and strapped on a pair of stilts which he was far better at using than barrel-walking. The children all cheered him on as he walked about amongst the hen coops and brewer's barrels.

He called over to where Mary and Peter were sitting......

"Peter, will ye throw to me the sickles that lie by the barn doors. Pray throw but one at a time." Peter walked over and picked up the three hay-makers sickles and tossed them upward. Dick caught them with practised ease, to the crowds delight, and juggled with them. The sense of danger brought oohs! and aahs! from the maids from the woolshed and dairy. He was a very popular lad. Peter returned to Mary just as the minstrels came to the sward and began to play. In no time the place was alive with happy folk dancing round the May tree. The rhythms made all who were seated want to tap their feet. It took little effort for any man to persuade the maid of his choice to get up and dance. The sunshine, the food and drink, and grand company, made pleasure for all. There were times when the players had to rest to regain their energy. This was when all ate and drank their fill from the trestle tables set before the barn.

Peter tried the ale and then the mead and brought some over to Mary. She preferred the mead as its sweetness suited her better. She glowed and looked so well and radiantly happy. Several folk came and asked about her health and condition.

The music began again. By the crude sundial set above the barn door for the use of the builders, it was the second hour after noonday. Mary felt the need to rise and walk about as she had sat long enough and needed to ease off the stiffness in her back.

Peter said, "Whither dost thou wish to walk Mary?" The music of the dance floated over the crowd and had a charm about it that Mary loved. She swayed gently in his arms. Then, as if she had forgotten how heavy she was, she pulled him to the May tree and joined the great circle dance.

All the company that was dancing held hands and the leader walked a circle around the tree. As the others followed a great spiral was formed. When the leader was close to the trunk he turned about and followed the line outwards. This made a double spiral, going in opposite directions to each other.

Mary and Peter were caught up in the rhythms and danced round the tree as if they were eighteen again. They wended their way to the middle and turned about and followed the lead to the edge of the dance. As they got to the edge Mary took the opportunity to leave the revellers because she was feeling a little weary. Peter led her back to the wool sacks. They walked there slowly and sat down, laughing as they had not done for what seemed years.

When they regained their breath, Mary said, "I have not done that this long time, oh I did enjoy it Peter."

She lay against him and they melted together in joy and happiness that showed to all who gazed on them. Where she had found the energy, Peter just could not imagine. He stroked her hair and sat holding her hand. She gazed at the silver ring on her finger, rubbed it to put a shine on it and held before Peter's eyes. He took her hand and kissed it on the palm and wrist. It made her wriggle and laugh.

She sat up with a little moan and rubbed her back but settled down again. Then she did it again and this time Peter became concerned. She gripped his arm hard and went a little pale.

" What is it Mary, dost thou have discomfort from the dancing?"

"Too much of everything Peter. Too much to eat and drink, too much joy and happiness. Too much dancing and too much........Oh...."

"Mary, what is it, what ails thee?"

She bent her head downward. He bent forward with her to hold her. He looked down at her shoes and saw water in a small pool at her feet.

"Peter... the baby....it has started.....my waters have broken....."

He called to Becky and Kitty

"Becky...Kitty... go and find Maria and Tilly if ye can and hasten, for the baby has started to come."

Mary sat back up straight again but her

breathing came faster as she gripped Peter's hands.

"I must stand up" she said earnestly. Peter stood up and Richard saw the stirring from a fair way off. He came running up to Peter and said:

"Is there ought I can do for thee Mary? Dost thou need a cart to carry thee?" She looked at him, grateful for his concern. She panted a bit, then regained her thoughts and said:

"Nay Richard, I could not climb into it, but I thank thee. The Baby is coming, and though I can walk, I would ask thee for thy arm on the other side of me. I shall walk to yonder barn with thy help and with Peter, for I know I must reach the hay in there to birth our child."

Peter took her left arm and Richard the right one and slowly with a few stops at Mary's commands, they arrived at the sweet smelling hay inside the great barn. Tables were rapidly shifted by all available hands. The minstrels had stopped playing and Mary asked why.

"The music will soothe me through my time. Peter, pray bid them to play, if they be not too tired." Richard left them and spoke to the musicians and the music began again. Mary sighed with relief as she was made comfortable on some linen cloth laid over the hay. The great doors were pulled to, but not shut and she was pleased that the dancing still continued outside.

"Dost thou need aught to eat or drink my love?" asked Peter.

"Aye I would like water Peter. I would take some herb posset, if anyone would make it for me. In my pouch there is a cloth bag with herbs in it. I have kept it for such a time as this. It do have rosemary, bay and raspberry leaves, all-heal and mugwort."

Maria and Tilly came into the barn and tended to Mary so see how far she was in her labour.

While they waited to see how frequent her pains were they tried to usher Peter to leave. He began to go outside but Mary said:

"Peter wither dost thou go, leave me not."

Maria said "It would be best if thou didst leave us Peter, for this is woman's work and thou mightest be distressed with what is to happen."

He was bewildered, and turned to the only one who must answer his torments.

"Mary what dost thou wish me to do. Name it, and whatever thou dost wish I shall do."

The pains came upon her and she held on to her last breath and flushed in her face. She panted and then gathered herself enough to say.....

"I wish for thee to be with me all through this. At times I may shout at thee to go away as if I never want to see thee again..........", another pain came and she tried to relax into it and then it went away......... "If this I do tell thee..... take no head of it, for it is not my meaning."

"Tell me how I may help thee through all this Mary!"

"Just to be here......... Oh! That was a big one..." she panted and sweat came on her forehead. Peter found a pitcher of cool water and soaked a cloth in it to wipe and cool her face. She was grateful and took his free hand in hers. From then on, their hands never parted. She clung to him as if they had been nailed together. She had a terrific grip. Each pain she had, he felt go through him too. She didn't scream and shout like Lydia had done and he was grateful. He felt helpless and just sat there holding Mary's hand. If only he could do something. Then he noticed that the women around him were also just doing nothing. They were sitting and talking to each other quietly. He wondered why nothing could be done to help the woman he loved who was going through such pain.

She had placed herself so she could push against the upright post that went high up into the roof. She gazed up at the play of sunlight coming through the tiles, and drew comfort from it. Two white doves cooed high up in the purlins and seemed to speak to Mary. She answered with her mind between pains. These came faster now.

Richard came into the barn to see how things were going. Tilly took the tyg from him. It held the herb posset that Mary had asked for.

"This is an exceeding good brew Richard, who did make it?" asked Mary.

"Ruth did this for thee Mary, she's a good woman." More and more pains came and Tilly and Maria cast about for some clean cloths. Mary told Peter to untie her white apron as she turned a little to one side between pains. He untied the bows and gave it to Tilly who smiled down at him and could not resist kissing him on his sweating face. "Not long now," said Maria. "Do not push yet Mary ye be not ready."

"I can see some dark hair... keep panting between pains Mary, thou be in good time, but push not too hard when I do tell thee. Over much and thou mayest do thyself some hurt". Mary nodded. She knew what to do as she had gone through this before. She was ready for the last mountain that she had soon to climb.

Peter's back was getting cramped so he

shifted about in the hay on the barn floor and was easier. Maria had taken off her apron also and Tilly had found some flaxen thread in the apron pocket that was Mary's. She never went anywhere without a flaxen thread. Outside the music still flowed and joyous laughter still came from the Mayday merrymakers. Several of the married women came to the barn-door to ask how things were progressing. There was a constant stream of folk.

Peter said little but watched in awe of this miracle which was unfolding before him. He was part of its beginning a mere thirty yards away in the woolshed last August and was now about to see the final miracle of birth.

Into his mind came the memories of the birth torments of Peg. Lydia's agonies, screams, mind-rending wailing and the terrible length of time it all took. He began to feel a chill come over him and he shivered. Mary squeezed his hand to tell him she knew what fears he had in his mind. The sun had dipped below the horizon and the shadows were lengthening. The musicians were still playing but more slowly now and the dancers were swaying gently to the music. One or two of the younger revellers were drifting homeward.

"'Tis time to push, Mary, I can see his head. He has long black hair." Maria's voice was gentle and calm but Peter could see the concern on her face. Mary gathered herself for the next pain and the next effort. When it came she pushed as hard as she could. She cried out with the pain but Peter could see that the baby's head was appearing. One more pain and he could see the baby's face. For a moment all was still and the child's head turned round a little as if looking about before Mary made her next push.

Maria said "Mary listen to me. When the next pain doth come, push thou but gently for the shoulders will be next. The child is nearly with us now."

Peter still sat on the hay-floor with Mary's hand still fixed to him. They both sweated with sympathetic effort.

Mary felt a big pain coming and breathed and held her breath. She gripped Peter and Maria told her to go easy as water came from her and then the child slid forth into Tilly's hands as she laid it on the apron she held ready. He was blue-grey in colour and the cord wound about his neck with a complete caul covering his face. Maria tore the caul gently and took it off while Mary rested between pains. Tilly took the caul and washed it clean and rolled it up carefully. This would be worn about the child's neck to save him from any chance of drowning.

Maria put her fingers under the cord by the chin and with care eased it from about the baby's neck. In a moment another push from Mary brought the whole afterbirth away and Tilly wrapped it up and set it aside. Maria took up the flaxen thread and tied off the umbilical cord a hand's span from the child and another a couple of inches further away. Peter saw with such joy, his son Adam with tight shut eyes, open his mouth and bawl as if he had been dipped in cold water. Maria took Peter's knife without him knowing it and cut the cord. Then she wrapped the baby in her own clean white apron and held him up for all to see.

"Adam is here with us Mary." His voice

quivered with emotion and Mary sighed and relaxed against the sweet hay.

"He was a blue grey colour when he first was seen Mary, but now he be crying for his mother, he is a goodly pink with this long dark hair." He pointed with immense pride and interest. All tiredness was forgotten and he then realised how thirsty he had become.

Mary took Adam and he soon settled as she rocked with him in her arms. Peter kissed Mary's head and straightened her hair. Tilly and Maria tidied up the surrounding hay and took away the birth remains. Maria decided the best way of disposing of it was to put it on the Mayday bonfire which was still burning brightly. As she did so she sent a silent prayer to ask the Lord to bless this child with good health and happiness.

Then they came back to the barn and the happy parents. Mary was sitting up and was talking to a queue of well-wishers as the word of the birth of Adam went around like a woodland fire. Maria shooed them all away as Mary needed to rest. There would be plenty of time later for congratulations.

Richard and Ruth stood aside. She was a mixture of happiness and sadness for reasons that she and Peter knew. Richard had only been told of her inability to conceive three days before the wedding of Mary and Peter. He loved Ruth no matter what she could or could not do.

She would have given anything to be that woman sitting in the hay with the gurgling baby. Richard tried to comfort her. Mayhap they could take in an orphan child or some such.

How could anyone tell or foretell what would befall them in the future?

29 ~ THE REVELATION

One evening after the childer had gone to
bed, Mary, Peter and Richard sat around the fire
talking over the day and planning for tomorrow.
Mary took up Peter's old habit to look for any holes
to repair. She felt a lump in one side and out fell
a folded piece of off-white linen. She held it up
and shook out the folds. It looked like a baby's
shawl and she could not understand why Peter had
it. It was very finely woven and someone had put
a great deal of work into it.

She smoothed out the creases and looked
closely and the pattern that had been woven
there. Around the edges threads had been drawn
out of the weave to make a pattern that almost
looked like lace. In the middle was a curious
roughness in the weave. Mary held it up to the
light and, as the light caught the fabric, she could
see that the yarn had been twisted one way and
then the other to make it look different. The
pattern was almost invisible but if she let the sun
shine across it, she could see that it looked like
the letters that the children had been learning
from Peter.

Peter looked around and saw Mary with the shawl
and said,

"I ought to have given thee this the day I saw

Grace, when first I did return to Briarmeade. It was the birthing shawl that I was wrapped in the day I was born and the day my mother died." Mary said, "There seem to be some letters here Peter but I cannot read them...... "

He fell silent. The silence hung about them for a long eerie minute. Peter's face deep in thought. He slid from bed and stood next to her.

"Mary take up the linen close to the window where the light from the side will make the pattern stand out." He stared at the cloth and saw the words:-

Hannah
+
Robert.

A sweat broke out on his brow. Grace had said his mother's name was Hannah but the name of his father went with her to the grave. Grace had also said that there was idle chat about his mother and the gentry. Grace and Rachel, who delivered Peter, had both been told to stay silent in all respects about the birth. Peter's mind was in a whirl. Surely his father could not really be Robert De-Vere.

Peter collapsed back onto the bed and his eyes were shut. Mary called to him but she could not awaken him. She damped a cloth and wiped his brow and he revived a little.

"Peter," said Mary, "what is it that has happened to thee. Is there ought that I can do for thee?"

Peter slid to his knees on the floor, his hands clasped, his eyes tightly shut in prayer, his breathing fast and shallow.

"Oh God. I thank thee for the revelation thou hast given to me this day. Much now be clear to me. Amen"

"Oh Peter, what has happened to thee, for such torment was on thy face after I did show thee the linen." said Mary.

There came a knock on the cottage door. It was Richard, who had come to tell Peter news of the day's work.

Peter drew breath and asked for water before he could explain.

Richard filled a tyg and Peter downed it in one draft. He sat back, sighed and held Mary's hand. She had pulled up a stool and sat beside him, her head on his shoulder full of warmth and love. Richard smiled at them and envied the love that was so clearly and openly seen between them.

Peter began in a low voice.

"What I now tell ye both is to be for yourselves alone to hold and tell no-one. When I was born, my mother, who was named Hannah, was told that I was stillborn and had not cried, so she told Grace to wrap me in that piece of linen and take my body to the ten acre field and bury me there where I had been conceived. She was in deep melancholy and gave up the will to live as she had no-one in the world to care for and no-one to care for her. She died shortly after the birth."

"Grace had recently given birth to Richard, here, and understood the state of her mind. As she laid me down to dig the hole for my grave she heard me cry. She carried me to her own home and, as she was able to suckle Richard with ease, she suckled me too and brought me up as her own child."

"We always thought that we were really brothers until told otherwise by Grace when I was of and age to understand."

"Now that I have seen the birthing shawl and read the message that my mother wove into it, I have the answer to many questions. She could neither read or write but must have been told the letters that she needed and she wove them into the shawl. The message be just three words, or rather names - Hannah and Robert. This doth mean to me that Hannah intended to take the name of my father to the grave when she thought that I was dead, but the mystery be now revealed for the Robert could only be Robert deVere Ashton, the master of Briarmeade manor."

"Afore ye think that I have any claim to riches, debts or property, remember that I was born out of wedlock and do have no rights at all here or anywhere. I have no ambitions for anything on the manor, and wish only to be the same as I have always been. I must then hold ye both to keep secret that which I have told ye. There be ever the chance that what I believe now could be in all wise wrong."

"The manner in which I was only banished and not imprisoned, then sent away to Ashingham Priory, given my pardon made under steward and cook. All this mayhap could account for the leniency that I have had from Robert de Vere. I can think of no other reason, and remember also that our cottage here be rent free. For all these favours be to ease his mind for the guilt he hath upon him knowing that I might well be his living son."

"True or not, I be settled in my own mind that

I am the same who hath returned to the friends I have always had, to work with and to love."

Mary held his hands and kissed them as if she had to make sure, once and for all, that he was here to stay. Richard pressed Peter's arm as if to say, "We all love thee, never go away ever again my brother".

ABOUT THE AUTHORS

They met during a re-creation of life on a country manor during the Tudor dynasty. Alkanet and Kester were waiting in a queue for their supper and got talking. They found that they both wrote short stories so decided to collaborate.   Hence 'Itch' was born. Alkanet is a housewife and mother-of-three, living in the west country and was writing her way out of depression. Kester had been writing prose and poetry for 40 years and is interested in old crafts, relics and the history of life in monasteries.

Proof

Made in the USA
Charleston, SC
21 April 2013